THE MAN IN THE
VELVET MASK

DOCTOR WHO – THE MISSING ADVENTURES

Also available:

THE MAN IN THE VELVET MASK

Daniel O'Mahony

DOCTOR WHO

THE MISSING ADVENTURES

First published in Great Britain in 1996 by
Doctor Who Books
an imprint of Virgin Publishing Ltd
332 Ladbroke Grove
London W10 5AH

ISBN 0 426 20461 1

Cover illustration by Alister Pearson

Typeset by Galleon Typesetting, Ipswich
Printed and bound in Great Britain by
Mackays of Chatham PLC, Chatham, Kent

Prologue

If

I am dead.

I died in darkness, in a lightless world where every sign that could guide me was hidden. The darkness ate my sense of time and place. It ate me. I died looking into the light, into the sudden blaze. I thought it was a sign. I died hoping. The knife that killed me was kind. It dissected me, almost gently. It was a moment of excruciating painlessness, a wet moment.

The world tumbles and the blood spins in my skull. A sticky red trail marks my passing. I'm dead.

'You're a failure. You can't be used. In mind, in body, you are worthless.'

He has a strange voice. It surprised me when I first heard him. A man of his evil should speak with menace, or deceptive calm, but he's thoughtful, guarding every word jealously. He built this labyrinth. His words followed me, whispered from the dark walls.

I failed him. I also tried to kill him.

'Unlike you, I can see. Darkness can be conquered, as can all things.'

He put me into the murder machine. I'm dead.

'I despise waste. I accumulate all manner of things. I am a collector.'

The world spins as I drop down a sharp incline. The dim light stings my eyes. I hit the bottom of the shaft, rolling. It doesn't hurt – how could it?

I know where I am. *His* world. His cavernous workshop, stranger and larger than I remember. He's here, a towering shape with a voice that booms from near the roof, making no sense. The words, slurred, mean nothing to me. They're drowned by the pulse of blood, seeping from my neck and staining the floor.

I'm so small.

He scoops me up. (My blood spills faster, guttering onto the ground.) Our eyes meet, and his are as cruel and controlled as I remember. I can't tell what he sees, whether he knows I'm still conscious, whether he cares.

He mouths something, lips moving in clumsy twitches.

'That's a good clean cut. *Very* clean.'

Darkness.

1

The Best of Times

The clock was an elegant distraction. It squatted high on the west wall, its gold eye surveying the entire library. It was a dark intruder jutting through the wall from another world, whispering endless machine poetry.

Tick.

Donatien Alphonse François de Sade – 'Citizen Sade' – found it irritating. The tiny noises ate into him, feeding on his nerves, mind and concentration. His thoughts grew vague. The machine entranced him, and he put his work aside. He had never worked well here. His finest writing had been achieved in quiet, solitary places.

Tock.

He had brought a number of books to his desk, knowing that half would be left untouched, the other half merely skimmed through. Something within him rebelled against the idea of starting work. He reached for the first volume with reluctance, cautiously weighing it on his palms before breaking it open. His fingers traced the smooth edges of the paper, stroking up and down in thoughtless motions. Soft paper, fine and fragile as flesh.

Tick.

The words were blurred shapes bleeding on the cream page. Slowly they focused, hardening into bold, angular auto-scribe letters. The scribe, Sade felt, robbed Shakespeare of his poetry, while the modern translations sacrificed a little of his power. Even this minor work – *Vortigern* – suffered, and that was a great shame. Sade's eye fled through the text, never still, never settling. Shakespeare no longer excited him.

Tock.

3

He sighed, breaking the silence between clock beats.

Tick.

Shakespeare struck the surface of the desk with a satisfying clatter. Sade rose from his seat, precipitating a chorus of squeals from aching furniture. The noise was a relief, breaking the tense silence.

Tock.

He began to pace the room, his footsteps interrupting the metronome of the clock. Sade grinned at the savage discord. This movement, this disruption, this energy, was more like him.

Tick. (*Click*.)

He strode past Shakespeare, Voltaire, Diderot, Laclos, Richardson, Machiavelli, Rousseau, Rabelais, Molière, even past Madame Radcliffe. None of them held the spark of interest for him. Some did not exist outside this room. Sade remembered the bonfires that claimed the authors' immortalities. Voltaire had burned, cream-flesh turning to black, to ash, to thick smoke. Rousseau had illuminated the night sky in a holocaust of words and paper.

Sade had liked the smell of burning paper.

Tock. (*Clunk*.)

He paused by the special section, *his* section. Everything he'd had published was here, in the authorized edition: *Justine*; *Les 120 Journées de Sodome* (in a much weaker version, he feared, than the lost original); *Aline et Valcour*; *Juliette*. Emblazoned down the spine of each volume was the title he had lost to egalitarian times, 'le Marquis de Sade'.

He turned away. These were ghosts. He had not written them.

The clock began to whirr and click and hum in anticipation of the hour. Sade stared up at it, marvelling at both the beauty of the engineering and the engineering of the beauty.

The homunculi emerged from their hiding-holes near the base of the machine, little actors moved by magnets

4

and the ticking of tiny cogs and gears inside their tiny bodies. Each hour was marked by a different perform-ance, a new version of play and passion. The midnight performance, 'the dance', was not the most exciting vignette, but for Sade it was the most fascinating.

Four sets of figures lined up and began to wheel around the stage beneath the clock-face. Their movements were so smooth, it was difficult to believe they were machines. To Sade, the clock and its tiny performers were the greatest of his son's achievements. The automata played out their routine as the clock chimed, then retreated back into the machine. Sade remained, staring. The clock had smooth sides that captured his reflection. He failed to recognize it. He flinched, then glanced again. This time he saw a familiar face, the heavy, hawkish features hooded by deep shadow, but fiery and alive.

There was still something wrong, something hollow in his chest. Something lost, something hidden, something calling him away. Discomforted, he moved, taking long, certain strides towards the door and the lift beyond.

Tick.

He would descend. He would find that which he had lost.

Tock.

The texture of the liquid was grey and unpleasant. There was no label on the dark bottle, and no telling whether its content was foul water or foul wine. Edith Cameo took an experimental sip from her mug and regretted it. The taste was dry and bitter, and she fought to swallow. Thoughtfully she poured the remains back into the bottle before setting off on her rounds.

The prison passages were deserted by this time of night, with most of the gaolers either asleep or enforcing the curfew on the Paris streets. At midnight, the cells became Cameo's preserve. For the span of their brief confinement, the prisoners were her charges.

She set out down the first passage, her hat worn at a

notably crooked angle, her pistols dragging heavy at her side, a sardonic smile tight along her mouth. She valued formality – in the correct time and place. Most of her charges were sick with fear, courtesy of Doctor Guillotin. No more control was needed.

Her first and least interesting duty of the night was to kill the prisoners in the six condemned cells. This took a little time, and left her with aching fingers. She killed 50 prisoners quietly with pen strokes on the appropriate clipboard. Tonight was different. As Cameo moved the short distance to Cell 6, something had changed. She caught it, just on the edge of her hearing. Her routine was punctuated by the whirr and grind of the elevator, the clatter of doors opening in a nearby passage.

Not the cells! No one should come here at night, when it's my world, and its creatures are mine.

I've done so very little. Such a small pleasure, hardly worth punishing.

She snatched the clipboard from the door of Cell 6 and pretended to study it, frantically. She knew the details by heart, but the trembling of the board in her hand made them strange. This was incriminating evidence, in a way. (She could hear footsteps moving along the adjacent passage.) She hadn't marked it yet, maybe if she put it back. Yes . . .

The footsteps stopped. There was a presence at the end of the corridor, at her back. She turned, warily, still clinging to the board, still smiling.

'Citizen,' she said. (Calm, she thought. Why him? Of all people?)

'Gaoler.'

Citizen Sade was an imposing figure. He filled the tight passages of the cells, cramming them with bulk and muscle and precise terror. He was dressed casually and his clothes lent him a raw, half-finished power. He had a demon's face, sharp featured with dark hair swept back from his broad brow. His eyes were small, hidden beneath the arch of his eyebrows. Cruel eyes – they pinned her effortlessly. Cameo remained cautious, if only because Sade demanded her caution. She attempted to stand rigid, but the weight of her body betrayed her, sinking her into a slouch.

'You're Cameo, aren't you?' Sade said. 'Citizen Cameo, the idealist.'

That makes me sound dirty. That makes me sound wrong. 'Citizen,' Cameo murmured. 'I'm surprised . . .'

'I have a good mind, a sharp memory.' He smiled, at last. His mouth might be a crack in the walls of hell, but the smile helped. When he spoke, it was hardly to Cameo. She preferred that. She liked to be overlooked and ignored, particularly in this company.

'I've been wandering.' His voice was long and lonely and nostalgic. 'I thought I'd lost something.' He lapsed into another brief silence, one which Cameo thought it better not to break.

'These cells,' he ploughed on. 'I was here once. Not in this building, in the original, the one the mob tore down. I've spent so long in prison. So much of my life.' There was a false pause before he continued. 'These are the condemned cells, yes?'

Cameo nodded. 'Everyone here goes to the guillotine tomorrow.'

'May I see?'

Cameo nodded again, hiding her awkwardness as best she could. She drew back the shutter on the door of Cell 6. Sade peered through, without enthusiasm, and withdrew quickly.

'There's only one,' he said, surprised.

'I decide who goes where,' Cameo responded, languid despite her inner panic. 'There's a special category of prisoner. I like to keep them alone, for safety's sake.'

'He's masked.' Again, an edge of suspicion to his voice.

'His name is not to be known. To me, he's the man in Cell 6, that's all.'

'Monsieur le 6,' Sade murmured.

'Pardon?'

'When I was imprisoned at Vincennes, my name was not to be known. I was Monsieur le 6.'

Cameo hmmed. 'I like that – I like the sound. Yes, that's what I shall call him.'

'But not for much longer?'

'No.'

Sade shrugged, a massive gesture with the whole of his body. 'I prefer being on the outside,' he said, after an aching silence. 'Good night, citizen.'

She watched him leave, holding herself still until she was certain he was gone, hugging herself as she heard the elevator groan into life. She sank against the wall, her shoulders rubbing wearily against hard stone blocks.

Alone again, Cameo completed the execution record for Cell 6, exactly as she had done on innumerable occasions before. She took it casually to the nearest message tube, which sucked the papers away, hungrily.

Cameo imagined her work, her almost-truths and tiny deceptions, being spat out onto the desk of a phantom official she would never meet. *I'm the only one who really knows what goes on here. I'm safe.*

She returned to Cell 6, just to make sure.

Monsieur le 6 sat motionless on the only bunk, his arms and legs folded, aged eyes staring out from the holes in the tight velvet mask. He had been there long enough to develop a prison posture. He rarely moved or spoke in Cameo's presence, but his eyes were sharp and strong enough to reassure her of his lingering sanity. Cameo regarded him distantly, wondering whether he was watching her through the shutter, or simply staring into space.

'Monsieur,' Cameo called, gently. 'Monsieur le 6?'

His eyes remained still. Nonetheless, Cameo could feel the focus of his attention moving to her, a weight shifting in the cell.

'That was the Marquis de Sade,' the gaoler continued, making her voice calm and hard – it was easier now. 'He gave you his name. How does that make you feel, Monsieur?'

Le 6 stared, but Cameo was used to this and refused to be unnerved. He had evil eyes. Cameo was quite glad that he was locked away, safely anonymous. She didn't want to know who he was. She was half afraid of knowing.

'I was in the condemned cell once before, under Robespierre. I'm grateful to Sade, for toppling the tyrant at least. But he's wrong – I don't prefer being on the outside, I just like it. You understand?' Hard blue eyes stabbed from behind the soft mask.

'Maybe not. I killed you again, tonight. I killed you with this,' she added, holding up her pen for le 6 to see. 'Tomorrow at dawn, there will be a new Monsieur le 6 in this cell, and you will be officially dead.'

Cold blue eyes burned. The mask smothered any other reaction.

'Goodnight, Monsieur. I'll see you again when you're another man.' She closed the shutter and left to attend to happier duties, relieved that the role of death had been passed to another.

In the dark of the cell, blue eyes shifted, throwing their gaze to the floor. Behind the mask, a face twitched and flinched, strongly enough to crease the velvet. Then the moment of expression vanished, and the mask folded back into blandness.

Le 6's lips twitched, feeble with disuse. His voice was weak. 'Tick,' he said. 'Tock.

'Tick. Tock.
'Tick. Tock.
'Tick. Tock.
'Tick. Tock.
'Tick. Tock.'

The TARDIS screamed, its engine-whine building to a crescendo as it struggled between worlds. Dodo Chaplet

9

could feel the ship straining, the anger and the agony itching in her fingertips. The lights snapped out and the heat drained suddenly, simply away. She wouldn't have minded if she hadn't been in the bath. Suddenly she was in darkness, squatting in still, ice-cold water that clutched at her skin, sucking her down. The surface of the water glowed a thin gold in the dark. Dodo propelled herself, half-washed, from the tub.

She dried and dressed quickly, choosing her clothes by match-light and without care. She couldn't make out the shape and colour of them, but they were functional. She hoped they weren't black. Dark clothes went with dark occasions, in her experience. The lights returned, at a subdued strength, when she was halfway to the console room. She still felt the cold though, and pulled her jacket tighter. It was almost as though there was a draught in the TARDIS, a puncture in a distant wall opening the way for an alien breeze. It occurred to Dodo that the ship might be decaying, the wheeze of the engines signifying imminent breakdown. She found the thought frightening and did her best to forget it.

The Doctor was already in the control room, slouched on a ribbed wooden chair in a dark corner, out of the glare of the console. Dodo didn't see him for a moment, and it came as a shock when she did. He was a tough old man – his body seemed to have hardened with age – but now he seemed fragile, almost withered, almost transparent, his bones and the bones of the chair visible beneath thin, tightened flesh. Dodo could see his skull beneath a film of flesh – cruel and eyeless and crowned with waves of white hair. He reclined in an awkward, forced shape, and his chest was still. He was, Dodo guessed, dead.

She glanced down, studying her feet. The Doctor, unseen, was not dead.

She raised her head. The Doctor, seen again, was dead.

She glanced down, studying her feet. *Can't believe it.*

10

Can't believe it. Not him. Not him too. He was an old man. Yes, but . . . He was an old man. Yes, but . . . I didn't think this would happen. Not like other people. Not the Doctor. What am I going to do? It couldn't happen to him, not to him. He was an old man! What am I going to do now? Can't believe it. Won't believe it!

If he can die, then so — If I can't see him (what?) dead (Yes!), then he isn't (what?) dead (Yes). She raised her head.

The Doctor mumbled and sat up and opened his dead eyes. He had, Dodo noticed casually, started breathing again. Her skull swelled up and threatened to burst, thankfully subsiding before she could collapse. Feeling nothing, thinking nothing, she grinned.

'Doctor?' she said. 'You worry me.'

He muttered again, incoherent words forming on dull lips. His eyes growled beneath his brow. As keen as ever, they flared with a fierce, inward anger. It was a while before he tried to speak again. Dodo spent the time patiently, wearing a sympathetic smile.

'My time is near,' he said at last, his voice trembling and weak. 'Yes, almost up, hmmm. I can feel it now, Susan. I've known since my last meeting with that Toymaker fellow. But now I can feel it.'

'Not Susan,' Dodo corrected him quietly, not expecting him to hear.

He cocked his head to one side as if trying to catch the echo of her voice and strip the sense from it, displaying a precise, bony profile. He smiled, and his formidable brow trembled with tiny nods.

'Yes, yes, Susan left . . .' He turned again, fixing her with a bulging stare. 'But you remind me of her so much. You are her reflection, distorted in a rough mirror.'

Dodo's smile thinned, though she guessed he was trying to pay her a compliment.

'I must not forget her, now of all times! I refuse to forget! Yes, yes indeed . . . Dodo, of course, Dodo and young Steven.'

'Steven's gone too.' Her face pinched involuntarily.

11

Steven hadn't been mentioned since his departure.

'Hmm, what?' His voice became harder and calmer, the barking tone he used to dismiss trivia. Strangely Dodo found this reassuring. 'Steven was always the more sensible of you two. You should have the kindness to leave too, young lady.' He rose from the chair, apparently uncomfortable at dictating from a slouch. Dodo stifled a giggle. 'Some things I will have to face alone. The TARDIS will be the only help I need.'

'You're not going to die, Doctor,' Dodo replied, the frustration in her voice betraying her own fear.

'Of course not!' he snorted. 'Not today. Not until I have seen where we are.' His face became rigid, defying her prophecy. It was an impressive effect, spoiled as he began to move, hobbling to the console. Dodo snatched his walking-stick from its stand and hastily shoved it into his hands. His thanks were slurred.

Well, Dorothea, you certainly know how to take care of him. It was strange, she thought, how such a frail old man could be so resilient. The crouched black shape creeping towards the console was a living paradox, capable in any crisis but feeble in the safety of his own home. He had travelled endless distances of time and space, but could barely stand without help. He could (almost) control a machine of the complexity of the TARDIS, yet found it hard to put two coherent words together. Whenever they found themselves out of their depth – in any time or place – Dodo trusted in the Doctor's ability to take care of them both. Now she felt frightened to take her eyes from him.

Once she might have said that danger brought out the youth in him. Now, it brought out the *life* in him. He seemed to have precious little of it left. He was pressing his hands to the console top, their flesh glowing a vivid red, as if drawing life from the instruments. His head was held high, eyes gazing at the scanner high on the far wall. Dodo's eyes joined his.

Alleyway. Wooden buildings, some stone and brick.

Night. No one about. It might be raining, though the picture was too fuzzy to tell. The TARDIS never seemed to land anywhere interesting. She looked away, bored. 'I wonder where we are this week.'

The Doctor's gaze remained fixed. 'Let's see, shall we?' He chuckled – an odd, but vital noise. Dodo found herself grinning again, genuinely happy now. The Doctor's hands moved across the console top. The scanner image magnified, focusing on a cold white patch on a drab wall. A cross-section of French words leaped onto the scanner screen, regular letters punched onto damp yellow paper.

'With any luck, this may give us some clue.' The Doctor patted his pockets, searching for his glasses – another weakness exposed.

Reluctantly, Dodo began to read for him. 'This bill was issued by the, uh, something-something-something Committee of – the next word cuts off but it's almost certainly Paris. Next line: elude the waters . . . beware of the waters?' She flashed the Doctor a shameful grin and was slightly nonplussed to find him smiling back. 'I think it's a health warning. There's a something disease something-something, then it cuts off. I can't tell more than that, sorry.'

'I thought you had French blood.' It was a benign admonishment. He was still smiling.

'Yeah, but I was born in London and I spent most of my French lesson time at school behind the gym learning to kiss that way.'

The Doctor huffed. Dodo wasn't sure whether this was a sign of amusement or bad temper. He was still smiling though, so she took it as a good sign.

'There's something else just at the top,' she said, glancing back at the scanner. 'But it doesn't seem to mean much. *Le 24 Messidor. XII.*'

'The Republican Calendar,' the Doctor explained calmly – and Dodo finally felt that she was back on safe ground, 'dating from the autumn of AD 1792. It was an attempt to remove the names of dead gods and emperors from dates. Assuming this notice is – hmmm – a recent addition, then I would say we are in early July 1804, around two or three years before the classical calendar was reintroduced to France. Hmm, yes!' His hands came together in a feeble clap.

'The Revolution was always a favourite period of mine from Earth's history – all the turbulence of the age crammed into five years in one tiny country. That said,' his voice grew heavier, 'if it is 1804, the Revolution is long over and that dreadful little soldier is ruining everything!'

'If it is 1804, and it is Paris,' Dodo ventured, 'then my great-great-great-how-many-times grandparents are out there. Possibly conceiving my great-great-whatever grandfather at this very moment.'

The Doctor gave her a sharp, strange look. She met his gaze innocently.

'Perhaps,' he said, 'you should change into something more appropriate for the time. A cloak or a shawl would be quite adequate cover. I don't intend to stay for long.'

I'd like to stay, she thought. If only for a little while.

'Run along,' he suggested, his voice cracking. Dodo nodded dutifully and darted out of the console room. She turned back and caught a final glimpse of the Doctor, standing slightly crooked to the side of the console. He was clutching his walking-stick in both hands, his knuckles twisting and tightening round the shaft. He looked better. He looked dignified. He looked lonely.

Dodo followed a familiar path to the TARDIS wardrobe. Once there, she spent half an hour searching for a suitable cloak.

Citizen Sade left the cells and descended.

He had found interesting things in the dungeons. There had been a faceless prisoner – now dead in all but the literal sense. There had been the spectre of an idealist – maybe the ghost of the Revolution itself. There had

14

been the gorgeous, crushing freedom that came with being on the outside of the cells. These were not things he needed. He pushed his face into his hands.

I am not whole!

The hiss of the lift mechanism was an irritant. Sade's fists battered on the metal walls, demanding an opening. His instinct had taken him to the cells, leading his search, but that instinct had been wrong. There was nothing there but the dead and their keeper.

I am incomplete!

The lift mechanism worked by clockwork, much as everything in the New Bastille. Nothing moved unless accompanied by a whirr, a hum, a crash, a click, a chime and the endless buzz of spinning cogwheels. Even the dullest sounds reverberated inside his skull, eating into his brain, into his sanity. It was his son's design.

The lift juddered, momentarily. Sade scowled, then frowned, then crushed his eyelids together to squeeze brief tears out of dust. This lift was a cell, a cell, a cell! Elegant (as cells tended to be), crushing (as cells tended to be), escape proof (as cells tended to be) and accompanied by an endless, hateful monotone buzz.

By the time the doors opened he was on his knees, overwhelmed by nausea. Brutishly, he crawled out, and fell against the nearest wall. He was finally free of the ceaseless ticking, surrounded by welcome subterreanean silence. Overcome with relief, he made a smile – a humourless hollow full of teeth. Then he stood, brushed away the dust and gazed round the invented wonders of Minski's laboratory.

The room was a lair. It was the den of some shambling, debased creature from the pages of Walpole or Radcliffe. It was an alchemist's study, cluttered with paper-strewn benches and incomprehensible apparatus full of inevitably bubbling coloured liquids. It was a medieval dungeon, dark stone walls swathed with ivy and sweating into gutters. It was a cathedral, high ceiling supported by gently curved stone arches. It was a perfect Hell.

15

It was a theatre.

Everything was sham. It was an illusion, designed to intimidate and confuse. Even the clutter was orchestrated. It was a lair of the very best kind of alchemist, a symbolic Hell containing a symbolic Devil of a far higher calibre than the pallid creature that the English worshipped. Nothing was ever done here without meaning or sense. Everything was precise.

Sade found his son at the laboratory's heart, where the façade slipped. The stone gave way to steel, to brick, and to the smooth, clammy fabric of Minski's own devising. Alchemist's junk was replaced by elegant clockwork devices whose various harsh tunes merged into a pleasing harmony and writhing, formless artefacts that seemed to have grown from between the cracks in the floor rather than manufactured. It was warm here, dry, clean, as it was meant to be.

Minski was slaving over a warm corpse. His shoulders were hunched over the low table, curved with a devotion to his craft. He was dressed plainly, simple clothes covered by a soaking wet leather apron. Sade watched for a moment, fascinated by his son's method. The instruments he was using were a mix of traditional scalpels and stranger tools. Minski fussed over them, slender fingers snatching at the most appropriate blade. He pursued precision.

Sade coughed, a gentle announcement. A shrug of irritation passed up Minski's back, ruffling the thin fabric of his coat. That was followed by a spasm of something more ambiguous. Sade stood patiently, suppressing the shapeless fear that had followed him from the library.

Minski turned at last, cranking his head up to match his father's gaze. He was less than half Sade's height, but he stood with an arrogance that defied his stature. He had the face of a child or an angel, soft boned and ivory skinned, topped with a flow of golden hair. He had black eyes, searching and burning eyes in milk-white irises. Sade had loved him once, though he no longer had sharp memories of that time. Now he respected him, partly from genuine admiration, mostly from genuine fear.

Minski stank of rancid meat. Dead blood was darkening on his face, caked in his hair. He offered Sade a pure white smile.

'Father,' he said. It was a barbed word, full of elusive meaning. Sade nodded appropriately.

'Is it anyone I know?' he asked, nodding at the corpse. It was a woman's body, quite young despite death, still lovely on her left-hand side. Minski had cut away the flesh and the limbs from the right, exposing ribs and muscle and failed organs. A thin red weal along her remaining thigh marked the interrupted incursion into the left. She had no head.

'A guard,' Minski replied bluntly, choosing not to waste his words. 'A failed test case. She turned her gun on me, so I put her in the machine. It took her head clean off.' His voice was too strong and too controlled for his child's shape. Sade nodded, though the slice through the dead woman's neck looked rather ragged from this angle. He let his eyes wander, no longer caring to look at the corpse.

He found her head to one side of him, impaled on the horn of an alien machine. Strands of dark hair rolled down the head, twitching in an impossible breeze. Beneath the curtain of hair were serene features, a familiar face. Sade sighed.

'You knew her?' Again, Minski was sparing with his words. There was little emotion in his voice, no relish for life.

Sade felt disappointed. 'Once or twice.' He nodded, stroking the matted strands away from the dead face. Her skin was still warm, still a healthy shade. Still alive, he thought, she's still alive.

Dead eyes snapped open, pupils swivelling upwards to fix on Sade.

'Death to the tyrant!' proclaimed dead lips. 'Death to Deputy Minski!'

Sade struggled to regain his composure. In the corner of his eye was Minski, wearing a fat grin on his thin mouth. His eyes flicked to his son, then back to the ranting, animate head. It swivelled manically on its spike, spitting in Minski's direction.

'The Louis were tyrants! Robespierre and his followers were murderers! But it is Minski who has drowned France in blood! It is Minski who has made her the enemy of the world! It is Minski who betrayed the Revolution! We who love France and the Revolution must destroy Minski before he corrupts them beyond redemption! As the old Bastille fell, so shall the New!'

Sade's jaw twisted, wordlessly. The talking head squeezed everything out of his mind; all his fears and ghosts seemed petty compared to this marvel.

Or this abomination. He wasn't sure which.

He couldn't bear to look away, or disturb the scene with harsh speech. He spoke softly to his son, through the corner of his mouth.

'You've restored her life, is that it?'

The woman's head spun to face him, hair lashing through the still air. 'Death to Sade and Minski! Long live the Revolution! Libertines! Eternity! Frugality! Gottle o' geer! Gottle o' geer! 'At's 'e way to do it!'

The head winked. Minski cackled at Sade's back. Citizen Sade himself growled, his cheeks blistering with embarrassment.

'It's an automaton, that's all.' Minski stepped between Sade and the head, waving a hand in front of its face. 'It's a crude thing. I can breathe my life into dead things, but not their own.'

Sade heard his fingers crack. He wasn't aware that he'd moved them.

'I came here,' he faltered, 'because I've lost something, and I can't tell what it is. Your clocks are driving me out of my skull!'

'You're tired,' Minski murmured. 'Go to bed. I'll send you a blonde.'

'No. Thank you,' Sade hmmed, the heat of his anger spurring him on. 'I need something from you. I need . . . I can't tell you what I need. There's a hole somewhere, I don't know where or what shape or *why*! But *you* can help me!'

'I'll send you a hole.' Minski was sighing, finger and thumb pinching the bridge of his nose from tiredness.

'I feel –'

'No. You are the Marquis de Sade. You do not feel anything.' He gave his father another sharp, upwards look. 'Not this wheedling self-pity, nor your cringing guilt. You are supposed to be a monster. Act like one!' He had put on a voice that Sade knew was intended to tame and to cage. Sade was overcome by calm despite himself.

'Go to bed. I'll send you someone to destroy.' Minski laid a reassuring hand on his father's arm, a well-meant gesture as he had to stretch awkwardly to reach. Thoroughly tamed, Sade turned to go.

'Oh, I have something unexpected for you.'

Sade turned, his tempered features cracking open with surprise. 'There's no such thing!' he replied, half joking.

'There is.' Minski's voice was subdued, perplexed. The brow of his child's face was knotted into an old, adult pattern. 'It manifested itself about ten minutes ago. There is nothing like it on Earth as far as I know.' He smiled quietly at the shared joke. Sade, unnerved by the implication, kept his face flat.

Minski pointed a languid finger at the wetscreen on the far wall. The picture was too fluid. The excess water sloshed around in its rigid metal frame and interfered with the picture, but it was clear enough.

'A blue box.' Minski interpreted Sade's thoughts. 'A trick box that appears from nowhere and denies the scrutiny of my scanners.'

'It could be witchcraft,' Sade mused. 'Or worse, it could be the British.' He could hear Minski twisting his head in disagreement.

'Mr Pitt and his associates can't do a thing without my knowing of it. Though I must admit, the slogans on the box seem to be in English. And witchcraft? No. This doesn't feel like their machines. This is . . . something rare.' Sade turned just in time to see an ecstatic radiance pass over his son's face. 'Something wonderful, maybe.' Minski beamed with childish passion, an ugly-beautiful smile that lingered in Sade's mind for hours afterwards.

'Go on Father,' Minski said, after a slow, deliberate silence. 'I'll send you someone.'

Sade retreated gracefully, disguising his eagerness to leave the laboratory. Unease growled beneath his ribs. He crushed it, aware that he had won a temporary silence, a moment of relief. Two pairs of eyes watched him leave – one pair of smouldering coals – one pair dead, unseeing, reflecting nothing, but moving in spite of themselves.

Citizen Sade left the laboratory and ascended.

The Pageant.

The dancers came slowly, in small groups, wearing ancient and honourable faces. King Mob was first, then the Ace of Spades, Jack Frost, Chaos and Old Night, Coyote the Trickster, many Kings Under the Hill, Doctor Faustus, Xeno's Arrow, the Wandering Jew, Everyman, two nameless gods of old Carcosa, Deadly Nightshade, Janus, Childe Roland, a gaggle of lesser saints, Don Juan, Kali the Destroyer, Robin i' the Hood, The Lovers, the Devil, the Deep Blue Sea and a hundred others. From pantheons and legends, myths, folklore, alchemy and infant science, they came. Their masks were paper-thin, hard with glue and gaudy paint. As they spilled onto the dancing floor, the colours began to melt, trickling down onto their robes of sackcloth and rotting leather, the many colours merging to form a dirty grey. It was a tawdry, pitiful affair. Only the Three Graces – Liberty, Equality and Fraternity – retained their dignity.

The dancers wheeled slowly, mumbling under the lights, harsh shadows cast on water walls. Tyll Howlglass purred in his dark corner, disappointed with the shabby display and the shabby debate. He stretched his spindly bone fingers, letting them crack with impatience. Presently, Larkspur detached himself from the Pageant by shedding his mask. He beamed grey at his fellow outcast, an intense and nervous shade. Howlglass responded with a burst of sympathy. Larkspur was young and easily disillusioned — still, he loved the archaic ritual of the Pageant, with its foreign masks and alien language.

Larkspur spoke first, in bursts of liquid light.

We're lost, aren't we? I was at Pageant's Heart; I could feel the sway of the debate. Even the Graces are becoming convinced of the need for war.

He was agitated, his aura-body corrupt with sharp colour. Howlglass was in too melancholy a mood to feel any irritation.

We remain subtle.

Larkspur was not reassured.

This rush to conformity . . . It is the System Operator? Not some flaw in ourselves? Howlglass?

Something new has happened, Howlglass hmmed, *in the Paris node. At the heart of the Operator's territory.*

Larkspur strobed.

There's something new under our sun?

The debate was on Pageant's Edge. The others are disturbed by its implications. Would you believe we are commissioned to deal with it?

Howlglass turned his bone fingers to the Pageant. The dancers were still now, their masks blurred beyond meaning. Slumbering ash scarred the dancing floor. The walls had hardened, darkened, into black rib bones forming jutting arches on the ceiling. Howlglass took his first step toward the stilled Heart of the Pageant.

Tyll Howlglass!

The cautious softness of Larkspur's tone alerted him. He turned back.

This is a very public place in which to fail.

Cynic Larkspur, Howlglass pronounced, silencing him.

After a short hesitation, Larkspur moved forward, joining his ally on the floor. They swelled through the ranked dancers, past faceless archetypes and lost gods, to the light pool. Howlglass paused at the pool's uneven coastline, stilled by a sudden fear, the fear that Larkspur was right, that failure now would turn the Pageant against them.

We remain subtle, he said, forming the reassuring slogan with the whole of his aura. Then he spoke to the pool, saying: *Mademoiselle Arouette?*

Their agent's aura formed on the surface of the pool, a cold ebony outline as all human auras were. The sudden sparks of colour bristling in the darkness always puzzled Howlglass. They sharpened his fear.

'What do you want?' Her voice was inappropriately raw in the Pageant hall. Disturbed, the pool's surface rippled.

Our apologies for disturbing you.

'Thank you, yes. What do you want?'

The pool agitated. This was not, Howlglass admitted, a good sign. Larkspur's robes rustled with unease from an embarrassed distance.

Your services are required. There is a thing you must do, Howlglass continued.

'There are many things I must do. Is this important?'

It may prove to be. A machine of strange proportions, a container, has appeared in the city within sight of the Bastille. There is a human creature and something other. Does this interest you?

'No.'

Howlglass became aware of the silence at Pageant's Heart.

They could lend us valuable advantage.

'You heard me the first time.'

Please?

The pool greyed and smoothed, no longer holding the human's reflection. Howlglass stared, his stoicism broken, a cavity opening beneath his ribs. He turned and surveyed the ranks of shoddy, second-hand gods, matching their hollow-eyed stares with a mask of failure.

Nothing further was said. Slowly the revellers began to move away, dribbling off the floor in clusters, robes rustling with disgust. Larkspur, defiantly faithful, remained. A handful of others lingered at Pageant's Edge, among them Fraternity, quietest of the Graces. No others.

The curtain fell. The Pageant closed.

Dodo felt conspicuous in her cloak. Its shape was wrong on her body. The Doctor had looked at her and pronounced that there was nothing outstanding or anachronistic about her appearance, but she had little faith in his judgement and anyway that was the problem. She wanted to be outstanding. She wanted to be seen.

Still, the cloak was warm enough, and more than adequate protection against the half-hearted drizzle. She'd made sure that the Doctor wrapped up well, hoping that he hadn't noticed her sudden undue interest in his health. The night air hadn't improved him. He wheezed in the rain, catching only short breaths and having to lean against the TARDIS door for support. His fingers fumbled round the key, trying without success to slide it into the lock.

'Let me help you,' Dodo said after a minute's wait. Paris's silence was unnerving, unexpected. She was used to bustling cities that never slept, where the encroaching dark was only another excuse to turn up your tranny, or head out. For almost the first time since she had walked into the TARDIS, she had a real feeling of standing in another age – the wrong age – inhaling clearer air than she had any right to breathe.

The Doctor's grasp slipped and the key hit the gutter with a faint clang.

'Let me!' Dodo insisted.

The Doctor was already on his knees, scrabbling wretchedly on the floor. His spine twisted beneath his coat, a bent twig on the verge of breaking. It was a relief when he straightened up, key in hand.

'I am not incapable.' There was no patience in his voice. His anger was directed as much inwardly as at Dodo. 'And I'm not a fool. I simply need time.'

Dodo nodded.

'I'll just wander off,' she said, half-sarcastically. *Wander off, get lost, get captured, get locked up. And if – if – he's managed to lock up the ship by that stage, Don Quixote can stage a rescue. He'll tell me to be careful next.*

'Hmm, be careful,' the Doctor pronounced, a reedy voice emanating from the hunched bundle by the door. 'Napoleon's Paris is as dangerous a place as any we have visited before.'

'Thanks,' she said, feeling guilty as she turned and set off into the darkness, past the derelict houses of wood and stone and shattered glass. She tried to maintain a steady, inconspicuous pace but failed. Every step she took was forced. Every movement and every footstep was out of place in the silent city. The alleyway meandered. The TARDIS was a constant presence in her mind, an imagined fixed point constantly related to her progress through the alleys. There was no point in getting lost.

She turned a corner and mislaid herself. The TARDIS was gone from her mind, washed away in a flood of doubt and confusion. She had reached the lip of the alley, an opening into a wide, clear, high space overlooking the city.

The tower was out of place. Dodo could easily have believed that this was the Paris of the early nineteenth century, but the tower denied that. It was an invader in the city, an ebony shaft stuck into the ground like a splinter. It was completely out of sympathy with its surroundings, proclaiming its own alienness. Not that it was ugly. Pinpoint lights broke its smooth walls, illuminating the dark tower like a morbid Christmas decoration. Its highest point was broken and jagged, just visible in the night clouds.

It jarred though. It was a discordant note in the city. It burned the earth where it stood. The circle of ground around its base was scorched scrubland, half-disguised with ornamentation. No buildings stood close to it, only shells of buildings – cracked open and gutted.

Dodo had a good view of it. She grinned and shook her head.

'Not Paris,' she sighed. She lowered herself onto a dry patch on the border of the shadows and the street. Watching the tower thoughtfully, she began to rock back and forth, grinning determinedly. 'Not 1804. What a shame.'

The Doctor pocketed his key at last and tapped on the TARDIS's solid door.

'Excellent,' he said to himself, punctuating the remark with a giggle. 'Well, Dodo, I hope you remember this in future. I am not as feeble as I, hmm, uh, appear.'

Dodo, of course, had gone. She had told him, very clearly. He remembered. Yes. He remembered quite well . . . A scowl played on his face, a twitch of defiance against his fading memory and weakening body. Deciding that it would be wisest to wait for Dodo to return, he hobbled over to the notice on the wall to inspect it more closely. He read it once, hastily, without thinking.

There was a pause. He read again, studying this time, weighing the words and meanings in his mind. His walking-stick hung loose in one hand, no longer remembered or required. The Doctor had found a focus for his failing energies. A puzzle to ponder, a problem to solve.

'Monstrous,' he whispered, placing a steady hand on the wall beside the bill. 'Yes, exactly the word.' He returned to the document one last time, to check that it was genuine. And, if genuine, then also monstrous.

If genuine, the bill had been issued by the Committee of Public Safety, ten years after the last, bloody gasps of the Revolution. The name and signature of the First Deputy were unfamiliar: 'Minski'.

The contents of the bill didn't interest the Doctor. It was simply, as Dodo had said, a warning about disease carried in dirty water. But the language was the rhetoric of the Revolution, hardly the tone of Napoleon's regime, five years into his rule. He scoured the notice, searching for more clues, his weak eyes sharpened by mystery and fear. His reading glasses remained in his pocket. There was, however, nothing more to be found. The bill was chillingly straightforward.

Somehow the course of history had been turned, as though its flow had been dammed. Monstrous was the right word. The Doctor doubted that this new course had been set upon more than a century before. The landscape had changed, and the differences were unsettling, but the terrain was still vaguely familiar. The flood could be reversed, the dam breached and time's true river restored. The Doctor pressed his fingertips together, fingers splaying as he wondered where to begin.

He was still ruminating when an impertinent hand fell on his shoulder. He turned, expecting Dodo and preparing to admonish her for creeping up on him. It was not Dodo's hand. It sat offensively at the end of a hairy, muscular arm. None of the faces the Doctor saw as he turned belonged to Dodo. A good sign, he thought, a sign that she might still be free.

They wore uniforms, or parts of uniforms matched together with working jackets and coarse shirts. They wore tricolour ribbons, lending them authority. They carried muskets, lending them power. These were the only items that mattered. Their faces ranged from grim introspection to callow amusement. The man who held the Doctor was smiling, not without sympathy.

The Doctor decided to bluster. The perfect response leapt to mind.

'What is the meaning of this? I demand you release me immediately!' He barked this with an officer's voice, resonant with cruel charm. His tongue chose the worst moment to give up on him, lying dead in his throat. He spat gibberish at his captors. At the back of the group, one man sniggered and waved a dismissive hand.

'Dad,' said their leader, his hand still resting to the side of the Doctor's throat. 'It's very dark and the curfew holds. You're under arrest in the name of France.'

'Leave him alone, he's just a soppy old git.' It was the man who had waved who spoke. He was leaning against the TARDIS door. None of the men seemed to have noticed the ship, which the Doctor considered a blessing.

'If I let one curfew-breaker go free because he's not all there, then this time tomorrow Paris will be crowded with babbling lunatics. We must,' the leader concluded, 'be scrupulous.' He huddled against the Doctor, pulling him into a conspiratorial hug and speaking in a false whisper that everyone could hear.

'There are still a few hours before the magistrates sit. That's time enough to come up with an effective excuse, so you might yet keep that ugly head on your shoulders. You've got a good act. It'll impress them.' He made an exaggerated wink and stepped back.

The Doctor glowered defiantly, clutching his lapels and tilting his head in an expression of arrogance. The effect was wasted on the soldiers, who exploded with guttural laughter.

'Get the cart and the gear,' their captain announced when the laughter had died away. His tone had changed, signalling an end to the joke. 'And have someone wax the Bastille. Tell Citizen Minski we've got his trick box.'

He patted the side of the TARDIS, appropriating it with this simple gesture. The Doctor's face trembled; he was impotent in the face of casual authority, angry and now afraid.

There was no clock in Sade's chambers. He rarely needed one.

He sat on the edge of the bed staring at the woman Minski had sent to him. She was a blonde, as promised, a member of the Bastille guard whom he recognized vaguely. She looked strange without the uniform, and without the look of impassive boredom that all the guards wore. She wore a robe, wrapped hastily round her shoulders with none of her soldier's precision. Since her arrival, her features had moved smoothly from bleary-eyed resignation to pure terror. That pleased Sade, as did the fact that she was solidly pretty, without being beautiful. She was excellent raw material. An honest face, framed by curls. A young face, almost a little girl's. A trembling face, faking calm. He gave her a cool, shattered grin.

He kept her still and silent on the fringe of the bed chamber for as long as possible, weighing her in his gaze. He was building up a steady, mediocre passion, but his true fire was dampened. Once away from his son, his doubt had resurfaced, larger and uglier than before. He tried vainly to attribute this melancholy to the darkness of his room, the austere decorations, the depressing architecture. In truth he felt haunted, pursued by an anonymous spectre that was beyond human definition.

'Come and sit on the bed,' he said, blandly, at last, tugging at the collar of his own robe. The girl blanched.

'You have a ferocious reputation, Citizen Sade.' She had a pleasant voice. Imagine her shrieking that name. Imagine her blindfolded, shrieking that name. Imagine her blindfolded and bound, shrieking that name. She would be near pure-animal then, her quivering mouth the last vestige of humanity.

It was hopeless. He felt no better. He tried a joke.

'You've been told I'm a pain in the arse?'

She almost laughed, but lapsed instead into quivering terror.

'I hear stories,' she suggested, retreating a little in fear of sudden death. 'You're a dangerous man, and this is an unsafe time of night.'

'I've never killed anyone. Not in the boudoir, at any rate.'

'No, but it's said that every woman you've had is missing something when you've finished. They're incomplete, in body or in their heads.'

Sade shrugged. He tried another approach.

'What's your name? Your – first name?'

'Juliette.' She spat it from between chattering teeth.

Sade smiled, recalling another Juliette, who was vice incarnate. 'That's not very appropriate. Why are you here?'

'Citizen Minski sent me.' She straightened as she mentioned the name, her fear turning into something defiant.

Sade smiled. Here was a line he could draw from her, something to exploit. 'Ah yes, my son, a very successful man. I'm very proud of him.'

'We all are, citizen,' Juliette chimed, nodding in agreement, her fear giving way to enthusiasm and a little excitement. 'Every man and woman on the Bastille staff. We live for him. We die for him.'

'That's duty,' Sade suggested.

Juliette's face twitched, a slight show of disrespect. 'More than duty, Citizen,' she insisted. 'We're not compelled to cover our rooms with his image, but we do. We're not compelled to march on 10 Thermidor in his honour, but we do. We're not compelled to love him.'

Sade was fascinated. He had never thought of Minski this way.

'Why?' he asked.

'Because.' Juliette proclaimed, as if that was all the explanation that was needed. 'Because! Because he purged France of the Jacobins in the space of an hour, with only one company of men behind him! Because he's right. Because he *is*! He's the Celebrity! He's the last Frenchman!'

Sade was startled by this fanaticism. It burned on her face, in her eyes, turning frightened plainness into an inferno of beauty.

'He's not French,' he whispered, a calming tone. 'You know that?'

To his astonishment, Juliette leaped across the room and sank onto the bed beside him, when only a minute ago she would have slit her own throat rather than move a step closer. This was a strange madness his son had inflicted on her. Minski was the source of most insanity these days.

'There are stories,' Juliette whispered, as if imparting a terrible secret, 'that he isn't human, in the way that you and I are. It's said that he's the child of Russian giants, kidnapped from their home in the heart of the volcano when he was a baby. The prince that stole him kept him hostage in a tomb no larger than a kettle, so that he would remain stunted among humans, so the giants wouldn't recognize their son if they came hunting him. But they didn't. The prince grew tired of feeding him, so he was sold to a circus, from which you would eventually rescue him.'

Sade almost laughed at this hopeless melodrama. The only thing that kept him sober was the sure knowledge that most of these lies had been fabricated by Minski himself, and embroidered in the telling. There were probably a good half-dozen more ludicrous variations circulating in Paris alone. He wasn't going to kill the myth.

'He's not really my son, not by blood. All my blood-children are dead.' He felt nothing as he spoke. His dead family seemed like ghosts from another lifetime, half-known creatures who were never truly alive. 'I adopted him, as you say. I taught him everything I knew.' He paused. 'He taught me more.'

Juliette nodded, her eyes shining. Sade studied her carefully, wondering if this could be sly trickery. Obsession with things — with stories or invented gods — was a madness he could understand. Obsession with people was another matter. But no, she genuinely believed. Genuinely felt, too.

He lay back down on the bed, then turned over and crawled snake-like on his stomach until he was out of her sight. The muscles in his face relaxed, no longer struggling to keep up with her faith. He pulled the robe from

Juliette's shoulders, baring thin white flesh and bony blades. He placed a hand on her neck, fingers stretching out to tickle under her chin. She began to shake again.

'Why are you afraid of me?' he asked, gently. 'Minski is my son in all but blood.'

'Yes,' she agreed, meekly.

'But you love him, and you're terrified of me.' Sade slipped a dagger from its sheath inside his robe and applied it crudely to the back of Juliette's gown, hacking at it down the length of her spine, tearing away strips and layers of cloth.

'Yes.'

'You'd let him do this to you.'

'Yes.'

Sade slashed at the gown, reducing it to rags and ribbons.

'But you're not him!' Juliette was babbling, terrified, protesting against the inevitable. 'You're Sade! You're Citizen Sade!'

Sade shook his head.

'No,' he said calmly, finally at peace with himself. 'I am the Marquis de Sade. I am a monster.'

2

Carry on Chopping

The soldiers moved the TARDIS onto the tumbril with little difficulty. Two of their number struggled to lift the police box, but most of the strain was concentrated on a system of motorized pulleys mounted on the cart. The Doctor rested against the wall and studied the operation.

There was an engine built into the tumbril, its lively mechanism exposed in places. Half-hidden pistons flexed apart and slammed together, gears rattled, metal cogs spun wildly, setting sparks flying through the machinery. A chimney jutted from the floor, pumping heavy gasps of coal-smoke into the night. There were no horses – the engine served more than one purpose.

The machine intrigued the Doctor. He wondered if its engineers had fully grasped the principles of the design they were working to. It was too ambitious to be a product of this time. The sight of it, of its *wrongness*, hardened his resolve.

He glanced down at his hands, folded across his stomach. They were still, steady, precise once again. The night air was warm against his skin and good to breathe. His mind felt clear and sharp again. Mind and body united behind him once more.

Men stood around him, sweating in the wet-hot night. Their muskets or pistols bristled, close to hand but lowered. They didn't think him dangerous enough to guard properly. The Doctor had decided against escape though. He wanted to be captured, to be taken to the heart of the paradox.

Lights ruptured the gloom. Soldier-shapes grew out of

the darkness, shambling warily towards the first patrol. The new patrol was much the same as the old, dressed in the same rag-uniforms. They were civilians, the Doctor guessed, volunteers or recruits of the Revolution. Their features were flattened in the harsh light of their lanterns – electric light, judging from the dangerous sizzle the tubes were giving off. They had a prisoner of their own – a tall, blonde woman whose sullen features were obscured by trailing strands of hair. There was an open wound over her left eye.

The new patrol's captain joined the leader of the first by the cart, where they exchanged curt, unheard sentences. The woman was prodded along at gunpoint, before a sudden blow caught her on the shoulders and sent her sprawling against the alley wall. The Doctor reached out, snatching at her shoulder and steadying her. She murmured something French, something grateful.

He caught a glimpse of her eyes, of round, blue, dried-out pools. They were innocent, helpless eyes that reminded the Doctor of . . . of a human woman he had once travelled with. He frowned, disturbed by his capacity to forget, and by the despair he had seen in the woman's eyes. She had cast her gaze downwards and half-closed her eyelids, disguising the pain. Blood oozed on her forehead, a thick patch of red that hid the wound.

'And who are you?' he asked gently.

The woman glanced upwards, giving him a strange stare, as if his question had been incoherent or meaningless. Her face flexed as she struggled with the idea. 'S– Sophie,' she said at last, smiling uncomfortably. 'Sophie.'

'Well,' the Doctor continued, his tone even and undisturbed. 'I am the Doctor, and –' He broke off, surprised to see Sophie flinch and fall back, despair translated into terror on her face.

The closest soldier was smiling, weighing a pistol in his hand. 'Not *that* Doctor,' he said, drawing a finger across his throat. 'You'll meet him tomorrow.'

The Doctor tutted and busied himself with Sophie's

wound. She trembled, but didn't resist, as he applied his handkerchief to wiping away the blood. It was a moment before he noticed the clean, unbroken skin beneath the stain. It was another moment before he placed his fingers to her forehead, finding the scarlet patch light and sticky to touch.

It smelled of sugar and water and raw vegetables.

It was red dye.

Dalville hugged the shadows at the alley corner, placing himself carefully out of sight of the soldiers. He made a cloak of the darkness, letting it cling round him like a costume. He became a shadow in the heart of shadows.

The patrol seemed unmoving from this distance. They were thin ghosts, blanched and dazzled by the electric blaze. They were dangerous ghosts, ghosts in great numbers, ghosts with guns. Dalville felt reassured by the shape of a flintlock under his coat. It was a wooden prop, but at least it was there.

The air beside him rustled, betraying impatient movement. Dalville glanced at his companion. A rare temper was fluttering across Bressac's face, hardening the normally vague and waifish features. His eyes were whittled points, focused on the scene before them.

Dalville spoke softly, calm words quickly lost to the breeze. 'Who do you think the old man is?'

'Another victim.' Bressac's voice strained to sound hard and hateful. It didn't work, and he soon lapsed back into the customary wistfulness. 'He moves like a chicken. We used to have one just like him on the farm. Scrawny, tough thing – if there'd been any meat on it, it would have tasted like leather.'

Dalville made weary nods of his head. 'This chicken? Did you cut its head off? No, please don't tell me . . .'

He looked back at the soldiers, who had succeeded in their task of loading a tall, bulky container onto a steam-cart. He wondered whether there was anything valuable or important in the box, or if this was just a strange and pointless exercise. It didn't matter. The steam-cart hissed and rolled away, heading in the direction of the New Bastille. The dry, smoky atmosphere that had filled the alley cleared with its departure, but Dalville refused to relax. He kept his eye on the remaining soldiers – on the old man, who had suddenly become animated and agitated – and on Sophie, whom he might never see alive again.

He looked away, upwards, searching for the stars.

'Four of them went off with the cart,' Bressac ventured. 'Maybe five . . .'

'Still too many.' He hmmed, not bothering to look at Bressac. 'And you know whose fault this is, don't you? Who had her up and running about Paris at this time of night? Need I ask?'

He could hear the loyal frown forming on Bressac's brow.

'Sorry,' Dalville added, calmer, shaking his head. 'Sorry.'

The patrol had gathered around their prisoners, forming another, oddly static scene against the alley wall. Deep ragged shadows flickered around them. Dalville watched for a moment, imagining striding into the middle of the crowd to demand Sophie's release. It would be worth it, just to send the ripples through *their* moment, to unsettle their authority. That would be something worth losing his head over.

He was disturbed by a sharp nudge from Bressac's bony elbow. Alerted, he glanced up, just in time to catch sight of the woman. She stood at the mouth of the alley, caught between the shadows and the light. She was not quite a woman, but no longer a child. Her hair had an unusual, regular cut that might have sat better on a boy's head. She was staring at the soldiers and their prisoners, smiling foolishly. Dalville stood for a moment, confused by her appearance. The girl's grin cracked. She moved forward, lips forming a cry of distress.

Dalville sprang silently in her path and snatched her into the shadows. He clamped his free hand across her mouth

35

before she could scream. Their faces were shoved together, uncomfortably close. She was prettier, close up, than he would have guessed from the distance. She had a charming face, full of childish naïvety that had not been extinguished by experience. Her eyes were glassy and afraid. She smelled *fresh*. A rich, soapy fragrance clung round her. It was a small detail, but one that stuck in his mind.

The silence ached. Dalville's fingers ached. (The girl's face ached.)

Soft footsteps approached, at last, followed by Bressac's voice.

'It's all right,' he said. 'They've gone.'

Dalville breathed, as if for the first time. He took his hand from the woman's mouth, rubbing his damp palm on the side of his coat. She flashed an imploring smile at him, displaying crooked rows of unnaturally white teeth.

'Please,' she muttered, 'they've taken my friend . . . the Doctor . . .' Her accent was odd, definitely not from any part of France he knew. It had a pleasant ring, whatever it was.

'The old chicken – man.' Bressac corrected himself distantly. 'Sorry.'

The woman nodded.

'They'll take him straight to the Bastille, and from there it's only a few steps to the guillotine. You couldn't stop them, not now.'

'The Bastille?' She seemed confused by this point. 'This *is* Paris, then?'

'True. She's not been herself lately, but she remains Paris.'

The girl nodded thoughtfully. Dalville glanced at Bressac, looking for help.

His friend shrugged, a glazed amusement prowling on his face. 'These are hostile times,' he chimed in from a distance.

'We're friendly enough. Too friendly sometimes . . .'

The woman's grin grew, becoming warmer, becoming friendlier. This was her face as it was meant to be seen,

36

glowing with rare strengths – simplicity, honesty and plain pretty innocence.

'I'm sorry,' Dalville said, dropping the smile and hardening his tone at last. 'The best you can do for your friend is to go to the tower in the morning and petition for his release. Nothing more.'

'They have one of our friends,' Bressac interjected. 'We're in much the same position as you. Her name was Sophie. I, incidentally, am Bressac, and this is Dalville, of the Fantômas Wandering Players.'

Pompous, typical Bressac, shuffling politely in female company.

'He means we're actors,' Dalville explained, 'of no fixed abode.' He took the woman's hand and then kissed it extravagantly, setting an embarrassed red flickering across her lovely features.

'Dodo –' she began, breaking off quickly. 'I mean, Dorothea. Dorothea Cha– Chaplette.'

'Charmed.'

'Nice to meet you,' Bressac added briskly.

'Perhaps, if you have no other arrangement,' Dalville ventured, 'you might like to share our hospitality for the rest of the night? No strings,' he added gently. 'Just as a favour to someone in a similar predicament?'

A wary light danced in Dorothea's eyes and she chewed her lip thoughtfully.

'OK,' she said, grinning brightly. 'Thanks.'

'And please, for the moment, don't worry about your friend.'

'Oh, I won't,' she said, enthusiastically, her voice full of faith and devoid of irony. 'He's in his element now. He could talk his way out of anything.'

Dalville conjured up his memory of the feeble old man. He looked again at Dorothea, radiating innocence. He looked at his palm, finding crooked teeth marks dug half-heartedly into the skin.

At last, a real challenge!

* * *

The viruses sat quivering in their thin glass tube, indifferent to the outside world. They resembled maggots — fat black maggots bloated to bursting point. They were, Minski thought, the only thing he had ever truly created. He imagined that he should love them, or at least find them beautiful. No. They were ugly things, fat, with scorched skins. They were a hideous means to a beautiful end, and he felt nothing for them.

He clasped the tube between finger and thumb and held the grubs up to the light. That set them moving. They wriggled away, swarming desperately to either end of the tube, escaping the sudden burning brightness. They were designed to hide in the shadows, burrowing blindly through wet darkness.

Minski tapped the tube gently, knocking one of the maggots from the end. It was still alive after hitting the ground, disorientated and wriggling frantically. Minski stepped on it, not clumsily but with the edge of his boot, slicing it into two neat, dead segments.

The severed head of the traitor gazed at him from across the laboratory floor, eyes bulging out of cold blue flesh. They flicked down to stare at his boots.

Minski was distracted by a low mumble from behind him. Half-cautiously, half in irritation, he turned, in time to see the woman on the operating table tremble restlessly, her head rocking from side to side. A panic stung him, as he realized that the woman was half-awake and trying to rise.

Clutching the fragile tube in soft, cupped hands, he trotted across the room to intercept her. He arrived too late, finding her eyes open, staring softly at the world around her. She was a young woman, one of the youngest he had ever operated on, and her fresh, just-woken expression drove a nail of guilt into him.

'Citizen,' he said, in as gentle a voice as he could muster. The woman smiled, then giggled, then began to shake her head, knocking tangles of hair over her face.

'Citizen!' she snorted. 'You can use my name now,

38

honestly you can . . .' Her words slurred and shifted, merging together. Minski breathed with relief, plucking out his moment of guilt. The effect of the sedatives held. The girl was conscious but still addled. She swung back towards him, eyes ablaze with horror and realization.

'Minski!' she screamed in a shrill, embarrassing voice that broke into sobs as soon as it had begun. 'I'm cut. Help me, I'm . . . I'm bleeding.' Her body began to thrash beneath the light cover, tearing against the bonds that held her down. 'I can't move! I can't *move*!'

Minski grabbed her face, pressing his thumb and fingertips into her cheek, stroking gently to calm her. Her skin was dry and hot – uncomfortable to touch – but he persevered. He drew his face closer and began to hum, whispering lullaby words into her ear. His voice was a taut, powerful weapon, turning and twisting exactly as he desired it. It soothed the girl back to the threshold of sleep.

'Do you love me, Minski?' she purred, body still now, head back on the slab surface, eyes fluttering heavily.

'Yes,' he said, adding a forceful sincerity to his tone. He kissed her once on the lips, tasting blood in her mouth.

It was strange, he thought, that he could fake this so easily. He couldn't remember a time when he had known any sort of affection. He had always been First Deputy, at the dreadful, isolated heights of French society. Before the coup, before the rule of Minski, there was nothing.

His eyelids fell, blocking out the room and the light. It was black behind his eyes, black and empty. Shapes grew to fill the vacuum, emerging from the dark. Old dreams blurred into one smooth vision.

There was the water, the river of my birth, the ocean of my becoming. I was not Minski then, I was nameless. I was a mass then, without reason or feeling. I grew in darkness, deep in the waters where the world crushes and every sound is flattened.

Get out of my head.

Other shapes floated in the water, living in the water,

*speaking through the water, mingling with the water. I am aware
of them, of their wishes, of their power and their plans. They
were shallow beings, I remember, not creatures of the deeps, not
like myself. They didn't feel for me. I wasn't something that
could be felt for then. Not Minski, not then. I was nothing.*

*Then I rose, towards the light, shooting up through the
river through headier atmospheres. Then I exploded, smashed
through the surface of the ocean. No longer cramped by the
darkness and the wet, no longer confined, I found the light. It
hung from the rocky roof of this new cave, a radiant beacon that
shaped the cave walls. It was my first contact with this dry world.
It transfigured me.*

Get out of my head!

I was Minski then. I became Minski.

*The beings are still there, in the water. They're rising, rising
to drag me back under. I shall merge with the water, cease to be
Minski, lose myself forever. They're under the water –* in my
head!

His eyes snapped open, suddenly furious.

The cave was still there, its walls distant, uneven shadows.
The ocean was still there. Shapes still flitted under the
surface, clawing up at him. He froze the water to ice with a
glare, turning its surface hard and dark. The hidden creatures writhed helplessly, caught like insects under glass.

'Get out of my head.' He was careful not to shout. He
made his voice as calm and as dangerous as possible,
letting the words smash against the walls of this illusion.
His hand leapt protectively to the chain that he wore
round his neck. Cracks broke in the ebony cave walls.
Hard, iron rods broke through into the damp, like
splinters jutting out of broken flesh. Plump maggot-
bodies slithered inside the rods.

'I won't be controlled!'

He stopped, finding himself staring at the grey, tilting
ceiling of his laboratory. He'd expelled the vision, driven
the creatures out of his mind. Victory left him feeling
light headed. He threw his face downwards, forced his
jaws as far apart as possible, and vomited onto the lab

floor. He wiped the flecks away from his mouth, feeling cleaner for the experience.

The virus-tube was clenched in his fist, thankfully unbroken. He wondered how close he had come to shattering the glass. It wouldn't have mattered. There were at least twenty more tubes, ready to use, and a hundred other fat black maggots growing in the incubators. His eyes fell onto the face of the sleeping woman, wondering whether she had heard his tirade, but not caring. There were already numerous apocrypha about his life floating around France. If one prostitute started assuring her clients that the First Deputy was prone to fits and hallucinations, it would be simply another story, absorbed into the myth.

He pulled back the sheet that covered her body, revealing the hole he had made. It was a messy incision, weeping blood, the closest he could get to her nerve centres without killing her. He placed the tube against the cut and snapped it open thoughtlessly. The maggots broke free, excited by the warm flesh-stench of the girl's body. They vanished into the wound, digging down towards the closest nourishment. Minski nodded and set about sewing the wound closed. He had small fingers and a delicate eye. His stitches were precise.

The girl gasped suddenly, a sleeping shriek forming on her lips. Her body tensed, then relaxed, and she slept on undisturbed. She would leave the Bastille tomorrow, return to her home and her work and – save for the occasional twinge over the next few days – would feel completely unaffected by her night with the First Deputy. Minski was pleased with the subtlety.

'They haven't given up.'

Minski looked up from his sewing, eyes darting round the room for the source of the voice. They met dead, sightless eyes, staring from the severed head of the traitor. She wore a grim, humourless corpse-face.

'They haven't given up, I said.'

Minski crooked his head to one side, offering the head

41

a lopsided smile. 'You speak for them now?'

'They've made me their mouthpiece,' the head continued, cold blue lips moving more naturally than they had done when his machinery had been the only animating force. They were goading him. He refused to rise to the bait.

'I see. Not content with sending me lurid daydreams, they've set talking heads loose on me,' Minski said evenly. 'What are *you* going to do, talk me to death?' He checked himself quickly, afraid that he was showing his anger. Twice now, he'd been assailed in the heart of his territory.

'Some of them would prefer to reason with you,' the head continued.

'True. Their numbers are dwindling, aren't they? A few ineffectual dancers on the edge of the masque? Is that your constituency?'

The head said nothing for a moment. It was brooding, stung by his words.

'I'll always be here.' Its eyes flicked downwards, gesturing at the heavy machinery on which it was impaled. 'My voice will be constant. I'll bombard you with reason and rhetoric.'

Minski allowed a sickly smile onto his lips. He paced towards the dead head, slipping the chain from round his neck and holding it before the ghost's eyes just long enough for it to be recognized. A chunk of metal hung from the chain, delicate and complex, gleaming with its own light. The dead head stared, lines of frustration forming on its brow.

'I have been looking,' he said, 'for somewhere safe to keep this.'

Minski popped it between the head's bloodless lips. He reached for his needle, digging its point into the flesh above the mouth, drawing a single drop of grey, congealed blood. Corpse eyes stared at him, fixing him with a frustrated stare.

A good try, Minski reflected, as he set to work sewing.

* * *

Garce hated Paris. He hated the stench of the city, the hideous architecture, the foolish citizens and the tortuous foreign geography. His skin prickled when surrounded by the overwhelming *Frenchness* of the city. There was nothing here that he recognized, nothing decent, nothing solid.

He wanted to be here when Paris burned. The flames would sweep away both the twisting, mean-minded streets and the Revolution's clumsy attempts at monumental architecture. The fathers and mothers and children of Paris would roast in their beds. The black ships would hang over the city, blasting the tallest towers with Hellfire. The Bastille would be the first to fall. Garce hoped he would be there, watching from some safe vantage point with a bottle of cool wine in one hand and a leptosome street-girl in the other. These, Garce suspected, would be the only things worth salvaging from the conflagration.

He pressed his back against the door, disgusted by the damp wood that was staining the back of his coat. Weak French woodwork, prone to rot in the slightest damp. He glanced out of the mouth of the doorway, then checked his pocket-watch, irritated by the lateness of the patrol.

He turned back to his companion, who leaned with calculated elegance against the wall and grinned foolishly. Sir Randolph Eging pursued the art of the fop. He spoke casually with an affected sing-song voice and a pronounced lisp, a strange sound emerging from his age-worn face and broken teeth. He spoke eloquently too, turning his religion and the service of his king into a devious philosophy. Garce considered himself a pragmatist and felt that Randolph's company should be thoroughly embarrassing. In spite of himself, he found it inspiring.

'Minski,' Randolph was saying – no, not saying, *reciting*, as though it were poetry, 'is a priest of reason. He's a damn silly fool, so diseased with enlightenment that he can't see the real world in front of his face. Are you following this, Garce m'dear?'

Garce grunted and maintained his vigil.

'Take bodies, m'dear. Minski says that he's studied bodies and found that everyone's made of the same stuff, itself built on a design of two taut springs, coiled and locked together. Damn fool. They're *serpents*, two little devil-snakes wound together. It proves that Satan lives in our blood.'

'Why are they wrapped together?' Garce frowned. 'The snakes?'

'Why do any two creatures coil round each other?' Randolph replied. He broke into his distinct laugh — a rattling, filthy cacophony that broke through the fakeness of his fop-voice.

Garce bared savage teeth.

'Blood and water,' Randolph continued, his tone sinking into the deep, harsh growl that was his real voice. 'That's where He lives. In water.' He tensed suddenly, a raised finger trembling over his lips. Alerted, Garce stuck his head round into the street, in time to see the Revolutionary guards turn their corner onto the thoroughfare. He swore bluntly.

The patrol had snared two prisoners. The first was a hawk-faced old man who strutted arrogantly, as though this were his city and these soldiers were a guard of honour. As he turned the corner, he stopped to sniff at the air, making a pretence of allowing the closest guards to catch up with him. The second prisoner was a decent-looking bitch who stumbled more than she walked. There was little to choose between them.

'Which one?' he asked. 'The old man, I'd hope.'

'The woman.'

'I can think of better uses for her,' Garce protested. Randolph shook his head.

'Look at them. Look at the way they hold themselves. There's no fear in him — not of decapitation, nor of death, nor of oblivion. But look at her — she knows what's coming and she's terrified. And that's what we need,' he insisted. 'Blood made sticky by fear.'

He already had the weapon in his hands, unfolding it ready to wear. Only Randolph was prepared to use it. The black flesh mask was a gift from their masters, a living weapon, a parasite. Garce had worn it only once, and it had left him weak and frightened. It had a silent presence that pricked at his soul. The sight of it sickened him. It was a hellishly powerful thing.

Blood made sticky by fear.

Garce thought for a moment, his features first grim then rueful.

'OK,' he said. 'The woman.'

He had the first part, the active part, the minor part. It was a flamboyant, diversionary role. He waited until the last of the soldiers had passed, slipped the first of his pistols from their harness, stepped from his hiding place, coughed and fired at the back of the trailing guard. The nameless man slumped to the ground with a disappointing silence.

The shot alerted the others, soldiers and prisoners alike. Garce already had the second of his pistols to hand, and put another ball into the closest soldier's skull. He died spectacularly, one half of his face exploding with gore, the other wearing an expression somewhere between surprise and resignation. He fell comically, legs flailing, onto his back.

There was something deeply unsatisfying about this kind of murder.

The old man stepped towards Garce, clearly expecting a rescue. Garce disappointed him by planting the muzzle of the still-smoking flintlock into his face. He collapsed, stunned, and was dismissed from Garce's mind. Garce seized the woman by her shoulder, dragging her in front of him as a shield against musket-fire. The other soldiers were already on their knees, their gun-barrels shaking as they aimed.

The next moment dragged infinitely, packed with the fear that Randolph might not appear. In that case, the musketeers would fire and kill both the woman and himself. Then the world would go on, careless of their deaths.

Randolph stepped forward before they could fire. He moved without haste. The deathmask covered the whole of his head, smothering his features into tight shiny darkness, but it had to be Randolph. No one else had ever worn the mask so comfortably. Familiar eyes, made hateful by their context, peered out through the metal-rimmed eye-slits.

The soldiers' guns turned away, training on this new presence. They had sensed something dangerous here. Garce could see the mix of fluid confusion and terror in their eyes. The woman he held was shaking, babbling desperate nonsense. He tightened his grip round her waist.

Randolph smiled. It was visible beneath the smooth, solid blackness. He spoke, a silent senseless word.

The soldiers screamed in unison, in harmony, in a chorus of ignorant fear and pain. Harsh white light blazed from their eyes and mouths. Their skins turned first red, then black, then hardened and split open, unable to contain the Hellfire within them. The street flared, lit by howling torches that burned out quickly and smelled of roast pork. They left only ashes and charred uniforms behind them.

Randolph tore the mask from his face, coughing a small ball of blood onto the ground. It was the only sign that the destruction had weakened him. Garce offered him a cool smile, then turned his attention to the woman. She had slumped in his arms, fainting so quietly he had barely noticed. He slung the body over his shoulder, surprised at the ease of it. She was as light as a gutted corpse already, but slightly warmer and more exciting to the touch.

'At least we don't have to drug her,' he remarked.

Randolph chuckled. 'She was destined to play a victim,' he observed, sagely.

He looked back once, to see the old man lying by the

46

wall close to the remains of his captors. He was unconscious, or dead, or simply lying low. It didn't matter.

Such a shame, such a great shame.

Bressac and Dalville were good people. Dodo knew that instinctively, which was just as well as she had no better reason for trusting them. They seemed friendly, in very different ways. Dalville was an energetic talker, capable of rattling on endlessly about nothing – he had done nothing else on the walk back to his home. Bressac seemed naturally taciturn, lurking awkwardly on the edge of the conversation, saying little but offering weak smiles whenever their eyes met.

She wished she knew more about them. Most of Dalville's conversation was spur-of-the-moment comment and second-hand jokes. Dodo didn't question him very far, but was glad of his company. He could laugh, shrug and whitter on about anything that occurred to him. He put a hand on her shoulder and squeezed with unconscious friendliness. He was the most normal – most human – thing she had found since leaving the TARDIS. Everything else in Paris was strange and wrong.

Dalville's chatter gave her a chance to piece together some of the history she'd missed, some of the reasons behind the wrongness. One name that cropped up again and again, crammed into an off-hand remark about the weather or the curfew, was Minski. He had ruled France, Dodo discovered gradually, for almost ten years. No other politicians or soldiers cropped up in the conversation. Minski was a single-handed tyrant.

She knew that was wrong. History wasn't her strong point – one of many things, she conceded, that wasn't her strong point – but she *knew* it was wrong. The French Revolution was still in progress, and that was wrong. The Bastille had been rebuilt too, on Minski's instructions. That was definitely wrong. There was another name too, or a title that passed as a name – the Marquis de Sade. It was familiar, but Dodo couldn't place it.

The Doctor would sort it all out. Probably.

Dalville's home was parked on a blackened wasteland, crushed between the plain grey walls of two warehouses. Clusters of crumbling, scorched bricks sat guard round the edge of the site. Caravans were parked in a haphazard order around the field – brutal, functional and wooden, decorated hastily in thin, freely mixing colours. The same name appeared on several, emblazoned like a warning-word in red: 'Fantômas'.

The site was half-awake. A fire was smouldering and dying in the heart of the caravans, illuminating dark human shapes flitting through the spaces between vehicles. There were other lights dotted around the wasteland, oil lights hanging from the side of caravans or left free-standing on crates or piles of stone. Dodo shuddered as they got nearer, realizing that she was walking into a fire hazard. The lamps gave off a sweet, musty stench that caused her to splutter until Dalville thumped her on the back.

'That's a typical reaction,' he told her, languidly.

'I didn't expect . . . .' Dodo said. 'I mean. Isn't there supposed to be a curfew on?' She winced, realizing that she'd made another slip.

'Well, yes,' Dalville replied, 'but the patrols don't bother us on site. They know we're protected.'

'Protected? By what?'

It was Bressac who answered. He pointed at the Paris skyline, at the black tower that jutted from the city, dominating it.

Dodo felt a lot better when she got inside.

The interior of Bressac and Dalville's caravan was as minimalist as Dodo had been expecting. The first room was cramped, square and undecorated, bare boards on display everywhere. The ground quivered beneath her feet, tortured wood shrieking as she shifted her weight. Three makeshift chairs and a table sat in the middle of the room, squeezing out the space. The wood was a warm varnished brown, friendlier than the cool white boards that made up the room. Battered, shapeless cushions were stacked on the chairs, coarse feathers sticking at odd angles from tears and holes. The table top was hidden beneath a sprawl of leather-bound books, flaking manuscript paper and half-empty mugs. The neck of a dark bottle poked out from beneath a pile of paper and an abandoned jacket. Someone – Dalville, Dodo guessed – had tried to bury this room in cheerful clutter. They'd succeeded.

Bressac lit a lamp, filling the room with oil fumes, much tighter and headier in the confined caravan. Dodo's attention was elsewhere though. There were clothes, costumes probably, hanging from a hook by an inner door. Real late-eighteenth-century clothes! Luxurious, colourful and bristling with detail, not like the drab brown things that the actors were wearing.

'Wow,' she said, reaching to touch the cloth and not quite believing the texture that rubbed against her fingers. 'This is great!'

'It's cheap rubbish,' Dalville told her, treading carelessly on her illusion. He checked the mugs on the table, tipping the dregs onto the floor where they dribbled away between the boards. 'Times are hard. Wine?'

'Oh, uh, yes, thanks.' Dodo replied. Why not? Be a devil!

'That's cheap too. Cigar? Snuff?'

'Er, no thanks.'

'That's good. We haven't got any of either.'

Dodo snatched a powdered, formal wig from amongst the costumes and dropped it on her head. 'How do I look?' she asked.

Bressac didn't manage to suppress an embarrassed smirk. Dalville looked up from pouring the wine, and gave her a calm, curious stare, a deep-thinking stare.

'You look gorgeous.' He drawled the words, adding emphasis to them. Dodo flushed, unnerved rather than embarrassed, and removed the wig. Dalville held the brim-full mug out to her silently. Equally silently she took it. It was a bitter, red wine that stung her mouth. She smiled, enjoying the taste despite its sharpness.

A curious, frozen silence entered the room. Dalville poured the dregs of the bottle into the other two mugs. The dribble of the wine was the only sound to punctuate the scene. Bressac stood in a corner, eyes flickering awkwardly round the room. They were a strange couple, starkly colourful against their austere surroundings.

Bressac was the taller of the two, Dodo 'noticed, finding it strange that it hadn't occurred to her before. He was skinny and gangly, as if he had been stretched out of shape at an early age. He was a little older than Dalville, she guessed, his face more angular, less childish. He had untamed, ash-blonde hair that never settled. Like Dalville, he was clean shaven.

Dalville was short. Comparatively speaking, he was short – he still seemed imposing to Dodo. He had a boyish face, soft and cruel with searching dark eyes. His hair was long and dark, but not wild as Bressac's was. Instead it flowed, sweeping back in dark waves at the base of his skull. His smile was wrong. It was tiny and fussy, uneven on his dark features.

He looked gorgeous.

'How about a toast?' Bressac suggested as Dalville passed him his wine.

Dalville's features flexed. His smile broadened with malice.

'To the misfortunes of virtue,' he suggested.

That set a grin on Bressac's face. Dodo, confused, added her smile to the mix. 'The misfortunes of virtue,' they chorused.

After that, the atmosphere eased. Bressac cleared a space at the table and they sat together, as a group. Dodo took another couple of exaggerated sips at the wine.

'Why are you travelling like this? I mean, shouldn't you be based at a theatre or something?' The actors swapped odd glances. Another slip.

'Citizen Minski,' Bressac explained, 'isn't very keen on

50

the theatre. He doesn't like the idea of so many people getting together in the same place. So he's banned public performances. All the theatres in Paris are closed.'

'We're stuck with touring the provinces, playing in tiny venues or in the open air,' Dalville added.

'Well,' Dodo shrugged, 'why come to Paris at all?'

'Because the Marquis is a great lover of the stage,' Dalville continued. 'And of actresses. Christ knows, he's had enough of his own stuff banned to know what *this* is like. He's persuaded Minski to allow a number of private performances at the Bastille.'

'We're just the latest,' Bressac muttered. 'It's good money. Sadly, we've just lost our leading lady.'

'Sophie?' Dodo waggled her eyebrows suggestively.

'Yes. I'll go to the Bastille tomorrow morning, kick up a fuss and put the fear of the First Deputy into the gaoler. They'll have to let her go.'

Dodo's lips fluttered. Bressac broke in, anticipating her question.

'I know. I'll insist they let him go as well. Either that or no play.' He frowned, before continuing. 'Who is he by the way? A relative?'

'My . . . teacher,' Dodo replied, smooth as she could manage.

'You're not from Paris, are you Dorothea?' Dalville said suddenly, the question she'd been dreading. She tried to speak, but Dalville beat her to it. 'In fact, you're not French at all.'

'No.' Dodo stared at the mug on the table, avoiding the gaze of either man. She found herself wondering when she had drunk so much of the wine.

'It's not that I'm bothered. I was just wondering . . .'

'I'm English,' she said, hopefully.

'We're at war with England.'

'American?' She tried again.

'And with America.'

'I've got French blood,' she said, a hint of desperation in her voice. 'Several pints at least.'

Dalville rose, sending his chair shrieking across the floor. His hands fell lightly on Dodo's shoulders, thumbs pushing up into the mass of her hair and rubbing gently at the base of her skull.

'We don't care where you're from.' He was whispering, his mouth so close to her ear that she could feel him speaking. She felt oddly better. 'Really. I'm sorry if I upset you. You didn't deserve that.'

His presence withdrew, leaving her chilly.

'It's OK,' she mumbled. 'Fine.'

'Do you want to get some sleep?' Bressac suggested kindly, his gentle voice warming her slightly.

She turned to stare at him through bleary eyes.

'You look tired.'

'I – I'm not sure.' She shrugged, displaying her open, empty palms.

'You are quite safe with us, if that's what's worrying you.'

'Of course you're safe! I'm a man of honour!' Dalville's extravagant roar was as warm as Bressac's whisper and far more exciting. His energy was infectious, sparking through her and invigorating her as he spoke. 'And Bressac's as bent as Bonaparte. He's not going to lay a finger on you.'

Bressac's face *clicked*. He scooped a cushion from his chair and hurled it at Dalville. It struck his shoulder gently, but he affected a stagger and threw his arms out to steady himself.

'Not tonight Josephine!' he yelled, teeth bared as though the flesh had been torn away from his mouth. Bressac's eyes rolled despairingly. Dodo heard herself giggling, a stupid childish squeak.

'It's not you,' she said, hardening her voice. Iron, Dodo, iron! 'I'm just thinking about the Doctor. He's probably worried about me.'

'You said he can take care of himself well enough,' Dalville interjected, sounding genuine this time. 'I wouldn't think it to look at him . . .'

52

'He's got the advantage. He can live without me. He's . . . He's . . . I don't know . . .' A yawn had built up inside her, choosing this moment to force her jaws open and burst loose. She clamped her hand over her mouth. 'I'm sorry.'

'Here,' Bressac said. He placed solid hands on her elbow. It was a simple grip, loose and without force. His fingers brushed softly against the fabric of her cloak, as if the touching scared him. Still holding her, he stood, raising her after him with little effort. Still holding her, he moved to the inner door, pulling her gently after him. They stepped through into a gloomy emptiness, half-lit by the glare from the lamp in the next room. Dodo tried to focus on the dark interior, but her eyes refused to settle and leaped around dangerously, blurring the room out of focus. She sensed more than she saw, feeling the wooden structure around her. The beds were set into the walls, four of them, stacked in twos on either side of the room. Modest curtains were fitted along the side of each bed.

'Ooh!' Dodo pronounced in the poshest voice she could muster, wondering if the wine had gone to her head. 'Bunk beds! Can I go on top?'

Bressac sat her down on one of the lower bunks and spoke into her ear, whispering, because the darkness seemed to demand hushed voices.

'Is there anything you need?'

'No, thanks.'

'We'll try not to disturb you. Get up whenever you like. I should have some good news for you in the morning.'

'G'night.'

He was gone. The door was pulled to, crowding out the last of the light. Dodo lifted herself wearily onto the bunk and pulled the curtain closed behind her. She undressed slowly, finding the experience an uncomfortable, dragging chore. She made a careful bundle of her clothes and kicked them to the foot of the bed, prodding at them every so often with her toes, just in case.

53

The mattress was hard and lumpy, its coarse texture scraping at her back. There were no pillows, and the only cover was a rough blanket, riddled with holes, some cut from the material in bizarre shapes. It was comfortable enough, given that civilization wouldn't be invented for another one hundred and fifty years.

Despite her tiredness, she didn't sleep immediately. Muffled conversation filtered through from the next room, its sounds dulled but still audible and irritating. She lay on her back, eyes wide open and staring at the dark-hidden wooden ceiling. She lay still, pondering over the Doctor.

She believed in him completely. She had a rigid, sustaining faith in his wisdom and his endless capacity for survival. He would be all right, anything else would be unthinkable, but . . . but he had left Steven behind. Not in bad circumstances admittedly, but he had still as good as abandoned him on an unnamed world in an unspecified time for no obvious reason. Somehow, she couldn't believe in that decision. Somehow, it wasn't right.

The conversation in the next room had rolled into silence. She breathed with relief and flipped herself over onto her stomach.

The Marquis de Sade. She knew the title from somewhere. Before she'd met the Doctor, perhaps, back in the gloomy-grey days of 1966. She had no real recollection of that life. It merged in her mind into an endless succession of identical experiences. There were fragments, pop songs and interesting bits of homework and newspaper headlines . . .

They slipped out of her mind, along with everything else.

Bressac pulled the door closed after him, softly. Dorothea's eyes had been aching and haggard, desperate for a long rest, and he didn't want to disturb her. He padded across the room to where Dalville was sitting, toying with the three empty mugs on the table.

'I think she likes you,' he said.

'That's just the wine. Any more and she'd have been on her back.' Dalville flashed a callous smile at him, all the more unsettling for seeming so thoughtful. 'She's very odd, a fish out of water.'

'English?'

'That's obvious enough,' he continued, a thoughtful melancholy entering his face and his features, 'but there's more to it than that. She's foreign to everything. It's as if she's seeing everything for the first time. She's an innocent.'

Bressac studied his colleague carefully, searching for a motive in his unhelpful features. They surrendered nothing, not altruism nor curiosity nor lust. Dalville was a good actor, better than Bressac.

'I give in,' he submitted, putting a satisfied smile onto Dalville's lips. 'What are you up to?'

'Look at her eyes, Bressac,' he replied, his tone strict and even. 'She's innocent, pure, virtuous. I value these qualities. I value them so much I want to destroy them. I want to corrupt her. That's all.'

Bressac glanced awkwardly at his fingernails. He was afraid it might be something like this.

'You fancy her, yes? You're just too proud to say it plainly.'

'No, no,' Dalville insisted, snorting. 'This isn't a lustful thing. I want to take her virtue apart, destroy it . . . to know it. Only through darkness can the light be perceived, and virtue can be embraced only in vice. I'm on a philosophical and spiritual quest into . . .'

'Her knickers?' Bressac suggested sourly.

'Her human nature,' Dalville concluded. 'We're out of wine, y'know.'

I need to clean my hands, Bressac thought, coolly. This is a filthy place to live in. The dirt's growing under my nails.

'Don't hurt her,' he said quietly. 'Please.'

'You don't understand,' Dalville insisted, his tone

earnest and horribly false. 'I'm not going to force her to do anything. You can't corrupt innocence by assailing it. I'll have to change the way she thinks. When she wants to cooperate with me, when she starts to *shock* me, then I'll have succeeded.'

'That's not what I meant.' He couldn't look into Dalville's face yet. It was always irritating when his companion started to rationalize his moods and tastes and loves, but this calm outburst was more depressing than usual.

'You disapprove?'

Bressac found the courage to look up at last. He was surprised by the eagerness he saw on Dalville's face.

'Yes.'

'Well, then, you can be my conscience,' Dalville replied. 'Now we all have roles.'

3

The Miserable Ones

Wearing the deathmask always left Randolph unsettled, robbing him of something vital that he couldn't put a name to. He paced the deserted bedroom of his hideout, paying careful attention to the sound of his feet on the floor.

It had probably been a rich house once, before its bourgeois tenant lost his head to the Revolution he had in all likelihood sponsored. Now it was derelict, stripped of all its furnishings and decorations. Randolph couldn't imagine this place being occupied or beautiful. Past and present seemed to have no firm connection, here as much as elsewhere. Randolph could barely recall the days before the Revolution, even in England. His memories were like a dim, nostalgic dream.

He was disturbed by the thump of Garce's boots in the passage outside, by the opening creak of the door, and by the appearance of his colleague's silhouette on the threshold of the room. Garce was a tall, broad man not given to small movements. He exuded solidity, appearing to Randolph as if he had been carved from a shard of dark wood. It was a deceptive shape – Garce was as nimble and quick-witted as any man. He dressed simply and wore his hair long, cultivating an inappropriate romanticism.

'She's ready,' he said. 'Would you care to join me, Sir Randolph?'

Randolph raised a finger to his lips, to his eye, to his ear and back to his eye. Garce's eyes flashed, recognizing the code.

'Garce, m'dear,' Randolph pronounced in his sweetest, falsest voice, 'all this running around has left me with a frightful headache. Do the thing without me; I must lay me a-down or I shall faint.'

'Right,' Garce said, spitting the word sullenly, the flicker on his lips betraying his understanding. Randolph forced a yawn from his untired mouth and shambled from the room. He descended the stairs leisurely, grumbling for the benefit of any mechanical ears that the French might have placed around him. Once he was free of the house, he dropped the fraud.

He hid in the shadowed overhang of the balcony for the moment, fingering the hilt of his sabre from frustration. He wanted to leave Garce enough time to return to the attic, to their victim, to the ritual, to distract the eavesdroppers. Randolph hated this level of espionage. It was damned impolite, and the French took the whole thing to indecent lengths.

Certain enough time had passed, he darted through the shadow across the street and into the gaping doorway of the opposite house. This was another abandoned wooden shell. The ground floor would be left untouched to foster that impression. Shutting off his feeling, only acting and reacting, he moved silently to the stairs. Garce's voice floated down from the upper storey – a distant, scratchy reproduction, filtered through Minski's mechanical artifice. Randolph traipsed silently up the steps, following the voice. Garce's unfaltering but distinct French accent was broken by occasional shrill, feminine interjections.

The voices came from the door of the bedroom directly opposite Randolph's hiding-house. By the time he had reached the landing, the voices were audible and the squeaky mechanical note in their tone was clear. He snuggled up to the doorway, peering through the slightest of cracks, seeing nothing clearly. He doubted that there would be more than three spies, but held back, waiting for the moment of supreme advantage.

The victim's metal voice whispered, breaking the musty silence.

'Why are you doing this?'

'I serve.'

Randolph almost shuddered at this. Garce had a precise and pleasant countenance – shorn of those reassuring features, his voice seemed cruel and base. All for the good, Randolph supposed.

'Why does it have to be me?'

'No reason.'

'I'll let you do anything, anything you like.' Her voice slid into a mumble, then into silence. It snapped back suddenly. 'But don't kill me. Don't kill me. Don't kill –'

Her voice cut into a harsh shriek, punctuated by a low chuckle – a human laugh, not modulated through Minski's machines. As the scream hit its peak, Randolph seized his chance and burst into the room, his sabre flashing from its scabbard. Two men sat inside listening, both dressed in drab and dark robes that half-hid flashes of blue and white uniforms. Their faces showed dumb shock, but they reacted quickly enough. They were trained men – hardly peasant rabble. Randolph threw himself at them, the woman's scream underscoring his violence.

His blade slashed across the throat of the closest man. The sword shone duller, its edge darkened with blood. He put its end into the eye of the second soldier before he could fire a shot. The blade twisted and snapped in the bloodied socket as he died. The woman's voice faded as the thrill of the moment died away. Randolph remained tense, aware that precious time was being wasted.

He turned his attention to the soldiers' recording devices, eyes flicking across panels of artless grey metalwork with exposed clockwork skeletons. He bared his teeth, repelled by this hideous extension of cold reason into life, seeing nothing that could be attacked effectively. His eyes fell on a tray of wax-coated metal cylinders. This was the medium on which the stolen sounds had been encrypted, hidden in the flickering scratch-lines on the wax. Here was something he could understand and destroy. He dashed the tray to the floor. The cylinders scattered across the floor, the wax surfaces breaking apart on impact.

A shape flickered in the corner of his eye, a dark blot moving on the street below. Randolph sidled up to the window, peering out through dusty, cracked glass. There was a man stumbling along the front of the houses, a white-haired old man. Randolph's eyes narrowed thoughtfully. It was the old prisoner that Garce had wanted to bleed in the woman's place, the fool who had been unafraid of death.

Randolph looked away, his gaze falling on the flintlock held in the corpse-tight grip of the soldier at his feet. It would hardly take an effort to aim one of the pistols through the window and blast a hole through the man's skull. At this time of night, a shot would attract little attention.

No. He posed no danger, and his corpse would draw attention to their hiding place. Besides, there was something pleasing about his appearance. It was surely a sign that the remains of the patrol were yet to be found. It was bad form to shoot a good omen. Besides, Randolph realized as he looked again, it was too late. His target was out of sight.

The Doctor's face still stung, an unwelcome reminder of the weakness eating away at his flesh and old bones. The pain was slight though, and he had more than enough incentive to ignore it. He was driven, spurred on by a purpose and a quarry and . . . an anger, yes, an indignant moral anger.

He had been on the ground when the Englishmen destroyed the soldiers. Had he been standing, he would have died with them, his fragile body splitting apart as the energy broke through him. The device they had used was an anachronism that demanded investigation. They had also murdered almost a dozen men without effort or remorse, and that demanded justice.

60

They had taken Sophie too. She had helped the Doctor when he slipped in the street, lifting him off the ground before the soldiers could kick at him. She looked very much like . . . like . . . like someone he had known once.

He followed them from a distance, deciding that in this case caution was wiser than indignant confrontation. His sight and strength were sharpened by the experience, hardened by his single-minded purpose. Their house, or the derelict site that acted as their base, was surprisingly close. He watched them slip inside with their hostage, allowing them a moment to get inside before following.

The Doctor cut short his first attempt, pulling back as the older, broken-faced Englishman re-emerged. The man stood vigil outside the house for the moment, a strutting stick-figure in the distance. Then he plunged across the street and through the door of the house opposite.

The Doctor set out once again, forcing movement into legs that had hardened in the moment's stillness. He was halfway there when the effort of holding his crumbling faculties together overcame him. He stumbled, sinking to his knees, pressing his hands against the nearest wall, not so much to steady himself as to draw strength from the wood. The air around him was warm, but it made him feel cold and brittle by contrast.

There was a dark rot in his bones, in his soul, sapping his resolve and turning his body against him. He wished Dodo were here. He needed someone now, not simply to help him, but to be with him. She would be another source of strength, far more vibrant and enduring than the relentless determination that had sustained him in his pursuit. He remembered telling Dodo that she would have to leave and hoped she hadn't taken it to heart. He hoped she was faring better than he was.

He rested until some strength returned, then forced himself onwards into the house, the flesh on his hands bristling and stinging as he slipped through the doorway.

This was a dangerous place, despite appearances. The building seemed derelict, a skeletal house stripped down to its rotting wooden bones. Layers of dust hissed beneath his soft tread, though judging by the abundance of boot prints across the floor, he was not the first to disturb the stillness. He moved further into the corpse, holding his cloak around him like a concealing shadow.

Careless footsteps rattled on the stairs, setting wooden boards creaking and dust flying. The Doctor slipped smoothly through a doorway, out of sight.

The stench of offal pursued Garce through the house, luring flies from their hiding places in the cracks between the wood. Most congregated round the corpse in the attic, but a few hissed round his head. He swatted at them with the barrel of his flintlock, irritated by their presence.

His clothes and flesh were sticky and red, the last vestiges of the woman's life clinging to his body. He'd kissed her just before she'd slipped away, finding the blood on her lips. No clean death for her, none of the instant simplicity of the deathmask. The taste of her lingered in his throat, a filthy reminder of what he had done.

Part of his hatred was an understandable disgust with the woman – for being a victim, for being weak – but this mingled with a curious, confusing hatred for himself. It wasn't as though it were *self* that drove him to do it. If it were self, he would have spared the woman and briefly loved her. It wasn't his love for Hell or his hatred of the French that spurred him. It was duty. It was the need to serve. Loyalty to king and country was a taut, inflexible rod driven through his soul.

His doubts remained. He thought he had heard someone skulking downstairs, but dismissed it as a figment of the mind, something to be overlooked if he wasn't to spend the rest of his life cowering from shadows. When the sounds came again, he took up his pistol and resolved to investigate.

'Who's there?' he yelled, easing his pace as he reached the bottom of the stairs. Something flickered in the corner shadows and he turned the muzzle appropriately. 'Out, son of a whore dog who was also your lover – oh, it's you,' he finished in English.

Randolph was smirking, his distinct chuckle rattling at the back of his throat. 'That's frightful grammar,' he said. 'I see you've become Lord of the Flies in my absence.' He plucked one of the hissing insects from the air and popped it between his lips. His throat bobbed, every detail apparent beneath his thin flesh. Garce felt nauseous.

'Are you finished?' Randolph continued.

Garce's eyes flicked down to his rank, sticky-wet body. Randolph made a knowing, crescent smile, wholly without humour.

'And you?' Garce prompted.

His colleague's smile slipped. The shrillness in his voice vanished, eaten by grim darkness. 'Two Bonapartistes are dead, and we'll join them unless we move on in the next hour. No time for you to get cleaned up, I fear. You've prepared the ceremony?'

Garce nodded dully.

They moved upstairs in silence. Garce had prepared the ritual carefully during Randolph's absence. The necessary organs had been taken from the victim and placed in damp red patches, their positions forming the corners of an invisible symbol on the bare bedroom floor. Randolph stared at the configuration for a moment, before giving a small nod of the head that set Garce glowing with pride.

'We'll do this quickly,' Randolph murmured. 'You have the stuff?'

Silently, Garce handed him the chalice, rim-full with thickening red fluid. Randolph held it with both hands, raising it to the sky momentarily. Then he flung it away, its shiny surface catching the light as it bounced across the floor. The blood spilled out, forming a dark, quivering pool.

'It's the Hour of Longing, the cat-time, the white-moment,' Randolph began quickly, casually spitting the words of the ritual. 'We summon Tyll Howlglass, whose secret name is Naranek of the Pageant. By the power of the True Creator, who art Below in Fire, profane be thy name, et cetera, et cetera, et cetera.' He shot Garce a sly grin.

Garce clenched his teeth together, wishing that for once Randolph could approach the ritual with the appropriate degree of respect. The Devil would be a wicked thing to cross and Randolph was foolish to mock Him. Even as the thought occurred to him, Garce recalled that the rituals had begun this way in his grandfather's day. They were nothing more than jokes, turned sour and serious by time. There was no dishonour in trying to best the Devil, surely?

The air grew chilly as the heat was sucked from the room. The blood-pool groaned, its surface blistering with tiny lights – white beams shot with pale pink lines. It was a disappointment, like most conjurings. Randolph was bowing extravagantly, still mocking the being they had summoned. Garce followed suit, putting more pain and respect into his stoop. Darkness flickered on the pool, a shadow-face flexing from Below.

'We don't require a sacrifice,' said Tyll Howlglass, his voice hissing disapproval through the pool.

'Ah,' Randolph spoke, his voice the dry tones of an old man with hard-worn experience within him, 'but we have our own sacred rituals which must be observed, even in this barbaric country. They are old rules, dusty with time and meaning. We would be fools to ignore them.'

'We need our orders, Tyll Howlglass,' Garce interjected impatiently. 'Forgive my haste, half of France is at our tail.'

'Secure yourselves, then contact Medmenham,' Howlglass's voice crackled. 'Use the ansible channel – Minski will be watching the secular media. The English government will require your knowledge if we are to have our victory.' The spirit's voice seethed, as though it resented the prospect. An odd, gravid silence followed, the shadow-face flickering in the blood-pool as if contemplating whether to speak further.

'Howlglass –'

'There is one other matter,' the Hell-voice cut through the silence suddenly, 'I tell you this as an individual, rather than as speaker for the Pageant. This is a confidence – blood-compact – you understand?'

Randolph nodded.

'Some new thing has appeared in Paris, a cunning box brought here by a human woman and . . . a man. It *intrigued* the Pageant,' contemptuous static hissed under the words, 'briefly. Nevertheless, I would like the box or its owners acquired, gently.'

'And where might they be found?' Randolph's voice dripped with obsequious honey.

'The man and the woman are lost to us, though neither has left the city. The box has been moved to the Bastille. That is all.' The light vanished, the pool breaking open and hardening on the floorboards. An odd smell filled the room, a scent like crushed flowers and autumn decay. Garce shuddered, suddenly nostalgic for the New Forest in September. Hell – if it smelled this sweet – would be unbearable.

'The Bastille,' Randolph echoed, his voice laced with dry irony. 'Perhaps we should knock on Minski's door and ask politely for our box back?'

'It's not our problem. We should ignore it.'

'No. Howlglass has overstepped his mark. He's dancing to his own tune now. I doubt his fellow demons would like that much, should they find out.'

'We swore a confidence!' Garce blurted, shocked.

' 's truth m'dear, but I had my fingers crossed, as you did.' A note of impatience had entered his voice, unprecedented emotion for Randolph.

Garce shrugged, nodding with profound understanding. To serve the Devil was one thing, to mock him was another. He would betray the Devil, if duty demanded it, and he would kill the Devil too.

The Doctor waited in darkness, straining to hear the conversation in the upper room over the sound of his breath. His lungs wheezed, snatching shallow gasps of air. Fortunately his hiding place was just below the room where the Englishmen were talking and their voices carried well. There was a third voice too – not Sophie's, but a distant rumble that the Doctor couldn't make out. He guessed from the other men's reactions that this third conspirator was speaking from a distance.

'So,' he muttered to himself, 'long-distance communication, radio perhaps, or –' he checked himself with a giggle, realizing that he was speaking aloud. He almost capped the silence with a clap, but thought better of it.

Eventually the groan of the third voice fell silent. The two exact English accents remained, cutting through the musty darkness. Their conversation became less interesting, but the Doctor already had the clue he required. He pressed his fingers together and hummed, delighted with what he had overheard.

He hadn't thought about the Bastille, though the soldiers had pointed it out to him against the Paris skyline on their journey there. He silently berated himself for overlooking something so conspicuous, so anachronistic, so heavy with symbolic meaning. It had to be the centre of the historical disruption. The TARDIS had been taken to the Bastille, and if the patrols were thorough about rounding up curfew breakers, Dodo might also be found there. He resolved to visit the place as soon as it became safe.

The men's voices grew muffled, their footsteps trailing out of the upper room and thumping down the stairs. The Doctor could no longer make sense of their words, but they came sparse and terse. He gathered that they were preparing to move out for good, and wondered whether it might not be a good idea to challenge them,

66

particularly as they still held Sophie hostage. Again he thought better of it. The hot gloom around him was stifling and tiring. He needed to rest now, to recuperate and recover his strength. He could hardly stop the men or help the girl in his present state. They could be thwarted and she could be rescued later.

This was selfish and it bothered him. He hoped it was a symptom of his illness and not of his self. He hoped that, when the change came upon him, he would be reborn a better person, cleansed of this stain. In the meantime, he would settle for the only redemption he was allowed. The cold, dusty floor wouldn't be the worst place he had rested and his cloak provided some warmth. When the Englishmen left the house, their voices vanished into the streets, replaced by a haunting silence befitting the dead house. They didn't return. The Doctor slipped into a light sleep, troubled by fragmented dreams and images.

He woke unexpectedly and before time, woken by the nudge of a boot tip to his shoulder. He was awake and ready instantly — a good omen, he felt, a sign of briefly restored health. He pretended to be sleepy and startled, rolling onto his back to get a clear look upwards.

He had been woken by a woman, dressed like a soldier in a strange, ragged half-uniform. The Doctor frowned, searching for the tricolour rosette, finding it nowhere. The woman herself seemed quite young, probably at the start of her thirties. She had a small, pinched face that could have been brightened by a smile or by laughter, but was instead lined and weary. Her dark hair was cut into short, ruffled, brutal locks. There was a grim thoughtfulness in her expression that reassured the Doctor that he wasn't facing a killer, and a grim pistol in her hand that warned him that he was. She knelt beside him, pushing the barrel under his chin, a cold 'o' prodding against his skin.

'Old man,' she spoke in a soft tone, a rural accent struggling against Paris sophistication, 'there is a woman's corpse in the attic. What can you tell me about her murder?'

The Doctor stared back at her, his strength and warmth seeping away.

'Sophie?' Her name, the only word he could form.

'She was a friend of a friend.'

Ideally he would have felt a turbulent rush of thoughts and emotions. It should have been a struggle to believe it, even to register it. No, he understood clearly and perfectly. The only thing he felt was a cold, stomach-sickness accompanying the realization that by refusing to confront Sophie's kidnappers, he had betrayed her.

This is a twisted history, a false echo of the real world. There is no danger in *acting* in this time, in this place.

'I didn't kill her,' he said calmly, shaking as though it were a lie.

'No,' the woman said, pulling her gun away. 'I know. It was English spies. But it's suspicious that you're here.'

'I might say the same of you, young lady,' the Doctor retorted sharply, finding more comfort in this line.

'I'm not a young lady. There are no ladies any more. I am Catherine Arouette, at your service.'

'That hardly explains what you are doing here,' the Doctor continued to bluster, adding an even-handed, 'any more than I. For all I know you might have killed that poor child upstairs yourself.'

'Ah, no, I did not.'

'How do I know you're telling the truth?'

'Because I am not a liar, citizen,' she replied sweetly. 'Because you are prepared to believe me. Life is sometimes simple.'

The Doctor blinked. Arouette smiled at him – a tiny, sad thing, but the first she had offered him. That was the only weakness in her face; everything else seemed grey and inscrutable.

'There are soldiers coming. They may decide to search these houses, in which case we will be found and guillotined for Sophie's murder,' the woman said hurriedly. 'Perhaps you'd like it if I drew them away?'

68

'I would be in your debt,' the Doctor said after a moment's consideration.

Arouette nodded and rose to her feet, pushing the pistol into her belt with one hand and drawing a short sword with the other. Its blade was a dark line in the shadows, neither catching nor reflecting light. Arouette weighed the sword carefully, seeming as comfortable using it in her left hand as the pistol was in her right. The symmetry was surreal, and momentarily the Doctor wondered if he were still dreaming.

'I've a good reason for doing this. I was warned about you, about your box and the human woman you travel with. You're not what I expected.'

'I never am,' the Doctor growled, allowing only a flicker of childish humour into his voice. It was the wrong time for that sort of thing.

'So, I'll distract the soldiers for you. I will see you again, I think. Don't try to look for me,' she added, turning to give him a manic, profile stare – more frightening for being sincere, 'for I am a master of disguise.'

She hurled herself out of the window and into the street. The Doctor lay still, listening. Within moments though, there were coarse shouts from outside, cries for help, the sound of boots pounding on mud and stone and gunshots, a volley of musket-fire that lasted only a second but reverberated in the Doctor's ears for an hour.

He waited before rising, before moving to the window and staring out across the bleak night street. Arouette had gone, the soldiers she had spoken of had gone, any signs of the struggle were hidden by the dark. The Doctor imagined he heard more shots, distantly, from nearby streets, but these could easily have been the echoes of the first volley.

'A strange woman,' he said sadly, hoping it was not an epitaph.

He decided to forgo sleep for the rest of the night. Sophie was dead in the attic – he was certain that

Arouette had told him the truth on that count at least. A wakeful silence was needed, to honour her memory. He remained at the window, maintaining his vigil until the sky was lit with tortured streaks of grey.

Citizen Cameo could tell that it was getting light. There were no windows in the dungeons, but she sensed the morning taking shape outside. It was usually quiet in the cells, but at dawn a new kind of silence pervaded the tunnels round the condemned cells. Chilly, sinister, complete – it was greater than the absence of noise.

Cameo knew the routine, though it still disturbed her. She patrolled the condemned cells every day before they were emptied, peering through the doors at sullen, shocked faces. These people were already dead. Stripped of their humanity, they were left with only an animal terror of the future. Some of the other gaolers thought they saw penitence in the prisoners' eyes – fear of God transcending fear of death. Cameo couldn't believe that, though she would have welcomed the comfort.

Cell 6 was the only respite from the tense, final inspection. Monsieur le 6 was proof of life beyond death. Cameo was his saviour, merciful and cruel. She drew back the shutter on his door in time to catch him writing. He was squatting on the floor, his back turned to her, his spine curving with effort, the bone-shape visible beneath his thin shirt. His shoulders were hunched, protective of the pen and paper in his lap. Realizing he was being watched, he straightened and tucked the sheets under his bunk.

Cameo grinned wickedly. It had been some months since she had discovered that le 6 was writing in his cell. He had been accumulating scraps of paper – flyleaves torn from the occasional volume she allowed him – ingeniously gumming them together to form a scroll. It was his most prized possession and he guarded it furtively, hiding his script in a cavity beneath a loose flagstone in the floor. Cameo had tolerated this eccentricity, until now.

She laid her gift on the floor, needing a free hand to unlock the cell door. It was a compact machine — much heavier than it looked. She hefted it back into her arms, cradling it as she burst in on le 6. She didn't bother looking at him. There would be nothing but smooth velvet and a sharp stare.

'I've brought you something,' she told him, placing her gift at the end of his bunk, where he could see it clearly. 'No man should die as many deaths as you without some reward. I got this from the clerks, as a present.'

Now she looked at him, at the dumb eyes and the shifting, clinging mask. It wasn't that he was ignorant or uncomprehending. He knew exactly what the toy was and how it worked. He knew also why it had been presented to him.

'It's an auto-scribe,' she explained. 'All the characters of the alphabet are set on the board. You press on them, and the machine will transcribe your choice onto the waterscreen. This has 27 litres of memory in which to write. If you need more, just say and I'll requisition some waxes.'

His mouth was twitching beneath the mask, the velvet dancing in imitation. His body shifted too, hunching and tightening, pushing fearfully into himself, away from the machine. Cameo smiled, amused and puzzled. It was strange, watching this man act. Every freedom she allowed him became another prison, every gift another bond, every concession another encasing mask.

He wouldn't write again. He wouldn't touch the machine. By presenting him with the means to write, she had killed the instinct in him. She found it fascinating that he should cooperate in his own torment — fascinating and repellent. 'Monsieur le 6' was a fine description of this man. It felt as though it had always been his title, that Citizen Sade was simply the first to add words to the unspoken name.

'So, you won't need this,' she continued, tugging the scroll from beneath the bunk. The muzzled eyes of le 6 flicked to it, at once protective and dismissive. It burned in Cameo's hands. She didn't look at it until she was outside. She hadn't meant to read it at all, but as she locked the dead man back in his cell, she realized that she might never have a better opportunity to decipher his thoughts.

I am here alone. The writing was tight and neat, an aristocrat's hand. *I am here at the end of the world, hidden from all eyes and beyond the reach of any creature. There are no more restraints and no more obstructions. There is nothing but God and conscience.*

Cameo's face crumpled, bitter tears swelling in the corner of her eyes. She crushed the manuscript and tossed the remains into the gutter where it could rot undisturbed. She left the cells hurriedly, pursued by the haunting silence.

There was a man waiting in her office, not a prisoner, not a guard, not an official from further up or further down the tower. Not – liberty, equality, fraternity be praised! – Sade or his gargoyle son. It was just a man – a young, frail creature with shocked features and hair like a cotton halo. He shuffled, wringing his hands out of fear. The austerity of the office imposed on him, cabbage-grey walls wringing the colour from him. Cameo perched herself prissily behind the desk and smiled at her visitor, anxious to show him a human face.

It was so long since she had spoken to a real person – since Jean had gone, three years ago. She had spent so much time here, among the dead and the also-dead. She welcomed him, struggling to put him at his ease.

'I'm looking for a woman,' he began, the words spilling from his mouth in tight bursts. 'A curfew-breaker, from last night. We're actors, the Fantômas company. We're to perform here, for the First Deputy. We have a dispensation from Minski himself.' He paused, his eyes shuffling round the office. He was making space around him – probably wisely, though Cameo couldn't help but feel stung. 'You haven't killed her yet?'

Cameo shook her head, smiling kindly at this infinitely distant human.

'If she was brought in last night, she won't have seen the magistrate.' He didn't seem convinced, so she continued, gesturing at the neat stacks of paper on her desk. 'Your friend is there. One bit of paper among equals. It might look like waste, but it ensures everyone gets dealt with fairly. The Terror is over. Nowadays, no one dies without trial.'

She studied his face again, finding little sign of reassurance. 'This woman. Does she have a name?'

The name he gave didn't appear on her checklist for the night's intake. She shrugged and offered him a resigned grin.

'She might have called herself Sophie,' he added wearily. Cameo's eyes flicked down the list, but both names eluded her. The man trembled, rocking on his feet. Cameo stared at him, wondering what could be making him so nervous.

She was spared the ensuing, awkward silence when the door crashed open and an apparition surged in, carried on a tide of babbling tricoloured guards. It was a gaunt, gangly creature, with skin only a shade darker than its snowfall of hair. It was cloaked in black, and iron eyes burned in the hollows of its skull, a personal death come to visit. Cameo folded her fat fingers together and relaxed, confident that she was dreaming.

'I demand to speak to someone in authority!' the death howled over the protests of the gaolers.

Cameo made flapping movements with her hands, waving the guards from the room. The actor lingered in the corner, squeezed to the edges of the room by the dark shape in its centre. It wasn't still, even now. Its head twitched and its fingers clicked, trembling with power. Not death then, just another man. Cameo was disappointed.

'I've some authority, a little. Perhaps I can help?'

'I am a regional officer of the southern province. I

had thought that I would be expected. It seems I was wrong.'

The old man's voice crackled. Cameo didn't like it, it was hectoring and too aggressive. The fragile actor also seemed upset – his twitching and shuffling had become more pronounced. Cameo felt a surge of protective anger.

'Who was it you were expecting to see? Citizen Minski perhaps?'

'He will do to begin with.'

Cameo rose and brushed past him to reach the door.

'I'll just go and find him for you,' she said, a honey-sweet curve on her lips. The smile she flashed at the actor was more honest. 'I'll check with the other gaolers. Sometimes they can't be bothered to fill in the proper forms. Don't worry.'

It seemed cooler in the passages, though Cameo knew that was impossible. The calm was no illusion. She felt steadier out here, away from the masked men and the old men and even the likeable young men. Life was easier with only the dead to worry her.

Both men were shadows on the wetscreen. One was a vast black shape with a white smear for a head. The other was a grey blur, all details lost as the screen surface shimmered and rippled. The silhouette hovered in the centre of the office, oblivious of the blur's attempts to approach him.

'I'm sorry about the quality,' the observer said.

'Not your fault,' her guest growled. 'My son realizes that water is a poor medium. He thinks it might be the tides.'

'Perhaps we should declare war on the selenites?' the observer suggested brightly.

Her guest almost smiled. 'We have closer enemies.' He broke into a frustrated, wordless growl. 'You were right to call me, but I can't see whether or not this is the man.'

A new shadow rippled on the screen, a profile –

distinct and hawkish. The observer recognized it and grimaced. She turned to her guest.

'Would you mind standing back a little, citizen? I, uh, think it might be your shadow . . . that's, uh, interfering . . . .' She breathed a little easier when the figure at her shoulder moved back. The picture sharpened, the abstract shapes gaining detail and depth, and at last their voices could be heard over the babble of the screen-stream.

'What? What?' The old man's voice was tiny and petulant when filtered through the security system, a comic squeak. 'Do I know you, young man?'

'No.' The young man's voice was equally shrill. The observer strained to hear and her right temple began to throb. 'But I know that you are the Doctor, and that you are the teacher of Citizen Dorothea Chaplette.'

'Dodo?' the old man squealed. 'You've seen her?'

'Yes. I am Bressac, of the Fantômas Travelling Players. Dorothea is staying at our camp. She's quite safe.'

The Doctor seemed relieved. He was trembling, though that might have been the screen. He touched Bressac's shoulder, causing the younger man to flinch.

'I am very glad to hear it.'

'She is very worried about you.'

'Nonsense. She has an abiding – and I might say thoroughly unwarranted – faith in my ability to survive. But you may tell her that I am safe.'

'Ah. I thought you might return to the camp with me?'

The old man snorted, his face bulging almost to fill the screen. 'No. I shall stay to explore the tower. You seem to me like a decent young man. I'm sure she is in no danger.'

Bressac shook his head, though he didn't seem convinced. 'Ah, there's something, um, else,' he continued, his voice falling into a low hush, though it still shook clearly from the screen. 'Last night when you were taken by the patrol, there was a woman captured with you.'

'It's him.' The observer's guest leaned forward, hissing into her ear.

'She's a colleague of mine. I worry about her. I don't suppose . . .'

The Doctor took his hand from Bressac's shoulder, stepping away surreptitiously, slipping his arms back into his cloak until he seemed nothing more than a patch of darkness once again. The observer kept her eyes on the screen, engrossed by what she saw there.

'I am sorry. We were rescued by two men who took Sophie away with them. And I'm very much afraid that' – the observer detected a slight pause, though again this might have been the screen – 'that I lost track of them. And her.'

Bressac was out of the range of the closer cameras, so there was no vision of his face. The observer could imagine it though – hope cracking into disappointment.

'I don't think we need to listen to any more of this.' Citizen Sade's voice sounded too close to be real. 'I'll have them arrested at once.'

'I'll stay and keep watch,' the observer said, adding, 'in case they let anything slip.' She stopped, realizing that Sade had gone and she was talking to herself. She turned back to the screen and the unfolding drama.

'There's not really much point in my staying,' Bressac was saying. 'I'll tell Dorothea that I've seen you. One thing, are you really an officer of the provinces?'

'That depends on where you stand,' the Doctor replied, emitting a low chuckle that could have been a child's if it weren't so deep. 'Truth, like many things, is relative.'

Dodo sat on the steps of the caravan, watching the sun creep across the horizon, spilling light as it went. The sun was sharp, but not bright. Paris seemed a new city, its spires and towers framed against a warm blue sky. It was a cool, brittle morning, in fine contrast to the sweltering night. Dodo shivered as the breeze tickled her bare shoulders.

She was alone. Without the players, the wasteland seemed drained of its spirit. All the caravans were brightly painted, but the colours were dull echoes of the real, vivid light. Theatrical masks were painted onto the back end of the next caravan, smiling and crying for her benefit. The name 'Fantômas' snaked between them in stark black letters.

She staved off boredom by exploring her mouth, running her tongue along the inside of her teeth, poking into gaps and cavities. Her imagination ran riot, turning chipped teeth into breached ivory fortresses. Her mouth was a damp inviolate space, almost the last place she could really call her own.

The door hinges creaked behind her. Turning, she saw Dalville emerge from the scented interior. He was dressed simply in a crumpled white shirt and muddy-grey breeches, a buccaneer-look that reminded Dodo of every crummy pirate flick she had ever seen. His appearance woke a strange nostalgia in her, for a different world, a different life. He looked good.

'You're up early,' he remarked, pleasantly enough. It sounded false. She turned her head down, shadowing her face rather than returning his smile.

'Bressac got me up, before he went to the Bastille.'

'Hmm, I see he got you a new costume.'

Dodo's eyes flicked downwards automatically, to the gown that Bressac had fished out of the company's wardrobe for her. It was sumptuous. She had fallen instantly in love with it and had been a little hurt when Bressac pointed out the stains, the frayed patches and the faded colours. She didn't care – it was gorgeous, old-fashioned and authentic. Dalville tapped warm fingers against her exposed, fleshless shoulder blades. She squirmed, enjoying the small contact more than she felt she ought to.

'I suppose he also gave you the run of our palatial wash house, and fed you before he left,' the actor rattled on, carelessly. 'He's a good man, very diligent. He can be very emotional as well. He reads too much.'

'Yes.' The word almost choked her. 'Sorry, it's very cold. Can we go in?'

It was night inside the caravan, the heat and the darkness caught behind closed shutters. Dodo pulled a chair into the corner, feeling comfortable in the obscure edge of the room. Dalville's cream-white shirt shone in the gloom, drawing Dodo's eyes as he moved to the far side of the table. He stood rather than sat, and shifted nervously. It was a good act.

'There's a little wine left,' he offered.

'I'm not used to it. I think it went to my head last night.'

'Maybe later,' he said. He might have been smiling in the darkness.

'It's like a grave in here,' he added after a dry, shifting pause. 'Would you like me to open the shutters?'

'No, no,' Dodo responded, 'not on my account.'

The silence rolled – an enormous crushing presence in its own right. Dodo could hear Dalville's artificial breaths from the opposite corner. He was concentrating on breathing, she guessed. She knew the feeling, like those strange self-conscious moments when she had to take control of her eyelids, afraid that she had forgotten how to blink thoughtlessly. Her own breaths were wild by comparison.

'Bressac, uh –' she began breezily, stumbling immediately. She'd hoped to make this sound natural, like just another drop-in scrap of conversation. She began again, with emotion this time, and emphasis.

'Bressac said that you want to corrupt me. Is that true?'

Dalville smiled, a cruel ivory gleam amidst the dark.

'Yes.' It was a muted, candid reply.

Dodo turned away from him. If she was going to burst into tears, she didn't want to be looking at him.

'Were you trying to get me drunk? Last night? Just now?' she added.

'No. That would be taking advantage of you. That's not what I want.'

Dodo looked at him again, but his shape seemed hazy in the dark. She felt the first wet beads forming on her eyelids.

'I — I don't understand.' It was a hoarse whisper, the only steady tone she felt capable of controlling.

Dalville didn't answer at first, turning instead to the shutters on the windows. He pulled them open, expelling the darkness from the caravan. The sunlight prickled against Dodo's face and naked shoulders, making her feel vulnerable and exposed. She hardened instinctively, blinking frantically to kill her tears.

'Why does anyone pursue beauty?' he declaimed. He had a subtle but strong voice that felt soothing and calm to her ears. His arms were held in an open, elaborate gesture, another reassuring sign. She began to understand how good he must be on the stage. 'To possess it? To cherish it? To *bathe* in it? No! We pursue it so that we might destroy it!'

Dodo looked away from him, still trembling but now with an unexpected feeling. She broke into a fit of bitter laughter — real heart-felt laughter, not childish giggling. When she looked at Dalville again, there was humour shining in her eyes and a slight confusion in his.

'I'm *not* beautiful. I'm short, I'm dumpy and I have bad teeth.'

Dalville's features barely flickered. 'All right, not classical beauty then. It was always a facile virtue. I don't know what you'd call it. Your innocence, maybe.'

'I'm not going to be staying here forever.' She crossed her fingers as she spoke. 'How long were you planning to take?'

Dalville shrugged and let his head loll to one side. It occurred to Dodo that he was giving her glimpses of his mime and his theatre, but not much of himself. She didn't know him. She wanted to. She brought her hands together slowly.

He bowed, mocking her applause. 'You understand what I'm saying?' he said.

'Just about.'

'That's my first victory.' He winked at her, straightening from his bow.

Dodo grimaced, sighed and shook her head wearily. 'You're an idiot.'

'No. I have been, and I will be again, but at present I am a murderous and cunning villain.'

'Ah,' Dodo replied. She couldn't think of anything else worth saying. Neither could Dalville. He leaned back against the far wall, watching her with sombre eyes. Dust shone in the gap between them, caught by the morning sun.

'It's stuffy in here,' he said. He leapt away from the wall, towards the door, pulling it open with a flourish. The sudden breeze helped ease the tension at least. 'Would you like to meet some of the others?'

Dodo nodded and stirred, then slumped back into her chair, gazing at him suspiciously. A question had lodged itself at the forefront of her mind, where it growled, wolf-like, demanding an answer.

'What are the misfortunes of virtue?'

Dalville's features twitched – a genuine expression, Dodo thought.

'We toasted them last night. Were you talking about me?'

To her surprise, Dalville burst into a fit of good-natured laughter. He dropped to his knees beside her and smiled, beaming up at her as though he were an eager child, imparting a secret to a baffled parent.

'You are *wonderful*,' he said. '*The Misfortunes of Virtue* is the play we're performing at the Bastille.'

'I've never heard of it.'

'It's the first performance, adapted from an unpublished manuscript. You must've heard of *Justine*?' Dodo shook her head, sending a ghost of disappointment across Dalville's face. 'It's one of the Marquis de Sade's sizzling bestsellers. *The Misfortunes of Virtue* is the original text. Everyone thought the Marquise de Sade had destroyed the only copies. But somehow Fantômas got hold of one. Don't ask me how.'

The Marquis de Sade again. Dodo still couldn't place it. She shrugged. 'Why not just perform *Justine*?'

'Because,' Dalville pronounced, rising to his feet and somehow lifting Dodo after him. 'Because *Justine* is a bit naughtier than the original and our audience is easily shocked. Because it's easier to dramatize and there's less talk in it. Because it's unusual, and we wanted to catch Sade's eye. Because.'

He took her wrists, leading her to the door and down the steps, never taking his eyes from her as they moved. Dodo stumbled after him, her legs shaking and buckling beneath her. The air outside made her feel a little steadier. She leant against the caravan wall and asked about the play.

'You're full of questions,' Dalville observed, tapping her on the nose as the Doctor might. 'It's about a girl called Sophie –'

'Sophie?'

'Yes. She goes through life being tormented and abused. Every evil character she encounters is rewarded for their sins, but she never loses faith in the need to be virtuous. At the end, she's struck by lightning and killed.'

'That's horrible.'

'Dalville and Bressac are villains. Bressac's actually a better part, but Fantômas's casting calls are immutable, so I have to put up with fewer lines.'

Dodo thought about this until her forehead throbbed. 'So, your name isn't really Dalville? That's just your character.'

'While he's my character, my name *is* Dalville. It's only a name thing, thank Christ, or we'd never get on.'

Dodo frowned, still confused, staring at the man before her and seeing two people. She slumped further down the caravan wall, one hand rising to her temple. 'You're going too fast,' she mumbled. 'It's hurting me. And who's Fantômas? I thought . . . isn't it the company name, or something?'

81

'Fantômas is our director, the man who holds us together in adversity, though you won't believe that when you meet him. This is a secular world, and he's the closest thing we have to God.' He laughed briefly and bitterly.

Dodo felt no inclination to join in. The sourness vanished from Dalville's face and he grinned at her. That was another honest gesture. It came from the real man, a man she hadn't met.

'Now, you've asked so many questions, I think I deserve this.'

He pulled her close to him, suddenly but gently, and kissed her. Then he released her, letting her sink – numb and weary – back against the wall.

She asked him to explain everything to her again, slowly.

So he did.

The dead were roused by the morning alarm at the Bastille. It was shrill and hard, reverberating off the stone walls, murdering the silence. The alarm-bursts were punctuated by the click of keys in their locks, of barked orders and shuffling feet as the cells were emptied. Sade led his soldiers into the prison concourse, an instant too late to avoid the crowd.

Grey-skinned, grey-clad, grey-faced prisoners shambled out of the passages, raising bony fingers to cover their eyes against the sun. Some were emaciated, their uniforms ragged and filthy, clutching their punchcards in nervous, rigor mortis grips. Others – later arrivals – seemed in better condition but still blinked as they stumbled into the light. They shared a common expression – a hollow-faced sadness, beyond hope and despair. A few heads turned as Sade and his followers burst in, but their eyes were glassy and disinterested. Peacock-coloured sashes stood out against the swirl of grey, the gaolers herding their charges outwards.

'Numbers 2b and 5s!' someone shouted above the

alarm bells, a strained desperation in her voice. '2b and 5s! Show your cards to the nearest guard! You don't want to be misassigned! 2b and 5s!'

Sade stared at the mass of humanity seething through the courtyard. He hadn't realized that there could be so many – not in one day. Some of these prisoners were being taken to camps on the north coast. Most would go to the steam-guillotine, though there seemed little point. They looked dead already.

Not wanting to wait too long, Sade plunged into the crowd, struggling through the tide of grey and broken bodies to the far wall. He needed to keep the momentum going, drown out his doubts with action, with the throb of blood through his skull. He shoved through the living mass, reaching the door to Cameo's office and pushing his way inside.

The gaoler was leaning back in her chair. She flinched as Sade entered, her face curling as though she had swallowed something disgusting, and she jerked to attention, knocking her hat and several file cards from the desk in her haste. Sade glared at her suspiciously – there was something instinctively disrespectful in her flabby features. She rose slowly to her full and unimpressive height. Sade was delighted by her dismay. She thought they had come for her.

The younger man was no longer in the office, though he hardly mattered. The old man was still here, looming across the desk to intimidate Cameo. He turned as Sade entered, and his eyes flashed as the soldiers piled in behind. Sade flourished his pistol, pointing it at the old man's chest.

'Citizen Sade?' Cameo trembled barely perceptibly.

'Cameo,' Sade forced a reasonable edge into his voice, taunting her for her fear. 'This man is an enemy of the Revolution. He's suspected of curfew-breaking and the murder of a patrol. My son himself wants to question him.'

The old man chuckled to himself, irritating Sade.

'Citizen . . . hmmm? Formerly known as the Marquis de Sade perhaps?'

Sade bowed slightly, humouring the old fool.

The old man smiled curiously – for a prisoner he seemed very pleased with himself. 'Yes, now that's very interesting. You might be the very man I came here to see.'

'You're under arrest. You'll be held here until the First Deputy is ready to interrogate you.' He turned to Cameo. 'This is a special case. I want him in solitary under your personal guard. Have you a free cell?'

'We're just clearing out. I'll have to check today's manifest –'

Sade raised a hand.

'Don't bother.' He turned to the nearest soldier. 'Put him in cell 6.'

'6?' Cameo wore an expression like shattered glass.

'It's free. You've just emptied it.'

Cameo frowned, glancing around her as if debating whether to take her objection further. Her face hardened eventually, her eyes fixed on the floor.

'Cell 6,' she said, in a dreadful, strangled whisper.

The old man went with dignity, which was some help. It reminded Sade of some of the aristocrats, who had treated imprisonment as a bad joke, a mild annoyance that would be made right before any real damage was done. They had kept their dignity right up to the moment when the drum roll stopped and the blade fell. Then, too late, they screamed like children.

As I would have done. The thought popped unwelcome into his head.

'Excuse me, citizen, there's one small thing I'm curious about.'

'Let's hear it then,' Sade murmured. He seemed harmless enough.

'Am I correct in thinking that Minski is your son? That was the implication.' The question might have been meant to hurt him, but it was put in an innocent, bookish tone. There was a gentle, inquisitive gleam in the man's eye, and Sade felt compelled to answer.

'He's my adoptive son, yes.'

The old man broke into a chuckle, a smile radiating out of his childish, ancient face. They arrived at the cell before he could give voice to any more of his nonsense.

Cameo made a fuss of opening the door, fumbling with her keys and ignoring Sade's harsh gaze. The prisoner himself put up little resistance, stepping through the cell door without encouragement. Cameo slammed the door after him, locking it hastily.

Sade frowned, wondering whether it was his presence that was unsettling her. 'He's trouble, but he won't be here long.' He fixed the gaoler a glare of thorough contempt.

She grinned foolishly.

'Keep an eye on him.' He turned then, dismissing the soldiers with a gesture and walking away.

Cameo's delirious, relieved voice followed him along the passage, heralding the return of his dark, gnawing doubts.

'Yes, citizen. Thank you, citizen. I will.'

4

The Phantom of the Theatre

The more people Dodo met, the more she wanted to be left alone. It wasn't that the Fantômas Wandering Players were hostile – far from it, she'd been hugged so often her shoulders were aching. They were much friendlier than she expected, but she still felt distanced from them.

They were a parade of faces and false names. Everyone in the company acted it seemed, taking turns to work behind the scenes, mending costumes or building props. Their identities blurred in Dodo's mind, merging into a smooth whole against which only Dalville stood out. They welcomed her warmly, but their jokes and their gossip and the talk of their lives were lost on her. She found herself nodding and grinning weakly at every half-heard comment. She was not – never would be – a part of this. Dalville was a welcome presence, usually at her side, steering her through the crowd, helping her at awkward moments. She wished she could keep him to herself, alone for a moment.

She had expected the players to be flamboyant and radiant, and was a little disappointed to find they were a collective grey – indistinguishable from the crowds that tramped past their camp ground. They were intense, seeming devoted to studying their roles. Her own costume, she realized with self-conscious embarrassment, was easily the most colourful dress on the site.

The heat grew sharper, turning the morning tense and dry. Most of the players came to sit outside, stretched out on the scorched earth under the sun, their faces buried in their scripts. No longer the centre of attention, Dodo cast round the site, searching for a quiet patch of shade she could withdraw into. Her attention was drawn to the company's piano – a battered creature with one leg too few, propped up against the wall of a caravan in a pool of shadow. She approached, welcoming the cool dark.

'Do you play?' Dalville called. He was striding towards her, the sun framed behind his head like an undeserved halo. It was a good sign.

'A bit,' Dodo admitted. 'I'm not very good.'

'You can't be much worse than our last pianist.' She could see the sweat on his forehead as he got closer. He sighed, and she noticed that his generous smile was formed by the heat pinching his face. 'He was guillotined. It was going a bit too far – they should just have chopped his hands off.'

She didn't laugh. Neither did he.

'Would you like a player? I mean, I know I'm not going to be here forever, but . . . I'm at a loose end. I could play this, if you want.'

'It depends,' Dalville hmmed. 'What do you know?'

'I can play the national anthem with one finger.'

'That's probably treasonable. Anything else?'

'The "Ballad of the Last Chance Saloon"?' she suggested.

'I don't know that one.'

'You're in for a treat.' Her fingers mimed across the keys, but she held back, briefly afraid that there might be a terrible difference between the pianos of 1804 and 1966 that would show her up as a fake, a fraud, an anachronism. Her hands formed a tentative chord. It died, stillborn in her fingertips.

'Dorothea!'

Bressac emerged from between two distant caravans, shouting and waving. He darted across the field, weaving between the clustered actors. He had been battered by the heat, his hair drooping sadly across his face. His light skin seemed blanched in the harsh sunlight.

'Anything happen while I was gone?' he asked, his voice straining in the heat.

'No,' Dodo replied.

'More's the pity,' Dalville added. 'Where's Sophie?'

Bressac shook his head, his weary smile stretching into a grimace. 'She wasn't at the Bastille. She didn't get there. Apparently the patrol was ambushed. I've spent the last couple of hours running round Paris trying to find out if anyone saw.'

His eyes flicked to the ground. Dalville's followed, his face darkening despite the glare. For the first time since she'd left the TARDIS, Dodo felt the pure thrill of panic.

'What about the Doctor?'

'Oh,' Bressac said, brightening slightly. 'You were right. He's in his element there. He's got the gaoler hooked, like a fish on a line. He's *frightening*. I don't know how you can stand to travel with him.'

'Is he safe?' Dodo asked. 'Is he with you?' she added, though not hopefully.

Bressac shrugged. 'Yes. No. I'm sorry, I couldn't persuade him. Sorry.'

'Stop apologizing!' Dodo snapped. 'You've nothing to be sorry for.'

'Sorry, yes. Sorry,' he mumbled. 'He knows you're here, and that you're safe' – he made an ugly glance at Dalville – 'comparatively speaking. So, it's not all bad news.'

'Bad enough,' Dalville purred aggressively, his lips curved into a sour pout. Dodo twiddled her fingers anxiously, warding away her ill feeling.

'*Very* bad.'

The voice came from close by. It was a rough, wise voice with a slight melodic edge. It seemed ageless and bodyless, an immaculate invader. Dodo looked around for its source. She found it in a man, squatting on the ground by the edge of the caravan. Dodo didn't recognize him – she *would* have, had they been introduced. She wondered if he had been here all the time, unnoticed.

88

He looked up, his eyes meeting Dodo's for the first time. As he saw her, she felt newborn, as though by looking he had created her. He had deep, grey pupils – still points in his elusive features. He wore a light grey beard and his hair was a cascade of silver. A floppy, broad-rimmed hat perched on his head, casting a grim shadow across his face. A ragged peacock feather jutted from the hat – a mischievous note of colour.

'Tragedy, in point of fact.'

He stood. It took a while. He wasn't the tallest man Dodo had seen, but he created an illusion of stature. He dominated from his imaginary heights. A grey cloak swirled round him, as though it were another part of his body, under his control. His clothes were archaic, even for this time and place. Dodo suspected that it was deliberate, and not only deliberate but sane and cruel. His torn tunic and ragged shirt were a parody of Dalville's dress.

'Tragedy,' Dalville growled. He spat on the ground at the player's feet, sending a tremor across the newcomer's face. It might have been disgust, or amusement, or both. Dalville hunched his shoulders mean-spiritedly, hugging himself in the player's shadow.

'Sorry,' Bressac mumbled, wringing his hands desperately. The player nodded, but his eyes were cold.

'We must assume that Sophie is no longer with us,' the player barked, swinging round to address the gathered actors. Heads turned across the waste ground, the scattered clusters suddenly combining into a group focused round this one man. He was a living flame, beautiful to watch, dangerous to touch, liable to spread. 'It seems you can't rely on anyone! However, the show must go on! We continue as normal. Any questions,' he rumbled, coming to an end, 'can wait.'

He stalked away, waving carelessly to the group at the piano. Dalville scowled after him. Dodo's eyes watched his back as he strode across the field, at once grateful and disappointed that he had gone. She knew his name. Instinctively, she *knew*.

'You offended him,' Bressac purred, addressing Dalville.

'Good.' Dalville's face creased, then steadied. 'He doesn't care. He's God. And we're mortals. He uses us and discards us, and he's not going to come down off his pedestal for anyone. Not for Sophie, and not for you!'

Bressac turned sharply and trotted away, in the direction of his caravan.

'Pride, pride.' Dalville shook his head.

'That was rotten of you,' Dodo suggested. 'I think he likes him.'

'Likes?!' Dalville faked an actorly astonishment. 'Dorothea, Fantômas is the love of his life. He could spend effortless hours studying the back of his head. There's nothing *likes* about it. Is something wrong? You've gone red.'

'I'm sorry,' Dodo gasped. 'It's just . . . When you said last night, I didn't realize. I haven't ever . . . uh. Oh.'

'Actually,' Dalville hmmed, 'I could spend effortless hours studying the back of your head.' He had crept up close behind her and bent to taste the nape of her neck. Dodo squirmed.

'Stop it,' she hissed. 'You're embarrassing me.'

'Good.' Dalville's reply was muffled, his mouth working greedily downwards to her shoulders and her spine. Dodo stiffened, faking tolerance. She looked round at the scattered actors − listless jetsam on the broken shore − certain that they were all secretly watching and secretly smiling.

Dalville's lips burned. She might have enjoyed it, if it wasn't so public.

Dodo caught sight of Fantômas swaggering through the crowd. He was an ominous grey shade on the horizon, growing more solid with each step. Dalville − alerted silently − looked up. His kisses grew cold on her back.

'I must apologize,' the director said, reaching them and bowing.

'First time for everything,' Dalville grunted. Fantômas smiled. Like his voice, his smile was too cunning to be taken honestly. Dodo was on her guard this time. His presence still tugged at her, like the pull of a whirlpool. She could drown in him.

This could have been the Doctor, as a younger man.

'I am sorry. I am very rude. Dalville, what is this creature?' A skinny, glove-wrapped digit shot out and caught Dodo under the chin. She felt her head roll, balanced on his fingertip.

Dalville shouted something unpleasant, in another world. Dodo barely heard it. Fantômas, if he had heard, paid it no attention.

'Don't touch me!'

Fantômas's eyes glistened, drawing another answer from her.

'Dodo,' she added softly, 'Chaplet.'

'Ah, a blushing virgin.'

Dodo grimaced, feeling the blood rush to her face.

Fantômas spoke again, whispering in a strange, painful voice. 'Savour it. It doesn't last. It's theirs in the end.'

Dodo blinked. The finger vanished from her throat and her chin sagged. Something sweaty and leathery was clamped on her forearms – Dalville's hands, she realized, clutching her protectively. Fantômas had stepped back and was rubbing his hands together, whistling thoughtfully.

'Innocence! That's what you have, Dodo. An unsullied faith in the world, in people, in things. I doubt you've ever known a single malicious or lascivious thought,' he declaimed, twirling round to address the audience of players. He half-turned to add a final word in a whisper the whole field could hear. It was meant solely for her. It was meant for everyone.

'Sophie.'

Dalville's fingers dug into her. For a moment, she didn't understand why.

Then she did.

Fantômas hadn't moved. He seemed to be laughing, soundlessly.

'No,' Dodo spat. 'It's stupid anyway. I've never acted in my life.'

'No?'

'I was in a nativity play once. I was Mary. I had a pillow stuck up my front and I rode into Bethlehem on a hobby-horse. I didn't have to say anything.'

'You, Mary, Sophie. Similar roles. Dalville will lend you a script.'

Dodo turned to Dalville, appealing to him. 'I can't do it. I *can't*. Tell him!'

Dalville pursed his lips thoughtfully. 'I think you'll do very well.' He leaned closer, pushing his head against hers and planting a whisper in her ear. 'He's usually right, when it comes to casting.'

Dodo pulled back, staring at him in disbelief. His face seemed random, a happy accident at the base of a kaleidoscope. As she watched, it splintered into beautiful fragments of colour, swirling against the grey sky.

'I won't be here,' she protested weakly. 'I'll be going soon.'

'When you go, you go,' Fantômas said distantly. 'We'll get someone else.'

Dodo slumped back onto the piano keyboard, sending coarse notes jarring across the camp site. Her hands went to her face, covering herself in darkness.

'Are you all right?' Dalville called. 'Sophie?'

'Yes,' she said, after a deeply felt moment. 'Yes, I'm fine.'

A cell was a cell was a cell. That was a truth the Doctor had learned through hard experience. This was better than some. It was hardly luxury, hardly squalor. The design was basic, functional, but not barbaric – four walls, bed, even a wash basin. It lacked imagination, but no cell required imagination. It was roomy, holding as much space as every other prison the Doctor had known – *not enough*.

In normal circumstances, he would have squatted on the bunk and cursed his fortune. He had the energy to keep his bluff going indefinitely – it was simply bad luck to be recognized so quickly. After a moment's self-pity, he would have relaxed and rested, and waited to be taken to Citizen Minski. In normal circumstances, in a normal cell.

This cell contained an oddity.

It squatted on the floor. It stared at the cell from behind an elegant velvet mask, of the same blue material as its clothing. It hadn't moved or spoken in the hours since the Doctor's arrival. At times, it was so still it seemed dead, unbreathing, perhaps never-alive. Its silence was almost resentful, as if this were its world, and the Doctor an invader.

Since the Doctor had been imprisoned, the gaoler's face had appeared at the window, glowering at him with monotonous regularity. She resented him as much as his faceless, fellow prisoner did. He understood now her irritation and her fear. The masked man was something secret and dangerous.

Hours passed. He rested, perched upright on the bed, trying to think.

'Now,' he said, striking his hands together, 'there is something very strange here, and I intend to get to the bottom of it.' He eased off the bunk and into a squat shape on the floor. His bones moaned as he forced them into the painful, unfamiliar posture.

The masked creature sat opposite him, staring.

'When I was imprisoned here, it was on the strict understanding that this was a solitary cell,' the Doctor continued blithely, hoping to coax some response from the unmoving shape. 'Imagine my dismay to find you here. I am a very dangerous prisoner. I value my privacy. Putting aside the distinct possibility that you are simply a figment of my imagination, or some variety of – hmm? – stuffed decoration, I should say that –'

'Tick.' The voice from the mask cut him off, simply.

'And what does that mean? Hmm?'

'Tock.'

'Tick,' the Doctor ventured.

The featureless mask glowered. '*Tick*,' it insisted. '*Tock*. Tick. *Tock*.'

'Tock,' the Doctor ventured again, breaking the flow this time.

The mask was silent for a beat. Then it screamed.

'Tick! Tick! *Tick*! Tickticktickticktickticktickticktickticktick! *Bang*!'

The Doctor nodded, chuckling to himself. 'So, you're a time bomb. Do you have a name?'

The mask was silent. Smooth, velvet silence.

'No? May I?' The Doctor reached out and touched the prisoner's face, not certain at first how he would react. The velvet crumpled pleasantly between the Doctor's fingertips, and the man remained still. Slowly, the Doctor eased it away from his face, letting it fall forgotten to the floor. His cell mate made no move for it.

Beneath the mask was an old face, a chubby face, an empty face. Time had worn it down, and years without sunlight had bleached it ice-white. It was smooth and expressionless, like the scrap abandoned in the corner. Unlike the velvet mask, the flesh mask had been marked by pain and fear. He had wispy hair, some strands of blonde still shining from amongst the grey. His mouth was tight, his lips chapped and broken. Only his eyes seemed unbroken by time. Something brooded in those watery blue pupils – an unyielding sanity, defying the mask and the cell and everything else around him. The Doctor realized that he was neither senile nor mad. He was silent through choice.

'I'm being foolish. I am sorry,' the Doctor said, easing his limbs out of the awkward squat. He got to his feet and sighed. The old prisoner was still silent, but the Doctor imagined that somewhere in that noiseless void, his apology had been accepted.

He had been here for a long time, this prisoner. He

probably should have been executed long before. Cameo must have been protecting him.

'I am going to try and escape,' the Doctor announced, coming to a sudden decision. 'My whole life is like this. I am imprisoned, I escape. I am imprisoned again, again I escape. My life is a sequence of cells, dungeons, oubliettes, caves and traps, again and again.

'You might ask why I bother,' he chuckled to himself, clutching his lapels and reminiscing. 'You might well ask. Are you listening to me? Good. Cells exist to keep the outside out. Their very nature demands our escape. A locked door exists only to be unlocked. I escape because I value my liberty. That's a good principle, perhaps the best I have, and if I cannot rouse you with that, then you, sir, cannot be roused at all!'

Silence. The old man's eyes rolled across him then fell still. The Doctor felt a moment's disappointment, then a moment's disgust, then put the wretch out of his mind, turning to the door.

'Liberty.'

The Doctor spun sharply. The nameless old prisoner still sat squat on the floor, his expression unbroken. Only his lips moved, twitching with words and sentences, and with meaning.

'There is no liberty. She's dead.' He raised his head at last, to fix the Doctor with a plaintive stare. 'I did it. I killed her. It was me.'

The noon chimes pursued Sade through the subterranean passages. The tunnels were icy and deceptively dark. Out of the glare of the sunlight, Sade might have forgotten himself and mistaken the shrill, distant peals for the midnight bell.

The darkest shadows were in the laboratory. Minski's wetscreen flickered on the far wall, casting a little light. Sade moved between unseen but familiar obstacles towards the glow. Minski stood beneath it, his head craned upwards. The glare lent his skin a trembling, silver sheen.

It seemed to Sade that his son was composed of unsettled water. Waves broke across him, he seemed to grow. The tide retreated, he shrank. He smiled at his father.

'Are you ready for the old man yet?' Sade asked.

Minski shook his head noiselessly. The silence was wrong, Sade felt, the motion should *crash* – like the sea against the shore.

'We have his box. He can sweat. Besides,' he continued, 'I'm distracted. There are English spies in Paris. They're using an ansible to communicate with their masters at Medmenham. They think they're unseen.'

Sade focused on the screen and the shimmering image there. He saw a cavern – a dark, dry place with jagged, natural walls. It was packed with men – a collection of old, gaunt faces with little to tell between them, so grey and raw that they seemed carved from the rock. They wore their robes and cowls uncomfortably. Their jaws wagged noiselessly. They were a solemn bunch, with a deep sobriety etched into their faces, but without sound they seemed comic and hollow to Sade.

'The reformed Hellfire Club,' Sade guessed.

Minski nodded. 'The whole of Mister Pitt's government is there. And its allies. That one' – he pointed to a scar-faced monk whose arm was held in a sling – 'is Alexander Hamilton. He's here on behalf of the Americas. There's also a Russian, and an Austrian. It's very cosmopolitan.'

One of the men squatted on the floor at the forefront of the image. His robes were tattered, shredded into rags. His mouth flexed into strange, ceaseless, babbling shapes. He fell onto his side and rolled on the ground, a mute howl forming on his lips.

'Poor, mad George Hanover,' Minski commented dismissively. 'He's ruled by his son these days. And his son is ruled by his butler. So it's said.'

'Shouldn't you put the sound on?' Sade asked. 'They look foolish.'

'I prefer it this way.'

'It might be important.'

'I know most of what they're saying. I had a hand in its devising, though they don't know that,' his son added, a glimmer of smugness entering his dry tone. 'They're discussing the invasion, the forthcoming attack on France.'

Sade experienced a surge of pleasure, an unambiguous delight at the prospect of open war. He kindled the hope that his age and position wouldn't preclude him from fighting. The field of war offered unimaginable opportunity for new experiences and atrocities.

'It's a trap, of course?' he asked.

His son nodded. 'The oldest of all traps.' Minski spoke in a gravel tone, each word delivered ponderously, in sparse patches. It was a hateful, ancient voice. 'They think they're all-powerful, that they cannot lose. But I'm all-knowing, and they can't win.'

The next thing he said made no sense to Sade. He wasn't even certain that it could be called a word. It was a sound, a noise. It was less than that, it was a gesture, made with the mouth, unsettling the air. The screen responded, fading into dull static. Sade, his moment of excitement passed, felt the world go numb and dark around him. Only Minski seemed real – the distorting light of the screen making him old and hunched.

'They worship Satan in England, and America,' Minski drawled, wheeling round to face Sade, plunging half his face into eclipse as he moved. 'And in Spain, the Italies, Russia and North Africa, and the Holy Roman Empire is holy no longer. They're afraid of the light, I think. They retreat into the deepest, darkest shadows. They are the nightmares of reason. Don't you agree?'

Sade's eyes shuffled round the room, searching for something else to latch onto. The darkness hid everything, except his son.

'I . . . don't know,' he admitted.

'You don't know? The great philosopher has no opinion?'

'I haven't thought about it much, not lately.'

Not since you came to power, my son. Not for ten years.

'Perhaps our enlightenment has displaced their religion?' Minski suggested airily. 'It's dispelled the shadows of heaven, and shown that they're empty. Godless, they retreat into superstition, into the unexplainable. They find Satan – or a creature that could be called Satan. What do you think?'

'Given the choice between believing in a goblin and our fellow humans,' Sade suggested with a wry smile, 'most of us would choose the goblin.'

Minski smiled too, though falsely.

'I am their enemy, and their allies' enemy,' he continued. Sade listened patiently. 'I've displaced God. Do you understand what I must do, to restore order to the world?'

Sade shook his head, though he knew what his son was about to say.

'I become God.' There was no madness in his voice, or in his eyes. There was no zeal, no glee, no emotion at all at the prospect. His voice was as drab and humourless as ever. That was the most frightening part of it.

'I will be a God of Reason,' Minski droned, 'a benevolent God. Everything will be for the best, in the best of all possible worlds. You agree?'

Sade thought, then sank to his knees, his eyes thrown to the floor.

'Father,' he said simply. It sounded right.

Minski stepped forward and put his hand on Sade's forehead. His palm was cool and its texture felt alien to Sade. He was forgetting, he realized, that this was Godflesh. Sade imagined his son in the part of a deity, omnipotent and banal, hiding behind darkness and façades, uncaring. It seemed plausible.

'My son,' Minski murmured. 'My son.'

The Pageant.

At the Hour of Scampering, Larkspur stood restless and

alone beneath the dome of light. He kept to the edge of the scene, away from the clusters of dancers. He had no wish to speak to others. And they, in turn, ignored him.

The pale glow of the dome was obscured by strands of darkness, weaving and twining together, forming complex patterns and webs across the sky. The light peered through occasional chinks but, as Larkspur watched, these holes were sealed, one by one obliterated by the gathering night. Beneath the dome, the Masqueraders were growing the seventeen airships required for the war. Larkspur was at once enthralled and saddened by the sight.

He was distracted by a soft rustling close by. Looking round, he saw a dancer strutting determinedly towards him, its long robes whispering as they trailed across the floor. Larkspur felt a moment's joy, suddenly lost to a cold, churning fear. This was not a meeting he desired.

Hello, Ahasuerus, he said, bowing simply.

Hello, outcast, came the reply. Colour and warm light seeped from the edges of Ahasuerus's mask. For a slow moment, Larkspur was reassured.

Then Ahasuerus's long, pale fingers went to his shoulders, smoothing out a fold in his robes. Larkspur's calm was shattered. He pulled back hastily, out of the dancer's reach. Several of his eyes spun, scanning the dome floor in case any others of the Pageant had seen. As far as he could tell, none had. He turned back to his companion, sharp and angry greys filtering through the lenses of his mask.

Have you no shame? he asked.

Not in this mask, Ahasuerus replied. Larkspur felt his lightbody bleach with despair. He slumped backwards, dropping into a squat on the dome floor. Above him, the twitching limbs of the black ships formed from the web, ignorant of the discomfort far beneath them.

I apologize, the mask said softly. *It's rare to find you without the company of Tyll Howlglass. I forgot myself.*

Larkspur nodded gratefully, but said nothing.

May I ask where Howlglass is?

He speaks with King Mob. He seeks support for our position.

He won't get it. Not from Mob. No one who could help you, will.

I know that. I told him that, Larkspur said softly, trying to hide his frustration. A thought struck him, and he rose to his feet to address his companion. *You could help us.*

No.

You could! Larkspur insisted. He realized his hands were on Ahasuerus's robes, trembling against the decaying fabric. He was briefly ashamed, but suddenly it no longer seemed to matter. He steadied his hands and tugged, drawing Ahasuerus's mask closer.

You could! You can see what is happening. We have become fragmented. Our enemy is turning us against each other, mask against mask! Do you really believe that we would be waging a war if our decisions were truly our own? We have never acted so foolishly in the past.

Ahasuerus's voice hummed wordlessly from behind his mask. *You believe that the system operator influences us?*

More. I believe he is making our plans for us.

Is this what you believe, or is it something Tyll Howlglass has said?

It is both! Larkspur insisted, then hesitated, wondering if perhaps he had made a mistake.

Forgive me, Ahasuerus said. His voice was kind — a reassuring, velvet black murmuring from behind the mask — but it filled Larkspur with despair. It was a voice for denying with, a voice that would say no. *I recognize everything you say as possible, and more than that, as true. But equally, the operator may be making your plans for you. We may all be playing his game. Such wonderful uncertainty! No. I do not support this war, but I cannot support you.*

Larkspur slumped back to the floor, despairing. He leaned upwards and spat his answer at Ahasuerus's mask. *Your neutrality could also be a part of the operator's plan.*

Inaction, not neutrality.

Whatever.

Again, I apologize. I must admit to having political motives. Howlglass's performance at the last dance — with the human Arouette — was far from reassuring. It looks as though she is barely under our control.

She is under no one's control but her own. Larkspur sighed wearily. *But she understands what is happening. Her actions may be her own, but they are reliable.*

That's as may be. Sadly, Howlglass has compromised himself.

What? Startled, Larkspur spoke sharply. He gazed uncertainly up at the mask of Ahasuerus.

With the two agents of the English crown.

Now they are a law unto themselves, Larkspur interjected, though reluctantly. He needed to hear what Ahasuerus had to say.

They have loyalties of their own, the other mused. *Unfortunately for you, Howlglass has been asking them to pursue your case. There has been a private dance at Pageant's Heart. The rhythm tends to having you and he expelled from the Pageant.*

Larkspur thought for a moment, his eyes darting across his face as he pondered tightening options, and new possibilities. He looked desperately to his fellow dancer. *Your advice?* he asked.

Get out of here. Go to the Paris node and direct your activities from there. Take Tyll Howlglass if you must. They may still bar you from returning, but at least you will have seized the initiative.

We would truly become outcasts . . .

You would, little one.

Larkspur found himself nodding. A sudden, desperate fear had fallen across him. He was grateful for Ahasuerus's presence. His mask was something reassuring and solid amidst the turmoil. It was something worth clinging to.

Thank you, friend, he replied, trying to work up the energy to beam a calm blue into Ahasuerus's eyes. He couldn't manage it, and instead he found himself staring limply down at his reedy, brittle fingers.

Larkspur, his friend said quietly. *There is something that could persuade me to take sides.*

Yes? Larkspur was cautious.

The box that appeared in Paris . . . The marvellous creatures it contained . . . If you could find them, and convince them to aid you in your cause, I would be persuaded. I feel some affinity with them. They're fellow travellers, so to speak.

Yes, of course. I will do my best.

Thank you. Ahasuerus's hand fell on Larkspur's shoulder, where it rested comfortably. This time Larkspur felt no need to pull away.

One last thing. Why did you choose the mask of Larkspur? What is It? Is It a warrior, a saying, a principle or a god? Is It female, male, epicene or other? Is It a wanderer, like Ahasuerus, or is It a trickster, like Howlglass?

Larkspur brought his hands together, his frail knucklebones cracking under the pressure. He answered slowly, painfully. *It is . . . vegetation.*

Ah.

I was misinformed.

No. No, the mask of Ahasuerus said, gently. *It is appropriate:*

> 'My vegetable love should grow
> Vaster than empires, and more slow.'

A human construct. It suits you.

And you also, Ahasuerus.

The dancer pulled away slowly, his cloak hissing as it stroked the floor. Larkspur watched in silence as the figure dwindled before disappearing from the dome entirely. He lowered his mask from his face into his hands, studying it passionlessly. His fingers felt cold and distant.

I still love you, he said wistfully, *very much.*

Above him, the finished airship withdrew from the appendages on which it had been suckling and rose through the dome into the world that awaited it.

* * *

'Sophie. I'm Sophie.'

She scratched the words onto the top of the script with a lump of charcoal. Her hand shook and the letters were thin and ragged. She steadied herself and added another sentence, in neater letters, below the first.

'What does that mean?'

It means I'm a part of them, no longer alone.

It means I'm not Dodo.

It means I have to stand in front of strangers and do things I don't want to.

She hadn't bothered to read the script. She was scared of reading, frightened that studying Sophie's lines would pull her into the character. She'd flipped through the pages, finding the dialogue and directions typed in neat, bold letters. That shocked her, and she remembered that in this France, in this history, things were not as they should be. The shock faded quickly; history didn't seem so important. She threw the script away, across the room.

'It's not what you think,' she told herself, 'but what you can remember.'

I only saw the first Sophie for a moment, but I remember her. She was tall and blonde and gorgeous. She was fab, just fab.

That's who I have to be.

She crouched on her bunk, huddled in a foetal ball, deep in the darkness. The door to the next room was closed, as were the shutters over the window. The light came thinly sliced, catching bristling dust particles in the air. She was locked in, alone with the stuffy heat and the stifling darkness. She felt safe like this, protected against the encroaching world.

Time passed, unmeasured and meaningless. She tried not to think, rocking her body gently and allowing herself to become seduced by the rhythm. She lost interest in the room around her, lost interest in looking and hearing and feeling. Shapes blurred in her head, vanishing with the time. She expelled them, retreating into her body, into her self.

The heat was a distraction. It was trapped in the

caravan with her, growing ever more intense. It was a humid, lazy afternoon warmth. It made her skin sticky, then clinging, then damp. She shifted on the bed as her gown hardened against her back and her chest and her thighs. The fabric peeled away slightly, but half-heartedly, leaving her feeling irritated and soiled. Sweat dribbled against her skin, and she felt dirty and ugly.

It felt good though, to be sitting there, alone.

She began to dream. She sat in the corner, still and awake and dreaming.

She dreamed of a tree she'd known as a child. It was a huge, gnarled oak that stood at the far end of the park. She used to play under it in the short but endless summer holidays. She learned its shape and the texture of its bark, she found every secret grip and discovered every sturdy branch. She'd tried to climb it once, but fell and cut herself, though not badly.

She'd been lucky. The same year a boy from another school fell from another tree in the same park and broke his neck. Falling, she had known exactly what he must have known, in the brief moment between the branches and the ground. Her mother had been upset and banned her from climbing again. The council cut down all the trees that autumn.

Her memories of this time were black ones, mostly.

The dead tree – which had been felled in 1957 and was probably no more than a sapling at this moment – appeared in the far corner of the caravan. It creaked and twisted in the dream wind. There was a face engrained on its skin, and, below the face, a torso hidden in the whorls of the gnarled bark. Its branches were arms, with spindly twig-fingers stretching across the room. It couldn't reach her. The gulf was too far. It screamed, the wind howling through hollow roots and branches.

The hinges of the caravan door shrieked, startling her out of the dream. She looked up sharply, expecting something hideous to be caught in the door frame. She found a familiar face, lonely and guarded but sympathetic.

It was perhaps the friendliest face she remembered recently. She struggled to put a name to it.

'It's very hot,' the man said, holding up a bottle and a mug. 'I brought you something to drink. It's bottled water, from Alsace.'

She nodded sullenly. She didn't want to move from her safe crouch in the corner, but she did, clambering out of the darkness to perch on the edge of the bunk. The newcomer was trying to be kind, and she didn't want to hurt him.

Bressac, she thought.

Her own name escaped her, and she almost panicked. Bressac helped her.

'So,' he said as he poured a carefully measured dose from the bottle, 'is it to be Sophie or Dorothea? Or Dodo even? I hear you prefer that.'

'Dodo, thanks.' She took the mug from him, taking a first, greedy gulp. Bressac stood and watched her, holding himself at an awkward distance, too scared to come any closer. After a moment, he began to fidget. He pulled open the window shutters, letting in the air and the light.

'We'll have to call you Sophie whenever Fantômas is around.' He paused thoughtfully. 'He'd only get upset. You don't mind?'

Dodo shook her head, taking another gulp.

'I know it seems a bit . . . a lot unfair. Fantômas is like that. He's a good man though, and he's usually right, and he's like that with everyone.'

'He's very persuasive,' Dodo said, feeling much livelier. She put it down to a combination of the open window and the invigorating water.

'He brooks no objection,' Bressac murmured darkly. He lowered himself onto the opposite bunk. He picked up Dodo's script and flicked through it though there was no concentration in his eyes.

'There's something very odd about him,' Dodo suggested. Bressac's pupils leapt up from the script, suddenly intolerant and humourless. 'I don't know,' Dodo continued lamely. 'If you look in his eyes, you see something serious that . . . well, it just isn't anywhere else! It's like he's an old man pretending to be younger, or a young one pretending to be older. It's something fake.'

Bressac threw the script onto the bunk. His lips curled. 'I know,' he said dolefully. 'I know exactly what you mean.'

'He knows me.' Dodo shrugged, scrabbling helplessly for words to express her feelings. 'I've been acting all my life, and he *knows*!'

'I heard you say — yell, in fact — that you hadn't acted.'

Dodo pinched her lower lip with her teeth. It went numb before she spoke. 'I grew up in one of the poorest parts of London. When my parents died, I went to live with my aunt. She wasn't rich, but she was comfortable. She was a real social climber, and everyone she knew was exactly like her. I spent the rest of my childhood shunting between extremes. I couldn't understand how they could exist together in the same world! I had to reinvent myself to keep up with all the changes.

'So,' she finished, realizing that she was almost shouting, and lowering her voice, 'I've acted all my life. All the world's a stage.'

'It's not.' Bressac tapped his nose thoughtfully. 'There's no rehearsal, no proper audience, no intermission, one performance only. Behind the scenes there are only more scenes. You can't tell if it's a tragedy or a comedy, but you know that, sooner or later, it'll be an historical. Daggers have solid blades and the blood is real.'

'You're cheerful today. Please could I have some more water? Thanks,' she added as he refilled her mug. 'I want to tell you something. Just you, because you've met the Doctor. You'll understand.' She tasted the water calculatedly, leaving a curious Bressac stranded on the bunk.

'We travel alone now, but until recently, there was another one of us, a man called Steven. He was a few years older than me. He'd been with the Doctor for a while before I met them.

'Recently, we visited another, uh, country, where we found two groups of people that the Doctor managed to reconcile. That's where we left Steven. The Doctor just dumped him and we were off before anyone could complain. I thought it was a rotten thing for him to do, and I resented him at the time.

'But now, I think I understand why he did it. When he met the Doctor, Steven was a prisoner. He hadn't seen another person in two years. I can't imagine that. I can't imagine how lonely he must have been. That's why I think the Doctor left him where he did. Because it was a place where he wouldn't ever be alone. It was the right place for him.

'That's where I want to be, when he leaves me. In the right place.'

She sighed. Bressac though was staring at her ear, his eyes blank and his lips trembling. Her head turned slightly to return his stare.

'I'm sorry,' he said. 'I was thinking – about what you were saying, and about myself. I ran away from home – I lived on a farm – just after the Revolution. Do you want to know why?'

'Yeah,' Dodo nodded, leaning forward curiously.

'It was boring!' He blasted her with his voice. 'It was provincial. I was this soft-skinned fifteen-year-old, full of life and energy in a slow and dead world. I could have any girl I wanted, though the more I tumbled the less I wanted. I wasn't unhappy, but it was dull, and there were magical things happening elsewhere. So, I ran away.

'A couple of years after I left, my family was killed for being too rich and too royalist. My mother was thrown to a pack of starved circus wolves. I wasn't there, because I didn't want to be there. And I lived.

'I met Dalville the day after Marat was murdered. Our first company was dissolved five years ago, and we joined the Fantômas Wandering Players soon after that. We stick together.'

Dodo frowned.

A cool, thoughtful expression formed on Bressac's face. 'I know what you're thinking, but you're wrong. Dalville is my friend. I can't think of him in any other sense. As for his attitude, well . . .' He coughed. 'You know what I told you this morning?'

'That he wants to corrupt me?' Dodo nodded. 'He's being quite honest about it. I don't see how he plans to do it though.'

'He's a bit vague about that, but he'll find proof of it everywhere. The world is full of signs and portents. It's all rubbish. The truth is that he fancies taking you to bed with him. He can't admit that, not even to himself, so he's turned it into a philosophy of action.'

'You don't have to protect me,' Dodo said kindly, 'or him.'

'No.' Bressac shook his head. 'Ignore me. I'm waffling. Rabbiting on. I can't help it. Sorry. Still, it proves my point.'

There was a false silence, no more than a moment. Dodo struggled to latch onto Bressac's gaze, but it eluded her, his eyes darting carelessly around the room. He was blushing and his grin was so severe it was in danger of becoming a grimace. Dodo wanted to laugh and shatter the humourless moment, but she thought better of it.

'Bressac. Have you told Fantômas what you think?'

'No one tells Fantômas what they think. It's not healthy.'

'I don't think you're going to get anywhere with him if you don't.'

'Ah,' he said. 'Yes.' He clasped his hands together and flexed his fingers. Dodo could hear the minute sound of his bones cracking. 'That would be a good idea.'

Dodo crossed the room to retrieve the script from beside him.

'I'd better read this,' she said bluntly, lacking the energy to elaborate on the statement. Bressac smiled at her and made for the door. Dodo slumped back onto her bunk, situating herself as comfortably as possible, caught in the light and the breeze from the window. She gave the title page a cautious glance: 'LES INFORTUNES DE LA VERTU'. She turned the page and began to read.

In the hours since his companion had begun to speak, the Doctor rediscovered his patience. He had soon realized that his customary bluff and bluster were unhelpful. His fellow prisoner would not be coaxed or cajoled, meeting aggressive questions with a proud, canny silence.

The Doctor still thought of him as a masked man. The mask was a rag, forgotten on the floor, but the old man's guarded posture and silence were unchanged. There was still a difference. Before, he had been a blank — a repressed and thoughtless object. Without the mask, he was transformed. His face flexed through a hundred different positions, savouring expressions he hadn't used for years. His eyes prowled greedily round the cell, exploring and conquering its space. There was a cold irony on his lips.

The Doctor was astonished by the extent of emotion humans could convey through their faces. Perhaps it was because their minds were so silent, so barren and isolated. There was more than emotion here though. The maskless man's face was a study of icy intelligence. Watching him, the Doctor felt that he was looking at his own reflection, in a spirit mirror with distorting glass.

The man spoke freely and quietly, though rarely in answer to the Doctor's slow and careful questions. His responses were oblique and instinctive, and the Doctor began to understand why Citizen Cameo was eager to keep him a secret.

'I am not a free man,' he said, after the Doctor had asked his name for the fifth time. 'I am le 6.'

'Hmm? What's that?' the Doctor asked, startled by this success.

'I'm called Monsieur le 6 by the gaoler. She says that the marquis gave her the idea, which is true. He is seminal. There are gaps in the air.'

'You mean Cameo, and Sade?'

The man who was called le 6 gave him an odd stare. 'There are gaps in the air,' he repeated cheerfully.

'Surely you must know their names?'

'What are names? Mine was taken from me. I am reduced to a number. I think there is some irony in this, though it eludes me exactly.'

'You don't recall your name?' The Doctor struggled to contain his impatience.

'No. Do you have a name?'

'I am the Doctor,' he sniffed, realizing too late that this was a trap.

'No.' Le 6 nodded and smiled. 'There are gaps in the air.'

This was the third time he had said this and the Doctor was intrigued. It was his last lucid moment for a while. He lapsed back into silence, though his pupils lingered, exploring the room around him. He seemed to find the plain squareness of the cell fascinating. The Doctor was left exhausted and frustrated. He stretched out on the cell's bunk, allowing the surface to absorb his weariness. He didn't sleep, but lay with his eyes open. He projected his thoughts and findings onto the blank ceiling, mentally working through the problem.

The problem was that this history was false. The solution, he had already decided, must lie at a pivotal moment in the recent past, when history was weak and malleable. Staring at the vast grey slate that was the cell's ceiling, he began to feel that he might be wrong, that there might not be a single point when the world was changed. He could sense the wrongness of this world, but he doubted there was much difference between the cause and the symptoms of the wrongness.

Minski lay at the heart of the problem, he was certain, if only because he had no equivalent in real history. He wasn't certain though – it might be Minski's adoptive father at the root of the problem. Le 6 had told him that Sade was 'seminal', though le 6's word hardly constituted proof. There was also the question of the alien mask, and the Englishmen, and the awkward technology that the revolutionaries seemed to possess. He couldn't see the connections. The problem was still too complex.

He hated it. He hated all the half-facts and shadow-truths. He needed to find sense.

'I don't have enough time,' he said, tasting the irony of his words.

'We are slaves to time,' said the man on the floor, his head unturned. 'Ticktockticktock,' he added. The Doctor rose from the bunk and squatted beside him on the floor.

'Do you know what is wrong with the world?' he asked.

'There are gaps in the air,' was the unhelpful reply. The Doctor wondered if it might not be an idea to follow this lead, to try and wrest some sense from le 6's madness.

'Why are there gaps in the air? Did Minski make them?'

A disdainful smile slipped across the old man's lips. 'Minski uses them. They were made by . . . by others.'

'You mean yourself?' The Doctor regretted the asking immediately. Le 6 clammed up again, silent and sullen as if he had still been wearing the mask. The Doctor clicked his tongue and began to study his knuckles – it helped relieve the tension.

'What have you done?!'

Cameo's shrill voice burst into the cell. The Doctor turned and saw the gaoler's face pressed to the window. She was a picture of aghast horror, her eyes bulging as she surveyed the scene in the cell. The window snapped shut almost as soon as the Doctor looked, and he scrambled to his feet when he heard the crack of keys in the lock.

The cell door swung into the room, followed by the horrified gaoler. She stalked into the room, though her rotund figure made the effect more grotesque than menacing. She tugged her pistol from its waistband and flourished it, stabbing the muzzle at the Doctor's throat.

111

Her contempt, it seemed, was aimed at him, but her eyes flicked constantly to the old man who sat cross-legged and still on the floor. Her horror was there.

'What have you done?' She spoke like a distraught beggar, tears swelling under her eyes.

The Doctor shook his head, baffled.

'He has set me free.' Le 6 said. It was the worst thing he could have done, as it prompted the hatred back into her eyes. She bared her teeth and swiped at the Doctor's head with her flintlock. He stepped back quickly, almost overbalancing in his haste.

'You've spoiled it!' the gaoler squeaked. 'You've ruined everything!'

The Doctor's lips twitched to protest his ignorance, but the sound died as the butt of Cameo's pistol struck his temple. He fell back onto the bunk, clutching his face. The gaoler slung the pistol aside and leapt on him, both hands rising to latch round his throat, thumbs pressing into the soft flesh above his windpipe. He seized her wrists and tried to pull them away, but she was strong and determined and her body was younger than his.

There was a short, deadly *click* close by.

For a moment, the Doctor felt nothing but a light-headed dizziness. Feeling returned to his neck gradually, and he realized that the gaoler's hands were no longer there. Her face loomed over him like a statue. Her grim, nervous expression could have been carved. Her shaking ruined the effect. Le 6 stood to one side of her, the discarded pistol in his hands, held behind Cameo's ear.

'Gaoler,' he said, 'as an individual I've killed no one. But I was once a soldier, the worst kind of murderer. Remember that.'

The Doctor eased his way out from beneath the paralysed woman and caught his breath.

Le 6 gave him an easy smile from the side of his mouth.

'Shall we go?' the Doctor suggested.

Le 6's mouth formed a silent yes.

'I should warn you,' Cameo said, 'that all the exits on this level are heavily guarded. They'll recognize you as escapees and shoot you down. If you want to escape, go up into the tower, or down to the tunnels.'

'That would be rather convenient,' the Doctor replied haughtily, 'for the search parties, young lady.'

'She won't tell,' le 6 said. 'She has a debt to repay.'

'Yes,' the gaoler agreed wistfully. 'Of course.'

The Doctor nodded his agreement, realizing that he wanted to remain in the tower – which seemed symbol and centre of the false world – if he could. Besides, neither he nor le 6 were young any more. A quick getaway was out of the question. The old prisoner seemed happy to be active though. His smile had become a cruel smirk stretched across his face. He was enjoying his freedom.

Dalville moved through the camp like a ripple on the surface of a pond. The evening sky was a charcoal smear, coloured red by the flickering fires that sprung up in the clear spaces between caravans. Dalville felt naked, invisible and eclipsed against the gathering darkness.

He saw Bressac, cuddling a bottle of wine on the steps of the wardrobe van. His friend's face was desolate and he decided it wouldn't be wise to approach. The other actors seemed unreal, offending shadows cast on the caravan walls by the fires. Their voices seemed more solid than their shapes – songs, laughter, stories and screams blending into a unique cacophony.

Dalville didn't recognize half the faces he saw as he prowled. The actors' ranks were swelled at night, by thieves, madmen, whores, radicals and lovers. They were the children of the dark, driven here by the curfew, plotting in their own ways to take back the night. Dalville felt at once a part of, and isolated from, them. Everyone felt this way, he guessed.

No. There was one who felt nothing human. Fantômas stood by the door of his caravan, surveying the scene from its edge. He stood close to the fire, seeming to burn with it, bleached orange by its light. Dalville had no desire to be watched and sidestepped out of his gaze. Fantômas might have smiled.

Dalville returned to his dark caravan in search of Dodo. He found her in the bedroom, straining to read her script in the dying light of evening and the glow of the flames that had sprung up outside. Dalville lit the room's lamp as he entered, but she recoiled. It wasn't the smell or the sudden brightness, he guessed. In the new light, he saw that she had been crying.

'What's wrong?' he asked, surprising himself with genuine concern.

'I've been reading *this*,' she said bluntly. 'It's horrible. It's evil.' Her features were raw – the hurt stinging on her face.

'It's only made up,' Dalville said, shrugging but secretly knowing that she had a point. 'It's not real. We're only actors.'

Dodo stared at him strangely. Her eyes flashed and she flung the script to the floor. 'It's sick. It's just . . . pain and sex and death.'

Perhaps she should have looked away then. She lowered her head, but she kept her eyes on Dalville, as if he was an ally she could appeal to. He felt encouraged. She was tiny and fragile and desperately desirable. It hurt to look at her.

'You know, the authorities vet all plays for unsuitable material,' he said quietly. 'Even Fantômas can't argue with the censor. They'll cut this one to ribbons. We're expecting someone from the Office of Public Safety any day now, and he'll have a blacklist as long as your legs.'

She flushed and her face trembled, but she seemed vaguely happier. Dalville asked if there was anything specific she would like changed.

'Yes,' she answered, dragging the reluctant word across her tongue. 'I'm in practically every scene, but that's OK. I can live with that. It's just . . . well, do I have to keep taking my clothes off?'

Dalville burst out laughing. Dodo's features pinched round her skull.

'I just can't stand the idea of being, uh, being *watched* by all those people, OK?' she protested as her skin turned a furious red. 'I don't see that it's p– particularly necessary.'

Dalville rested a hand on her shoulder. It was a bad move – the bare flesh rippled under his palm, both pleasant and unsettling.

'Dodo,' he began (another bad move, he'd meant to call her 'Sophie'). 'The reason why you have to strip off so often is that Sade is a man, that Fantômas is a man, most of your audience are men, and we are all – without exception – out to get you.'

'Even you?'

'Me? I can't wait.' Her shoulder was cold under his hand. He tried not to think about that.

'I don't want to be looked at,' she said sullenly.

'Not even in private? Not even with a husband, or a lover?'

'I –' She stopped herself quickly. 'That's not the point. You're trying to confuse me. Besides, you said yourself, the censors will cut it out.'

'The censors are men too,' Dalville warned her, before falling silent. He wanted to end this topic of conversation. Like the stark and bony shape under his fingers, it was uncomfortable. The more he thought about it, the less he wanted to see her before an audience that would violate her with their eyes.

Some things should be private.

He went to the window in search of cool air. The orange-tinted scene that confronted him nearly sent him reeling backwards from surprise.

'I don't believe it!' he exclaimed, beckoning to Dodo. She joined him and they watched together, in silence. Fantômas was squatting on the steps to his caravan. Bressac stood at a respectful distance, clutching a bottle and stumbling in an awkward arc around the director, his shadow cast large over Fantômas and the caravan doorway. He moved with a stutter, each motion seeming hesitant and forced. He seemed to be talking to Fantômas who, in his turn, seemed to be listening patiently.

'Did you put him up to this?' Dalville asked cautiously.

Dodo murmured a no.

'It must be the drink,' he mused.

Fantômas raised a finger to his lips – a small but extravagant gesture that stilled and silenced the actor. Then he rose from his crouch, and his shadow rose with him to cover the nearest wall in darkness. He placed a friendly arm round Bressac's shoulder and led him up the steps to the caravan. It took an age, each step an eon passing, but eventually they were there. The door closed behind them. Dalville began to breathe.

'He's pulled.' His voice was distant and numb in his ears. 'He's pulled *Fantômas*! There is no God.'

'I think he's in love,' Dodo said. She was leaning against Dalville, her slight weight comfortable and deadening against his forearm. A cool hand patted his back warily. The awareness of her proximity was pleasing and startling.

She's shocked me. An odd thought, it didn't mean anything.

'I think you've lost your chaperon for tonight,' he said cynically. Her hand didn't budge.

There had been no alarm when they left the cell. Monsieur le 6 was calm. He tucked the stolen pistol into his waistband and strolled nonchalantly down the passage. His face flickered through a number of expressions before settling on a disarming smile. Only his uniform and his uncertain gait marked him out as a prisoner. Despite his stigmata, the Doctor felt reassured by his company.

The problem was solved when they stumbled upon a deserted guard post. Le 6 appropriated a long dark coat which hid the distinctive uniform, and a powdered wig which added a sense of dignity and office to his decrepit shape. In these clothes he looked like a bureaucrat, crumbling like the buildings where he worked, on a visit to the heart of the Revolution. The Doctor no longer thought of him as the man in the velvet mask. He was le 6 now, completely le 6.

Finding a lift, they descended into the roots of the Bastille. The Doctor would have preferred to go up, but le 6 had insisted otherwise. So far his suggestions and guesses had served them well. Either he was lucky, or he had an intuitive sympathy with his surroundings.

'You are a remarkable man,' the Doctor had suggested.

He shrugged.

Eventually it was the Doctor's weakness that called an end to their exploration. He ached. His flesh ached, his bones ached, the blood surging in his arteries and veins dragged wearily. He fell against the wall, and might have collapsed if le 6 had not been there to carry him to the nearest room. This was a barren, dusty place with four undecorated walls painted grey. There was not much to tell between this room and the cell they had escaped from. The Doctor slumped on the floor, raising his hands to his head to support the intolerable weight. Le 6 stood close by, chewing on a cold chicken leg he had liberated from the guard post.

'You are very kind to an old man,' the Doctor told him.

'Yes. I think you're many years older than I am.'

The Doctor stared at him curiously, wondering if this was meant as an insult. He decided not.

'Quite right,' he snapped back. 'I have led a restless life.'

Le 6 nodded sagely and returned to gnawing at the last scraps of meat from the bone. Unlike the Doctor, he had an appetite, a primitive hunger.

'I wonder what these levels are for,' the Doctor said at

length. 'We haven't seen or heard anyone since leaving the cells.'

'This is Minski's domain.' Le 6 tossed the bare bone away, following its passage with wistful eyes. 'The site, it's said, of unimaginable horror.'

'What sort of horror?'

'If I could tell you, they'd hardly be unimaginable. Minski encourages the stories, which suggests they're false. Worse, it tells us they're not true.'

The Doctor smiled at the fine distinction. He asked le 6 about Minski. A few new facts would be helpful and he trusted le 6 as a reliable narrator.

No one knew where Minski came from, where he was born, who his true parents were, or how he had come into the company of Sade. His first public act came on the day that Robespierre had been arrested. Somehow – le 6 was short on detail – Minski had arranged to take over first the revolutionary authority in Paris, then throughout France.

Minski ruled absolutely, through a hierarchy of officials and authorities, through the creation and control of new machines, through his own charisma. He had shuffled out existing political and economic groups and had ruled alone and unchallenged for ten years. It was suspiciously simple.

The Doctor's head reeled with delirious facts. There were too many clues. He needed to focus to make sense of them.

'I am pleased to find you in a more lucid mood,' he began, trying to rise but finding himself trapped by age and gravity. Not for the first time, he missed Dodo, but he was thankful enough to know she was safe.

'I become clearer as I move closer to the heart of who I am.'

'Are there still gaps in the air?' the Doctor asked.

Le 6 half-smiled, half-sneered. His eyes trembled though, betraying fear. 'There are,' he said, 'chasms between atoms, cosmic gulfs large enough to contain the universe yet too small to see.' As he spoke, his body rippled and straightened, as though he had been relieved of a great burden of knowledge, but the Doctor sensed that there was something more. The old man confirmed it with a languid nod of his head.

'There are beings that live in the cracks between worlds, like rats in the walls of a house. I met them. I dealt with them. This world is theirs, their creation.' His next sound was a dangerous, half-hysterical giggle. 'It's a tawdry imitation, no substance, just a crust of papier mâché. Only their science supports it, in the gaps, in the gaps in the air.'

Le 6 smoothed the folds of his coat down and shuffled aside. He left a silhouette behind, a le 6-shaped gap in the world, a le 6-shaped window into space. The false, paper-thin walls rotted when they touched the solid shadow, and the air buckled and warped.

The darkness was far from empty. There was a mechanism in the gaps within the world. Through the window the Doctor could see shapes both vague and solid, extending infinitely into the space between atoms. He perceived a distant, shaky outline, but had more sense than to try and follow it.

'There,' le 6 said from the other side of the gap. 'The world machine.'

The Doctor focused on the details of the machine, forcing himself to focus. The mechanism was a marriage – a miscegenation – of cogs and coils and pulleys and pistons and springs and tiny, flawless diamonds. Each detail ground, turned, tugged, pumped and flexed in harmony with its surroundings. The Doctor's eyes leapt from one part of the machine to another, concentrating on only one part at a time. It would be foolish to try and conceive of the whole machine. It was large enough to destroy his mind.

It was a landscape of different parts, locked together, working endlessly and without purpose. It had only one voice, one tone.

Tick, it said. *Tock*.

'The world machine,' le 6 said. He stepped back into his shadow, blocking the Doctor's view of the relentless, hideous machine. Relieved of the vision, the Doctor relaxed. He didn't know whether to feel elated or disturbed by what he had seen. Here at last was the source of the problem.

He didn't have the first idea of how to deal with it.

'There are gaps in the air,' le 6 said, quietly. He slumped into the far corner of the room, resuming the crouched position he had worn in the cell. There was no sign that the air around him had ever been broken.

The Doctor acknowledged him with a weary sigh. 'There are gaps in the air.'

5

Some Minor Alterations
to the Dialogue

Dodo was woken slowly by the sound of the rain battering against the caravan. Each droplet smashed quietly against the wood. Together they formed a crash of thunder that rattled the thin walls.

She lay still but awake, listening to the rain. The cascade echoed, trapped by the caravan's rickety structure. The reverberation gave the rain an edge of power and menace, and Dodo was thankful that it was trapped outside while she was wrapped safe beneath the covers of her bed.

She didn't want to move, though she felt far from comfortable. The air was tight and rank and humid. The rain hadn't killed the heat, but had turned it sour. The bedclothes felt soiled with sweat, the sheets ruffled, the pillow bristling with loose hair. Her back was sore between the shoulders, a scratch mark left by Dalville's fingernails the previous night.

This wasn't her. This wasn't now. This was something she'd read once and now remembered dimly. None of the small pains felt real. So she lay still.

She was alone. The space beside her was empty, dead space full of dead possibilities. She lay still, allowing broken shards of remembrance to rise to the surface of her mind. There was Dalville's shadowed face – a cynical grin and intense eyes shining out of the dark. There was the warmth of his palms spread across her back. There was his voice, sharp and soft, glass crumbling back into sand. Her own voice was squeaky and stupid, echoing in her skull.

She had asked whether he believed in love at first sight. He was amused.

'Love is a conspiracy,' he'd said, 'invented by the Church, florists and anyone else who stands to profit from it. It's a tame euphemism for passion, romance and writhing bodies. You've gone red again.'

'But,' she'd said after a mild coughing fit, 'you could say that a couple's eyes could meet across a crowded room without it necessarily being love at first sight.' Long-winded, boring Dodo, she'd thought. Then more coughing, further blushes. Then there was the kiss. He'd held her tight and close, putting his hand as far down her spine as he could reach. The scratch happened, dug into her by careless, probing fingers.

It was a passionless end to the evening. With hindsight she felt cheated. She'd slept in her gown for safety's sake. That had seemed so important the night before, now it was just silly. She wondered exactly whose desire she had been scared of, Dalville's or her own?

She had dreamed about him. He was a stretched, elongated phantom with dark, cancerous fingers that scarred her flesh wherever they touched her. She'd dreamed of making love to him in a dry, stifling darkness. Her body blackened and rotted wherever he stroked her. Dalville was a hazy shadow in her dream, communicating with her through his fingertips, caressing and corrupting her. She remembered it without feeling.

The rain wasn't easing up. Her surroundings grew ever more unpleasant, and she doubted that she would get back to sleep with the barrage hammering against her ear. She pulled back the curtains and rose into the silent twilight of the bunk room. She fumbled briefly in the dark to find the lamp.

The glare filled the room, startling Bressac who was sitting on the lower bunk opposite her own. He recoiled, falling back into the darkness, but the stark light pursued him into the corners of the room. The thin yellow glow jaundiced his skin, haunting his pinched, frightened

122

features and setting his eyes glowing red. Dodo smiled at
him.

'Good morning,' she said brightly.

He sat up and rearranged himself but didn't manage a
smile. His eyelids were grey and heavy. It might have
been exaggerated by the light; he seemed tired, even
depressed.

'Have you been there all night?' she asked.

His lips quivered, the first sign of a smile, albeit a bitter
one. He nodded heavily. 'I waited until I thought you'd
both be asleep, longer than I had to.'

He shrugged and fell silent. Concerned, Dodo moved
closer. He slipped back, his body melting further into the
warm shadows.

'Is something wrong?' she asked — a stupid question —
the best she could manage at short notice. 'Is it anything
to do with Fantômas?'

'Fantômas, yes,' Bressac muttered. He turned to her,
holding his head crookedly so that she could see the pain
forming in his eyes. 'You were watching last night? I
thought you might be, and Dalville . . . . watching me.'

Dodo reached out to touch his shoulder and reassure
him, but her hand wavered in the space between them.
Something told her that he didn't want to be touched, or
even approached. There was a dangerous distance around
him.

'What happened?'

'We went into his caravan. I've never been there
before. It's full of rubbish. He seems to collect everything,
every piece of junk he can find. It's a museum to
everything we throw away. It's rare for him to let anyone
in. It's his territory, hallowed ground.' He related this in a
dull monotone, his eyes fixed on the opposite wall. Dodo
fought the impatient urge to turn and see if there was
anything there.

'We only went in to talk. Just to talk,' Bressac continued, tilting his head to look at her. The toneless hum
of his voice began to crack, nameless emotions quivering

123

in his voice. 'I told him exactly what I thought. I think he knew a lot of it already. And when I finished, he touched my face and whispered something. D'you want to know . . . ?' He looked at Dodo again. A noiseless 'yes' blossomed on her lips.

'He said, "Bressac, I am not the man you think I am".'

'Is that all?' Dodo asked quickly. Too quickly – it came out sounding crude and tactless, but Bressac didn't seem to notice.

'Yes. Then he asked me to leave, to forget about everything. Do you know what that's like? To be asked to forget something that's kept you alive? Like asking a priest to forget God.'

Dodo shook her head, though something in his words set off a sympathetic resonance inside her. She knew what he must feel like. She *knew*.

'I refused,' he continued. 'I didn't want to be rejected without a good reason. And then he did something. He did something to his face. I don't know what it was, I don't want to know, but it changed him.' He snatched at her arm and pulled her closer, spitting the words at her.

'*It changed his face!*' he hissed. 'It was only for a moment, but after I saw it, I couldn't speak or move. Fantômas led me to the door and locked me out. To be honest, I didn't want to go back.

'Everything changed,' he said. 'It was the worst moment of my life.'

He released Dodo's arm and stood up, knocking the lamp from its hook as he rose. It dashed itself across the floor, fragments of glass and flame scattering across the bare boards before fading into the grey gloom. The first note of a scream warbled in Dodo's throat, flattened into silence when she realized that the fire hadn't caught.

'That was lucky,' she whispered.

'The universe is kind to you,' Bressac replied.

'I'm sorry,' Dodo said 'about everything . . .'

'No. *I'm* sorry. I'm always sorry.'

There was a crash, the thump of boots and muffled

voices from without. The door hinges squeaked, and a rectangle of morning light opened across the room. Dodo froze as the light fell across her face, the brightness cutting painfully into the corners of her eyes. She turned, or felt herself turn. She saw, or dreamed she saw, Dalville caught in the door frame. He was immaculate, fresh faced, precisely dressed and formally posed. It wasn't like him.

This false Dalville was followed by a stranger figure, a man dressed in severe black, dusty black, funereal black. Already a small man, he walked with a slight stoop, an invisible weight pinning down his shoulders. His bones clicked together as he moved, and he was always moving. He seemed decrepit, decayed, dry with age. He wore moon-lensed glasses that caught the light and glowed. Dodo looked closely, seeing a youthful, charming face hidden behind them, and a mane of dark hair obscured by his tall, black hat. A young man, she thought. She was a little upset by the deception, by his clothes. He was parodying age and illness and death. She felt insulted.

Dalville gazed at her and smiled sickly. Something genuine loomed in the fake's eyes, appealing to her desperately before slipping back under the surface. Dodo glanced at Bressac and saw a cautious smile on his lips. The caricature met his gaze and nodded brutally, acknowledging him.

'You've met Bressac, of course.' Dalville had an earnest tone to his voice. It didn't suit him. 'This is Citizen Chaplette, our new Sophie. Er, Sophie, this is Citizen Debord of the Office of Public Safety, the Revolutionary, uh, Censor. Ha.' He clapped his hands together and gave off an inane, toothy grin.

'Ah.' Citizen Debord's voice was dry and cracked like a paving stone. It hung in the air, refusing to die away, festering. If Dodo hadn't been so alert, she might have mistaken it for smooth charm. 'This is the young citizen who doesn't want to take her clothes off.'

'Yes,' Dodo and Dalville chorused emphatically. Debord gazed at her over the top of his spectacles. He had a squint, though Dodo couldn't tell whether this was genuine or an affectation.

'This is a much smaller girl than the one she replaced. She had long golden hair, I recall, and more of a chest.' He smiled, perhaps meaning it encouragingly. Dodo was dismayed to see that Dalville nodded brusquely and mumbled his agreement. Strangely, it made it easier to control her feelings. She bit her lip and met the censor's gaze, returning it with anger.

It seemed the best course. The only alternative was to burst into tears and crawl miserably under the bed.

'I don't see that this changes much,' Debord continued, his hollow voice betraying no feeling. 'You see citizen, it is my job to excise material which offends the common morality. Immoral ideas are wounds on the body politic. I am the leech. I stem the wounds and suck out the contamination.' He made claws of his fingers.

Dodo shrugged.

'The Office of Public Safety does not consider it immoral to allow displays of female nudity on the stage, nor does it contribute to the spread of immorality. Furthermore it is proof to the theatre-going citizen — though not, regrettably, in Paris — that our activities are not mindlessly opposed to beauty, and that France is a free society in spite of its censors.'

Dodo maintained her stare, though it was difficult to contain both her anger and her disbelief at the same time. Debord seemed ignorant of her. He plucked the spectacles from his face and began to polish the lenses. His eyes were tight, peering glints in dark sockets.

'I suggest,' he added blithely, 'that it would be more entertaining if you were to dye your hair blonde for the part, and perhaps deepen your bosom with appropriate and unobtrusive padding?'

She almost screamed. She contained it, painfully.

'Now.' He restored his glasses and turned to Dalville. 'I will rouse your colleagues. Citizen Fantômas has agreed to meet on the field in an hour, where I'll present the changes the Office of Public Safety requires to the text.'

'Is it a long list?' Bressac's voice rumbled. Dodo had almost forgotten he was there, a brooding half-shadow at her shoulder.

'No. No. Some minor alterations to the dialogue, to make it suitable for performance at six o'clock on a weekday afternoon.' He turned and lurched from the caravan, clicking his limbs together like a deranged insect.

Dodo closed the door after him, turned to Dalville and swore into his face. The china-smooth expression of the fake shattered, the reality oozing through the cracks.

'You did that deliberately!' Dodo shrieked. 'You set me up!'

'I'm sorry.' Dalville, thoroughly real now, wrung his hands together and grinned wryly. 'You can't argue with the censor.'

'That wasn't just wrong,' Dodo said bitterly, feeling the tears coming at last, now it was safe to show them. 'That was hypocritical, insensitive, ignorant, superficial, filthy minded, evil! He's the stupidest man I've ever met.'

'Apart from me?' Dalville cocked an eyebrow. She shoved him, pushing him back onto her bed. He suddenly seemed innocent and helpless.

'Including you!' she spat, still too angry to forgive. Bressac stepped forward and put his arms round her. She pushed her face into his chest and began to cry freely. His hands settled limply against her back, trembling wherever they touched her alien form. His voice was a warm growl from above.

'You don't have to do this,' he said. 'There's never been a company revolt before, but if enough of us stick up for you, we can force Fantômas to cast someone else. Is that what you want?'

Dodo stared up at him through wet, stinging eyes.

'No,' she said. '*No!* I can't back out now. I have to do it.'

* * *

Monsieur le 6 slept. The sleep of humans seemed alien and simple, and the Doctor envied him. The vacuous and serene expression that had formed on le 6's shattered features proved that. He was human, he was allowed to forget and to heal. The Doctor's weariness gnawed at him, scraping sharp fingers along the inside of his rib cage. Sleep wouldn't banish that.

He cleared his mind, and watched le 6, but it didn't help. He was distracted by the whispering of the world machine. Now he was aware of it, it seemed obvious, every second punctuated with a click from the threshold of reality. The noise bound him to the present – every tick, every tock, dragged painfully, a reminder of the painful pace of real time.

The world machine should have been helpful, but it seemed just another piece of evidence on an over-stacked pile. Odd clues sat together suggesting a shape, a fragment, a partial meaning stretched across five dimensions, but nothing complete. He needed a map, a guide, a key to wrest sense from it all.

The TARDIS was close. As the night drew on, its ghost had burned behind his eyes. It called to him as it had done when he had lost it in the fourth universe, or during the long months he had been separated from it in China. He had once told Dodo that it was an instinct, though he hadn't been certain that he was telling her the truth.

(No. It wasn't Dodo. It was another, from before or after her time. His human companions were jumbled in his mind, their features and characters mapped on top of one another. He would call her Dodo, until he remembered.)

Dodo should have been here. Dodo could have redeemed him.

He left le 6 sleeping and went in search of the TARDIS, choosing his path instinctively like a blind man moving towards the heat of a candle flame. The architecture of the Bastille cellars was hazy in his mind. He hardly perceived the walls, the tunnels and the steps. He simply moved towards his goal.

He found it in a large chamber on the same level. He hurried towards it, stumbling and almost tripping in his haste. He placed trembling hands on its battered blue walls, drawing strength from its solidness and from the power that hummed through it. The veins on the back of his hands stood out, throbbing beneath fading skin.

'Fragile,' he said, patting the box thankfully. 'Things fall apart.'

After checking that the ship hadn't been tampered with, he turned to inspect its surroundings. In his hurry to reach the TARDIS, he hadn't paid the chamber much attention, allowing it to blur in his mind into the shapeless mass of Bastille rooms and passages. It was the smell that convinced him to look around, a curious mix of abattoir, opium den and hospital. The stench of dried blood mixed with a hazy atmosphere and the obliterating anti-tang of wet acid disinfectant.

The TARDIS stood on the outer edge of the laboratory, where it seemed quite incongruous among pieces of gothic paraphernalia and equipment. The Doctor sensed that this place was a distraction. It was too seedy, too decadent to be real. The smoke hung heaviest here, wafting between the intricate glass instruments and the sinister furniture. The Doctor moved through it, into the heart of the lab.

If anything, the antiseptic ugliness at the centre was worse. It made the splashes of unreason vivid by comparison. The patches of dried blood on the edges of the stark white operating tables, the plastic tubs packed so tight with wriggling maggots that they seemed filled with an oozing black liquid, the head of a young woman impaled on the horn of an elegant black machine – her lips sealed with a map of crude stitches. All pointed to the work of an evil imagination. The Doctor regarded them coolly.

He was more impressed by a large grey viewing screen

suspended from the ceiling. He was intrigued to discover that the surface of the screen was not glass or perspex but water, stretched across a wire frame like a film of soap. There had been a similar machine in le 6's cell. It puzzled him.

Warned by a vague, bristling instinct, he turned, afraid that he was being watched. He saw no one and was on the point of turning back to the screen when he realized, and with realization came a cold sense of horror in his stomach. The severed head was staring at him from across the laboratory, turning smoothly on its spike. Its eyes were wide and pleading. As he watched, they blinked.

The silence rumbled. The stillness itched. The Doctor gazed at the head and it returned his stare. He reached slowly for a tray of medical implements on the nearest table, fingers easing round the cool metal of a scalpel. He moved towards the head and began to work at the stitches in its mouth. His hand shook and the blade left ragged gashes as he worked at the thread, but the eyes seemed to show no pain and the wounds were dry.

When he had finished, the severed stitches hung limp from dead blue lips, decorating the head with a loose moustache. It spat at him with its free mouth. Something struck the floor with a crack of metal. The Doctor's eyes followed the sound, finding a small key on a metal neck chain. He picked it up cautiously, disturbed to find it dry – almost dusty. Pocketing it, he looked again at the head. A painful smile had blossomed on its lips.

'Can you talk?' he asked.

'Not now,' it said in a normal, though wavering tone. Its eyes flashed sideways, towards the laboratory door.

A boy had wandered in through the open doorway and was gazing open mouthed at the scene around him. He was dressed smartly, the severity of his costume matching the serene innocence of his features. The Doctor rushed forward, waving frantically.

'You mustn't come in,' he said protectively. 'This is not a place for children. There is too much evil in here.'

130

The boy's eyes fell on the Doctor and flashed with amusement. At first the Doctor thought it was hysteria, but it was too cool and controlled for that. Soldiers appeared in the doorway, a better dressed, better disciplined mob than the patrols or the gaolers. Their pistols were held naked and threatening.

'I've seen you before,' the child said with the voice of an adult. He strolled past the Doctor to the TARDIS and placed a sacrilegious hand on its surface. 'I think we have a lot to talk about. Ah, but you don't know me.' He bowed sharply, snorting and clicking his heels for emphasis.

'I am Minski.'

At daybreak, Sir Randolph Eging left Garce sleeping in their safe house, and wandered out alone into the labyrinth of Paris. The rain spattered against his unprotected head and shoulders, dribbling over his eyes and turning the surrounding alleys into a blur of browns and greys. He tramped oblivious across the churned, muddy paths and through the swollen puddles. The air was heavy and sodden, drowning out the usual scents and stinks of the streets. There were few citizens in sight, and most of those were in too much of a hurry to spare him any attention.

Alone in Paris, lonely in Paris, Randolph began to enjoy himself.

Garce, he knew, despised the city. Garce hated most things French – it was in his blood. Randolph was not so sure. If it were the wish of his king, he would happily bring down destruction on the city, but he would do so without pleasure, without hatred. Paris perplexed him, fascinated him, drew him through its intricate structure, into streets and alleys laid out like a spider's web. It could be an unpleasant place, true, but it would never be dull.

That was his weakness, he realized, the one patch of exposed flesh on his flank. He would be sorry to see the city die. It was such a small failing, and one he was determined he would not surrender to.

Finding himself hungry, Randolph approached a street vendor who was roasting meat over a fire under a makeshift shelter. At first sight, he assumed the vendor was a midget, but was shocked to find it was a child, probably no more than ten years. He smiled, amused by his reaction, and wondering at the city's ability to surprise him.

The girl was wearing a heavy coat against the rain, but beneath there were layers of tattered, ragged clothing. A scar dropped down the right side of her face, tracking across an empty eye socket. The wound where her eye had been was small and puckered, a tiny pair of lips on the verge of a kiss. Her remaining eye rolled like a glass ball in its socket, scanning him efficiently, weighing his shape and manner as he approached.

Randolph was momentarily intrigued, but let the matter pass. His eyes flicked to the tatty sign at the vendor's side, the brief list of prices and choices. The transaction was achieved wordlessly. Randolph passed her a five-tenths piece, dropping it into the tin mug at her side, where it rolled slowly, briefly before clattering into stillness. The girl rammed an overcooked lump of meat into a grey lump of bread and gave it to him. He took it in one hand, holding his palm open as she passed him a few one-hundredth piece copper bits of change. It was a precise and sterile exchange. Randolph offered the girl a broken smile, to lighten the atmosphere. The wound on her eye socket twitched gently, but she made no other response.

Randolph bit into his snack, searching for the meat beneath the layers of damp bread and burned flesh. He found small traces of it, at the raw centre of the charcoal. The taste was weak and unfamiliar. He felt the lines on his face tug into a curious frown.

'What is this?' he asked. The girl grimaced and shrugged. He persevered.

'What am I eating? Cow? Pig? *Goat?*' he ventured.

'Cat,' the diminutive vendor said plainly.

'Cat?'

'Miaow, miaow,' the girl added, making odd gestures with her hands.

Randolph finished the meat off in front of her, to prove that he was open to new experiences. The rain streamed down his face as he ate, forming tiny oceans in the folds of his face. He made no effort to wipe the droplets away. They rolled to the extremities of his features then fell away, plunging like tears into the wind.

'Would you believe,' he asked the girl as he finished, licking his fingers clean as he spoke, 'that I am a murderer? I have killed an inordinate number of treasonable Williams, a Lady Johanna, and at least one seditious Erasmus. I have killed so many, but they were all *tedious*. Do you believe that, m'child?'

The vendor looked thoughtful for a minute, then shook her head, her long, ash hair flailing in the wind. She remained tight lipped and silent.

'And I have learned as well as killed,' he proclaimed, raising his voice against a sudden blast of wind and water. 'Twenty years ago I studied at Ingolstadt and Mirenburg. I was a member of the Illuminated Bavarian Conspiracy for a time, rubbing shoulders with Weishaupt and Von Frankenstein and the others. And I met an olive-skinned woman who claimed to have seen Atlantis fall, and she taught me that I wouldn't live forever.'

He paused, conjuring faint memories of taste and scent and texture. Moments of flesh beneath his fingertips. Warm instances, long turned cold.

'I've never loved,' he continued slowly, 'but I've known the passion and the torment of love. I have desired from a distance but said nothing and let the vital moments pass. And now I have eaten cat-meat. I've had a good and varied life, all told.' He leaned forward and hissed into the child's ear. 'Leave this city while you can. Death is coming.'

The girl regarded him with a stone face, then shrugged. He accepted her silence gracefully, turned on his heels and walked away. The image of the girl jammed in his memory for the rest of the day – the one eye open and staring coldly, the other forever missing, sealed in a permanent wink.

He cursed himself for not asking about it. He should have asked. If he could live that moment again, he would ask.

The rain lashed all around him, beating on the roofs and walls of the houses, on the soft earth beneath his feet. The storm attacked the city. Randolph hardly felt it.

The rain hammered the camp site, smearing the cheap paint on the walls of the caravans and turning the ashen earth to grey mud. It drenched the assembled actors, who huddled in their doorways, wrapped in colourless cloaks. It drowned Citizen Debord, transformed into a black smear by the drizzle. They held their breath, waiting for him.

Debord was chatting with some actors on the opposite side of the field. He looked like a huge beetle with a horny black shell. His arms twitched wildly, extravagant gestures trapped in cramped limbs. Dodo couldn't make out the men he was talking to, but she doubted that she would remember their names. They were still strangers. She had nothing in common with them.

Still, she belonged with them.

She perched on the steps of her caravan, in the wet. She found she could ignore the blasts of cold droplets across her face and arms. Fat beads of dirty water fell from the caravan eaves, striking her shoulders and trickling down into the folds of her clothes. Her hair felt filthy, damp and matted. She could live with it.

The door scraped on the steps behind her. She recognized Dalville from the sound of his feet and of the air as it moved round him, but she looked anyway. He was dressed in black, which seemed a less severe colour on him than it did on Debord. A fragile rosebud sat in the cup of his hands.

'For me?' she asked. He nodded seriously and passed it to her. She held it protectively on her palm, out of the grasp of the lashing winds. Dalville lowered himself onto the steps beside her, his body rubbing tight against hers. She welcomed the added warmth. He was silent at first, and still.

'Dodo,' he said at last, 'if I were to tell you that I bribed Debord to insult you, what would you do?'

'I'd call you a liar.'

'We're a depthless people,' he said, nodding bitterly.

'No. You're worse than that,' Dodo murmured, sounding harsher than she intended. 'At heart, aren't you just another randy actor?' She patted his lap cautiously. 'Yes,' she added. She smiled wistfully.

The rain drummed against the caravan and against their bodies. Dalville put his arm round her and rested his head against her shoulder. His fingers were warm and wet, digging under her gown and tracing the line of her ribs through podgy flesh. The rose remained on her palm, growing pale and limp as the rain assaulted it. She relaxed, blissfully happy despite the rain.

The moment was perfect. It should have lasted forever.

There was a commotion on the far side of the camp site. Dodo sat up and nudged Dalville in the ribs, drawing him to attention. Fantômas was prowling through the ranks of the players. He was a vital shape undiminished by the grey rain. He shone with solid colour where Debord blurred into darkness. Their two shapes collided violently at the heart of the field. For an instant, Dodo felt a pang of sympathy for the eclipsed censor.

'Ah ha!' Dalville leapt to his feet, turning to help Dodo up. 'We'll see some fireworks now. This is going to be fun.'

Fantômas's appearance sent a murmur rippling through the actors. They stirred, forming a crowd. Dodo and Dalville joined the throng, standing together at the back. Dodo glanced through their ranks searching for Bressac, but he eluded her. She hoped he wasn't still in the caravan, brooding in the darkness. Finally he appeared in the corner of her eyes, near the edge of the crowd. His face was turned downwards, shadowed, grounded. Everyone else's attention was on Debord.

No, Dodo realized, not everyone. Fantômas stood by the censor's side, but his eyes were elsewhere, staring outwards across the crowd. His face gave away little, but he seemed bored by the proceedings. Debord, when he spoke, addressed the director, but spoke to the whole crowd. His voice was a sand-dry monotone, but it carried across the field with strength and harsh authority. On a better day, Dodo might have been impressed.

'Citizens, I would like to present a short list that my office has drawn up.' He waved a sheaf of sodden papers in the air over his head, where they flapped desperately in the wind. 'These detail a small number of negligible changes that must be made to the text of your play before we can pass it for performance. You will doubtless want to dispute them, but I must tell you now that our position is not –'

'No.' Fantômas shrugged.

Debord blinked heavily, taken aback by his reaction. He began again, quieter and cautious this time. 'These changes, though negligible, may considerably alter the tone of the piece.' He was daring Fantômas to fight.

Again, the director shrugged. His face wrinkled, perhaps disgusted, perhaps bored. 'They're only words. They're not sacred. I'll make any changes your office requires.' He waved at the assembly of actors. 'You can discuss it with them if you care to.' He dropped out of sight, plunging into the crowd.

'These changes, while negligible, might also require a complete rewrite of the play!' Debord yelled over a renewed burst of heavy rain. His sharp features were blunted. 'Entire scenes may have to be altered.'

Fantômas had reached the edge of the crowd, slipping easily through the cracks between actors. He spun round

136

to face his accuser, mocking him with a bow full of extravagant theatrical flourishes.

'Whatever you see fit!' he called. 'The triumph of virtue, the misfortunes of vice! Who said the play had to be like the book?'

The silence of the crowd broke, shattering into a babble of confused conversation. Debord screamed for silence but the combined chorus of rain and chattering actors muffled him. He seethed impotently at the centre of the tumult, unable to restore order. Dodo glanced up at Dalville, finding a perplexed grin wavering on his lips.

She swung round to follow Fantômas's back as he retreated. He moved like a doll, like a marionette, jerky and self-possessed. He swaggered towards the edge of the camp site, where two hunched figures were waiting. They wore frayed monks' robes and cowls, their faces and hands hidden in the shadowy creases of the cloth. Their shoulders were rounded, their heads lolling forwards heavily. Dodo couldn't imagine faces or the bodies under the robes. They seemed no more than dusty and tattered clothes. Fantômas bowed as he reached them, an honest gesture for once, and straightened up slowly, without his usual flourishes and effects, without his strutting arrogance.

'Strange man,' Dalville croaked, putting his arm back around her.

'He wants to get his play done.' Dodo shrugged, glancing curiously over her shoulder at Fantômas and the monks. The director seemed to notice her gaze, then shook his head, leading his crumbling companions away. 'But it won't be his play. It'll be scraps of his play, cut up then stuck back together by the censors. It'll be their play.' She pinched at Dalville's thigh, alerting him as Debord came staggering through the crush towards them. The crowd clamoured round him, and he tried to swat them away with his papers. He looked wretched. The rain began to feel warm on Dodo's skin.

'We've known Debord since he was human,' Dalville hmmed, 'Bressac and I. It's hard not to feel sorry for him. I suppose I'd better go and sort him out.'

'You do that,' she said. 'I've got something to do anyway.'

She left Dalville to his fate and made for the director's caravan, hoping to reach it before its owner. The churned muddy landscape made the going hard, and the vans were laid out like discarded wooden building blocks, forming a maze of false passages and alleys. She arrived too late, barely in time to see Fantômas ushering the monks through his door. They climbed the steps clumsily, as if the art of walking were alien to them. One stumbled, nearly falling back onto his colleague until Fantômas's arm lashed out to catch him. He half-dragged the shapes inside, then glanced out across the camp. Dodo was in plain sight, but he didn't acknowledge her.

She trotted forward eagerly, darting round the walls to find the window. She crouched beneath the sill, straining to listen. Immediately there was a stab of guilt in her chest. She had rushed after Fantômas on an impulse, intrigued by his friends and his odd behaviour. She was just being nosy. It was something she was good at.

After a moment's thought, she realized that she was afraid of being caught eavesdropping, of being caught eavesdropping under someone's window in the pouring rain. Her cheeks stung, embarrassment squeezing out the guilt. She listened harder, throwing herself into the act of spying, losing herself in it.

The voices she caught were muffled. She guessed that the director and his guests were in the other room, or at best standing well away from the window. The inner door squeaked distantly, thumping against the wall. Then the voices grew stronger. Fantômas's rich voice carried through the window, but it was stripped and lean, the naked sound from beneath his theatrical mask.

'I imagine we're isolated now?' he was saying. There was no discernible answer, but he ploughed on. 'Minski's

138

always been good at exploiting our differences. I'm just surprised the others can't see it.'

'They see war as the only hopeful course.'

Dodo felt a rush of blood to her head, though whether it was fear or exhilaration she couldn't tell. It wasn't a human voice she had heard. Each word sounded like a symphony crystallized into a single sound, a hundred voices murmuring to form the note. Aliens! she thought. Aliens like the Monoids, or the Refusians, but here on Earth! Aliens in the nineteenth century! It didn't seem to make sense. She fought back her excitement and kept up with the voice.

'They don't believe an invasion could serve the operator's interests.'

Even through the window it was unique, rippling in her ears and her soul, disturbing sleeping memories and feelings. Sensations of Dalville rose to the forefront of her mind – his taste, his touch, his smell, his sound, his aura.

'They could be right!' Fantômas's voice seemed brutal and human by comparison. He sounded sceptical.

'No. The operator's command of the project machinery is too complete, too subtle. The invasion plans could hardly exist without his knowledge. They can only be put into effect with his sanction. If there is war, even if it is waged against him, it will be at his behest.'

The speech set Dodo's mind chiming, her fingertips tingling with ghost sensations. It was the love of her mother, the itch between her shoulder blades, the tension between two separate lives, the horror known by spiders washed away down plug holes, the seminal unions of her ancestors back into prehistory. It was the nameless void she had felt just once, when she saw the Earth explode, taking her birthplace and her grave with it.

She tightened herself, containing the scream.

'Friend Howlglass,' Fantômas sighed, a sprinkling of showmanship returning to his dull voice, 'have you tried putting this to the others?'

'No. We are now excluded from the Pageant.'

Memories of her future were shaken from her skull. She forgot quickly and gratefully. Inside the caravan, Fantômas clicked his tongue.

'Another biscuit?' he offered.

'Thank you.'

A cold hand wound out of nowhere and clamped across Dodo's mouth. Panicking, she bit into the palm. It tasted like old leather, like stale wine. The hand was wrenched sharply away, leaving stray strands caught between her teeth. Casually she noticed that there were too many fingers clawing at her face. Beneath the leather was something misshapen and mutilated.

It was the second alien, she guessed. It was wearing gloves, she hoped.

The hand tugged on her jaw, pulling her head gently round so she could see her assailant. Its face was close and visible beneath the cowl. It was lumpy and unbalanced, thankfully hidden by a mask of the same leathery fabric wrapped round the monk's hand. There were lenses sewn into the mask, on its temple, its cheek and by its chin – triple moons glinting within the cowl, catching the light. Its face was decorated with grey, lustreless metal – perverse jewellery impaled through the mask. There was a flash of colour on its forehead, a livid butterfly-pattern scar that swirled and shifted through a spectrum of reds.

'Dodo Chaplet?' it asked. The mask-flesh rippled, but the beauty of its voice cancelled out Dodo's nausea. 'I am Larkspur.'

(Her face reflected close and dark in Dalville's eyes. Her eyes shining.)

Another arm seized her round the waist. She didn't struggle, but closed her eyes and allowed the monk to drag her into Fantômas's caravan. She wasn't certain whether to be terrified or awed. She didn't have the opportunity to scream. Larkspur's laboured breaths growled at her ear.

When she opened her eyes, she was inside. Larkspur stood behind her, pinning her arms behind her back. The other monk – Howlglass, she remembered – stood against the inner door, his hood thrown down exposing the full effect of his mask. His seemed more spartan, less decorated and with fewer lenses. The scar on his forehead was a pale green, larger but still symmetrical. In the poor light of the caravan, it seemed less like a mask than a face.

Fantômas was at his side, smiling widely and savagely in his domain. The room was cluttered with piles of books and antiques and decorations and old junk. It forced out the space, turning the already tiny room into a claustrophobic cell. Fantômas was at the heart of it, a demented priest in a temple dedicated to rubbish. His face seemed less kind and less human than the masks of his friends. Unable to run, Dodo glared at him.

He held something out towards her, a white disc that shone like a tiny star on his glove. There were regular brown lumps stacked on the disc, shapes that she recognized but couldn't name.

'Biscuit?' he offered.

She fainted.

Much to his surprise, the soldiers had not returned the Doctor to his old cell in the Bastille dungeons, but had taken him up to the heights of the tower. They had put him in a large, airy chamber where he was surrounded by art and opulence. One wall was constructed entirely of coloured glass and finely wrought metal. The window tinted the morning light, lending it warmth, despite the cold grey fingers of rain smeared across its outer surface. The Doctor approached it, taking a long glance downwards to the ground.

He paced across the room to the doors. They were oak, decorated with intricate metalwork and gold finish. The handles rolled smoothly into the shape of his palm, as if they had been tailored to fit his hand. He pulled down and tugged at the doors. They were locked, of course.

So, he concluded. Another cell.

His eyes rolled round the room, inspecting the hollow

luxury. He tutted, disgusted by his extravagant but barren surroundings. There was no furniture in this beautiful prison, and he felt it was beneath his dignity to squat on the carpet. He stood defiantly, waiting for his captors. The silence and the strain of standing exaggerated his wait. It was probably no more than ten minutes before he heard footsteps in the passage outside, but his legs were already buckling beneath him. When the door opened to admit Citizen Sade, he was almost relieved.

'I want to apologize,' Sade said, stepping across the room towards him. He had a very even tread, the Doctor noted. He was a large man and his body bristled with brutal energy. His face seemed set in a mask of calm superiority. Only his dark eyes – hooded by the cruel shape of his brow and nose – suggested anything less than inner certainty. 'I should not have treated you as I did, as though you were a criminal. I'm sorry.'

He seemed unfinished. The crudeness of his shape was betrayed by careful movements and delicate speech. Even his clothes were plain and informal. The Doctor doubted that he was as powerful as he appeared.

'Well,' the Doctor tried to sound affable rather than cautious. It wasn't easy. Sade appeared as he had always imagined him – sly cruelty embodied. 'No harm has been done. Actually, I am not entirely sure about my . . . shall we call it my current status? Yes, indeed, that's most appropriate.' He trailed off into silence, allowing the mist to cover his eyes.

'Well?' he snapped, blasting Sade with his eyes. 'What do you think?'

'I think you're a guest.' The aristocrat seemed unmoved by his bluff. He was, if anything, rather languid. 'Of the honoured variety.'

'And what happens to your honoured guests?'

'At this time of day, we feed and water them.' He put an arm round the Doctor's shoulder and whispered conspiratorially. 'My son has strange tastes. He will offer you wine and meat which, unless he insists, might best be left untouched. I've gone veggie m'self,' he added wistfully. The Doctor grunted and tugged himself out of Sade's grip, certain that he was being guyed.

'I have always imagined you as an indulgent man,' he said brusquely.

Sade nodded silently and sprouted a secretive smile.

Further footsteps came from outside, the disciplined crash of boots thumping in time against the floor. The doors were flung open to admit a retinue of soldiers with Minski at their head. Sade moved away, bowing slightly and retreating into the corner.

The Doctor was a little better prepared for this second meeting with the First Deputy. Minski's frail form was decorated this time, not extravagantly, but enough to convey a sense of power. His clothes were formal, restrictive and dark, a patchwork quilt of sterile blacks. His pale skin glowed alongside the blackness. The Doctor coughed and adjusted his cravat in a futile attempt to seem unimpressed.

The dwarf nodded to his father as he entered, but barely turned his head. Sade's returning bow seemed insincere. The Doctor made a mental note of this antagonism, in case it proved useful later. He paid little attention to the soldiers at Minski's heels. In his experience, guards, like cells, tended to be of a similar type across the universe. Minski's retinue was small and wore gaudy, elaborate uniforms. They were all women.

'Doctor,' Minski said, smiling generously and trying to sound genial. The dry adult voice cracked incongruously out of the boy's mouth. 'I'm glad you could join me.'

'I was unaware that I had a choice,' the Doctor murmured.

'Indeed no,' Minski responded. 'We are all butterflies broken on the wheels of destiny.'

The thought that he was being ridiculed crossed the Doctor's mind again, but Minski's eyes were grey and serious. He turned, gesturing to his followers. The Doctor watched with mounting amazement, growing distaste, as the soldiers piled into the room and threw themselves onto the carpet. They crouched on their arms and knees, lowering their heads between their elbows so that only their backs were prominent. The Doctor's baffled gaze flicked between the cluster in the centre of the room to the three crouching women on the periphery.

Minski killed his confusion when he sat, perching himself proudly on the back of the nearest chair. The shape – no longer wholly human – trembled under the sudden weight, but the woman made no other complaint. The First Deputy gestured for Sade and the Doctor to follow suit. Sade smiled broadly, but the Doctor caught a moment of hesitation in him. He seemed uncomfortable, lowering himself onto the closest back.

The Doctor looked to the last of the living chairs. He thought about the ache in his legs and about the effort it had cost him to remain standing all this time. His eyes followed the curve of the soldier's spine, rippling stark through the fabric of her tunic. He turned to Minski, to the squat gargoyle whose eyes flashed with delight at his guest's dilemma.

What he needed was a good solid staff to lean on. He didn't need to sit, despite the ache. He could make a stick of that. The pain could *support* him.

'No?' Minski asked airily, false indifference hiding false disappointment. He was relishing the Doctor's discomfort, squeezing pleasure from the moment. He gave another gesture, which brought a fresh wave of servants flooding into the room, bearing trays, bottles, plates and utensils which they arranged neatly on the backs of the cluster of soldiers at the heart of the room. The table swayed and a sigh of discomfort emerged from one of its mouths. The Doctor felt an edge of anger sharpen his pain. The food arrayed on the human table was an impressive selection but it did nothing to waken the Doctor's appetite. Quite the opposite.

'Let's not be formal.' Minski leant forward and seized a

fork between his thin fingers. He stabbed it in the air, pointing at various delicacies. The Doctor regarded each with growing nausea. 'Guests first. Help yourself.'

The Doctor had the sudden urge to step forward and dash the trays from the table, to spill their precious contents into worthless mounds across the carpet. He wanted to bellow and shout, denouncing Minski as a petty and decadent tyrant. He kept calm, overriding his anger with the simple thought that he wouldn't have the strength to wreck the table, that his voice would accuse Minski in the feeble tones of a weakening old man. It would be an opportunity for Minski to mock him. The pain in his legs stabbed upwards, driving spikes between his ribs.

Minski wore a smug smile. His face was a white, cancerous blister.

'I'm not hungry,' the Doctor said, the effort leaving him gasping for breath. Sade shuffled uneasily on the back of his chair.

'Well, let's dispense with breakfast. I've arranged a small display that might interest you,' Minski droned, making another sign with his hands.

'Why are you doing this?' the Doctor asked.

Minski looked up, startled. 'I'm sorry?'

'You seem a very calculating young man. You must have a reason.' The Doctor felt oddly satisfied at having seized the initiative. Minski appeared genuinely perplexed by this new enquiry.

'Well,' Minski leant back, an arm emerging from under the chair to steady him. 'It depends what sort of scale you're working on. If you mean, "Why am I doing this to France?" or, "Why am I doing this to the world?" then the answer is simple.' He waved his arms vaguely, and leant forward sporting a fat and knowledgeable grin. 'All this, everything, the whole world, is a machine.'

'A machine?' the Doctor echoed, remembering coldly le 6's revelation.

'A clock.' Minski slapped his hands together, grinning.

'A clock?' Sade became the echo, adding a note of distress to the words. His brow furrowed and he leant slightly towards his son.

'A *cuckoo* clock,' Minski pronounced, addressing his father.

Sade fell back, his face buckling queasily.

A new burst of rain drummed against the window. The mood of stalemate was broken by the arrival of another soldier. She scuttled into the room, bowing respectfully to Minski before approaching Sade. Whispers were exchanged, out of range of the Doctor's hearing. Sade rose, his expression a cocktail of weariness and relief. Free of her burden, his seat sagged.

'There's something I have to deal with,' he said, vanishing hurriedly through the door and away.

The Doctor felt the intensity redouble as the First Deputy's attention fixed solely onto his guest.

'Our brains work like clocks,' he continued, 'clicking away as they balance and regulate us. We are a clockwork people in a clockwork world. Once I became aware of the machine, it was my duty to understand it, and then to control it. That's what it means to rule, to be master of the machine.

'On the other hand, you might mean, "Why am I doing this to you?" Again, simple. You have no place in this world. You're like a speck of dirt that falls through the cracks in the machine and clogs up the gears. I want to know what it is that gives you that power.

'I want to learn about your trick box. I want – I need to understand it.'

His voice was trembling by the time he had finished, and his eyes glared hungrily out of his undisturbed features. The Doctor was taken aback by the ferocity of his answer, forgetting himself so much that he nearly sat down. He had glimpsed something terrifying in Minski.

'You can come in now,' the creature with the child's face called. He turned back to the Doctor. 'This is what I want to show you.'

Another figure came through the door, a woman dressed in a simple grey robe whose hem brushed against the floor. She trod gracefully but steadily, her eyes fixed on the far wall. Her blonde hair hung long and loose against her back. She smiled and nodded to Minski, then bowed to the Doctor.

'This is the first of my achievements,' Minski said, almost by way of an introduction. 'She's very simple. The work became more complex later, though by that time I'd realized that I was going up a blind alley.'

The woman smiled again, bowed again, nodded again. The Doctor studied her features, wondering what it was that disturbed him. She wore a permanent expression of serenity, her features unruffled by thought or emotion. Her eyes were glazed and unblinking, staring innocently back at the Doctor. Finding himself embarrassed, he looked away. The woman smiled again, nodded again, put her hands to her head and peeled the skin from her skull.

Beneath the flesh was a hidden face, fashioned on a smooth bronze plate. It was dead, without eyes or muscles, conveying nothing. The flesh mask in the woman's hands still twitched through basic expressions, tiny muscle-mechanisms bristling on the inside of the skin.

The bronze-faced false-woman dropped her grey robe, exposing naked machinery in a frame of elegantly sculpted metal. She stepped back and began to dance. Her movements were fluid and expressive, her clockwork guts spinning frantically inside her bronze ribs and skeleton limbs. A gyroscope spun in her abdomen, keeping her balanced. She whirled and dived and leapt across the floor, spinning in between the quivering furniture, the Doctor and his host.

'Magnificent, isn't it?' Minski said. 'It took me two years, starting from scratch, to build automata that might pass for human, that would bleed if you pricked them. It wasn't until then that I realized I had been approaching my problem the wrong way round.'

'It is quite beautiful,' the Doctor said wistfully,

enthralled by the movements of the clockwork dancer despite himself. 'Isn't that enough?'

'No,' Minski replied. 'No, of course not.'

Sade breathed heavily, sucking in the dry air of the Bastille passages. The walls swirled around him deliriously, a kaleidoscope of greys and blacks. The relentless beat of the clock had returned, throbbing inside his swollen head. The ticking came faster than before, blurring into a shrill, unbroken note.

Winding through my life, clock-hands spinning, eating my remaining minutes in seconds. Hissing towards the chimes, the chimes will kill me!

The guard who had fetched him had said there was an intruder on one of the subterranean levels. He had been cornered, but they needed someone to take charge of his capture. Sade had descended, eager for the challenge. He hadn't expected the violence, the gunshot crack and the pain-burst in his arm.

He had lived with the fear of death. It was strongest at nights, when he was locked away and alone, when the only noise had been the fragile beat of his heart under his ribs, a reminder that Death was coming for him. They were the fears of a naif, of another, less learned man.

A soldier's face, a pretty woman's face, never the part worth watching, rose before him, lips flickering sound-lessly. She was asking if he was all right, though he wasn't certain how he could hear. Her hand touched his shoulder, sending a spasm of pain crashing through him. He moved his head to look, seeing her hand come away coated with blood.

'I'm bleeding,' someone said faraway.

'You've been shot,' the soldier said.

The chimes rang out across the inside of his skull.

Death seemed strange, a cruel practical joke played on the unready. He wondered what the precise moment would feel like. He had left so much unspoken and undone. Too late now.

'I'm dying,' he said.

The soldier smiled gently. She seemed to be standing vigil over him, like a guardian, or a ghoul. 'The ball went straight through your shoulder,' she said. 'Your arm's broken and you've lost some blood, but men have walked away from worse.'

'Thank you,' he replied.

She was the messenger, he remembered. He had followed her because she had a shapely rump. She'd giggled when he squeezed her in the lift, and seemed quite willing to return to his rooms after the intruder had been arrested. That was before he had been shot, and planning for the future hadn't seemed foolish.

'What happened to the man?' he asked.

'The others are chasing him.'

'How long ago . . . ?' he asked vaguely. Mere minutes she said. She'd sent for a doctor, she said. He told her she was kind, then lapsed into silence.

There! He's there with his back turned to me. I step forward, flintlock in hand, and call to him to surrender. He turns. I see his face. He sees mine.

There is a silence that lasts forever.

He screams. The pistol in his hand ejaculates. A clap of thunder. Voice and gunshot melt together.

He'd been a short man, chubby and old, dressed up to disguise his shortcomings. His wig hadn't hidden the thinning flecks of blonde-grey hair. Sade couldn't recall his face properly, only the anger that deformed it. His eyes had blazed with jagged rage. His tiny mouth had twisted bitterly as he screamed. He had recognized Sade. He *hated* Sade. He had no face.

'Le 6,' Sade said, as though it were a revelation.

'Sorry?' the soldier was puzzled and leaned closer. Her warmth seemed proof that he was not yet dead. The echo of the chimes died away.

'I know him,' he said simply. 'He should have been killed. He should have been killed a long time ago. Where is he now?'

149

'He escaped onto the next level down.'

'Good.' Sade clutched at his shoulder. His fingers became damp quickly and clawed at numb, broken flesh. Living flesh, though — warm flesh dribbling warm blood. He cradled himself, thankful for his return from the brink of death. 'Chase him into the labyrinth. Chase him into the murder machine.'

6

A Clockwork World

The Doctor's instincts sang as he drew closer to the TARDIS. Her voice called to him through space, poignant and vulnerable. The ship, with her quaint shape, her monotonous squareness, was a reassuring sign that some things remained inviolate, outside Minski's domain. He steeled himself, resolving not to yield the slightest detail about her to the First Deputy.

The Bastille tower was bustling with people as they descended. There was a scattering of soldiers but most seemed to be minor officials, their dark uniforms decorated with embarrassing tricolour blossoms. The Doctor was surprised to see so much activity. He had expected Minski to live alone and isolated, shielded from the world by bricks and mortar and cold steel, a brooding recluse ruling from the highest turret. There was a false note here.

Sade was waiting for them at the entrance to the laboratory, one arm wrapped in a crisp, white sling. Minski shoved past him, scuttling over to stroke the walls of the TARDIS. Unable to bear the sight of the son, the Doctor turned his attention to the father.

'I hope that's not as bad as it looks.'

Sade shrugged. A crease of pain flew across his face, replaced by the usual sardonic smile. The anguish lingered in his eyes, blazing points of white inside the black. The Doctor felt curiously benevolent. Sade's darkness seemed wholesome against Minski's bloodless gloom.

'A flesh wound,' he said smoothly. 'There was some trouble. No longer.'

'I want to see inside.' Minski's drab, sandy voice cut

151

across them. He looked up from his inspection of the TARDIS, but his palms lingered against its shell and his eyes flickered hungrily. 'How can I get inside?'

The Doctor trembled, too weak to contain his disgust.

'You must have a key,' Minski insisted.

A small lump of metal twitched in the Doctor's coat pocket. Not the TARDIS key, he realized suddenly, but the one he had taken from the lab earlier. It burned in his pocket, vivid in his mind.

Steel, he thought. Steel and concrete. Do not break, not bend, not shatter. He chanted the fortifying mantra to himself. Minski smeared his hands across the TARDIS, setting his chubby fingers picking at the lock.

Steel and concrete. Steel. Not weaken, not sway.

'I won't threaten you,' he said lightly. 'I won't torture you. You'd turn the pain against itself. It would harden you. But I believe you have a friend in Paris, a young woman. I know where to find her. Perhaps she has a key?'

Fire.

Minski's mouth was twisted into a victorious smile, a broad grin sliced across his flesh. It was full of childish cruelty, incongruous on his child's face. A silent rage ignited inside the Doctor, searing and scorching his defences. In his imagination, Minski burned.

Sade stepped between them, blocking the Doctor's view of the TARDIS. Briefly relieved, the Doctor sagged, recovering himself before Minski reappeared. Sade's back was tense, his spine trembling under his shirt.

'This is going to have to wait,' he said, a slight waver in his voice giving his pain away. He glanced cold-eyed over his shoulder at the Doctor, perhaps warning or suspecting. The Doctor made his own face a blank.

'There was an intruder loose in the Bastille.' The words rolled languidly from his mouth, smoothing away the painful cracks. 'It's not a problem. He's dealt with, but I'm worried.'

'Why?' Minski snapped. His fingers knotted together, flexed and cracked.

'I saw his face,' Sade rumbled, oblivious to his son's irritation. He looked again at the Doctor, another hooded, indecipherable glance. 'I saw his face and I didn't understand it.'

The child's face darkened and stretched tight across the child's skull. The Doctor drew a little pleasure from Minski's stinging expression.

'All right, we'll talk.' The tyrant spoke harshly, clicking his tongue. If it weren't for his voice, the Doctor might have mistaken him for a child again. He was smouldering with shapeless, childish outrage – directed at the parent who distracted him from his latest toy. If it weren't for the voice, and the power he commanded.

Minski grabbed Sade by the arm and pulled him to the laboratory exit.

'I'll be back in a moment Doctor,' he called. 'If you need anything in the meantime, ask the guard on the door.' The Doctor nodded silently.

Alone at last, invisible at last, the Doctor let gravity take its toll. He relaxed against the wall and allowed himself to sink, the gangrenous pain in his legs seeping out onto the floor. A sigh escaped him, hanging briefly in the stagnant air. This was a moment of relief, a moment to savour.

There was a small, hard, metal shape in his hands, twisting between his fingertips. He stared at it lazily, not quite able to focus on it, or find a name for it. It was a tiny item, with a thin chain hanging from one end. He must have taken it from one of his pockets, without thinking.

'Key,' he said, allowing himself a wide smile.

He turned it over and over in his palm, studying it with scientific intensity. It was ordinary enough, perfectly normal for this time and this place, but it fascinated him. It was something about its texture or its weight, or the odd way in which it caught the light. He held it up and it seemed to change, losing its shape. For an instant it was transparent and he caught a glimpse of complex circuitry and throbbing organic components trapped inside. Startled, he leapt up, and the key slid back into its original shape.

'Key,' he said decisively. He caught it in a tight fist before setting out through the façade into the heart of the lab.

The head was still there, grinning morbidly from its spike. It gave him a gentle blue smile that disarmed some of its horror.

'We have some time,' it croaked as the Doctor approached, its voice losing some of its smoothness. 'Sade's personal problems go deep and dark.'

'I imagine they would.' He adjusted his lapels and flexed his fingers, fidgeting while he decided the best way to begin.

'Ah,' he said at last. 'What happened to you?'

The head grinned wryly. 'Nothing happened to me. I've always been like this.' It sighed – the Doctor's eye was caught by the paper lung pumping inside the workings of the machine beneath it. 'There was once a woman who allowed herself to be abused and experimented upon by Minski. She was really an assassin, a traitor sent to kill the tyrant. She was caught and lost her head to Minski's murder machine.

'All her knowledge is crystallized in here, in her dead brain. When Minski reanimated it, he created me, inheritor of a woman's dead thoughts. I know her,' it finished, 'but I don't remember her at all.'

'I see,' the Doctor lowered his head, studying his fingers. The key hung by its chain round his wrist, an enigma dangling in thin air. It seemed less important, all of a sudden.

'Did Minski sew up your mouth?'

The head shook slightly, as though it were trying to nod. It bit at its lower lip, tugging out a strand of blue thread.

'Why?'

'There were other voices, speaking through me.

154

They'd help you, but they've retreated into their dark corners. That key you have is important to them. It's their only way in, I'm told.'

'Indeed?' The Doctor hmmed, holding the key up to the light once more. It remained an ordinary key. 'In my experience, young lady, keys are seldom as important as the locks they fill.'

'I'm not a young lady,' the head murmured. 'I never was.'

'No. Of course, no. I am sorry.' He stretched out a hand, letting his fingertips brush against the smooth metal object on the chain. It bristled under his touch, and he caught a brief sight of something greater caught in its structure. It was extremely advanced technology, for a mere key . . .

'Extraordinary,' he giggled. 'I do believe there is more to this than meets the eye.' He touched the key again, holding it between his fingers, willing the change upon it. The metal warped in his hand, spilling out of the key shape, changing colour and texture and tone, growing rapidly against his hand. It was no longer metal, but organic. The gnarled surface was soft and wet and pulsed as it grew. The fluid material spilled across the floor and solidified, and leapt into the air in defiance of gravity, freezing hard as it reached its apex. The key billowed outwards, hardening and darkening grey-green. It became an arch, growing out of the laboratory floor, a portal leading into darkness.

'The key contains the door. Wonderful!' the Doctor clapped with delight.

The head regarded it with a sardonic eye, impressed and suspicious. 'Where does it lead?'

'Outside this space-time, at a guess,' the Doctor speculated, shrugging. 'Possibly it's the main gate back into normal space. Possibly not. There is only one way to find out.' He gave her a mischievous grin.

'I'm sorry I can't come with you.' the head replied, without irony. The Doctor acknowledged it with a nod and a bow, then stepped through the archway. The darkness enfolded him.

At the heart of darkness was the machine. It ticked.

Fantômas's bedroom seemed more cramped than that in Dalville's caravan. It shouldn't have been. There was only one bed – a wooden frame whose only pretence to comfort was a couple of frayed blankets and a pillow – and a writing desk crammed into the far corner. Despite this, Dodo felt confined. The shutters on the window were closed and the shadows ate into the corners, swallowing the free space.

The aliens were with her, their bulks seeming to squeeze the room tighter. Howlglass hovered beside her, his shadow a long dark spar across the dwindling light. Larkspur perched on the bunk at Dodo's side, a gnarled hand resting on her shoulder. Perhaps it was trying to reassure her, perhaps warning her to keep silent. Dodo felt calmer than she expected. The being's touch was warm and tentative.

Fantômas was gone. Within minutes of Dodo's capture, someone had come to the door, forcing the director to bundle allies and prisoner into the bedroom out of sight. Dodo wasn't the slightest bit sorry to lose sight of him. She'd even brightened up a bit when she recognized the caller's voice as Dalville's, certain that a rescue was on hand. Larkspur's grip on her shoulder tightened slightly, a warning pinch.

'I've brought the list of changes,' Dalville began, his voice drifting in from the next room. Even if it wasn't a rescue, Dodo felt heartened, and a little excited. 'It's very long.'

'It's what I was expecting. What are the important points?'

'Debord wants a happy ending, so we'll have to marry Sophie off.'

'She can marry Dalville,' Fantômas interrupted, barb-voiced.

Dalville coughed nervously before continuing. 'She can't get struck by lightning, so we'll save some cash on the special effects. Several major characters have to change. The debauched friars will have to become comic friars and we have to give them jolly songs to sing. Debord says its OK if we make them cannibals, but we can't make reference to flatulence. That sort of thing.'

'Anything else?' Fantômas yawned, audible in the bunk room.

'We have to cut Bressac out completely,' Dalville replied. No, Dodo thought, replied was the wrong word. Dalville *accused*.

'Have you told him yet?'

'No.' His voice was shaking, fear laced with fire. 'Bressac is the best part in the entire play. If you let them write him out . . . Well, it was a good performance you gave on the field, but some of us think you've let us down.'

'That's right,' the cold reply came without a pause.

Shocked silence filtered through the door. Dodo strained, trying to catch the sound of Dalville breathing.

'Is there anything else?' Fantômas added abruptly, 'I gather you're quite friendly with Sophie. Any special pleading on her behalf?'

'No.' Dalville growled. 'Take the list. Just . . . take it!'

Feet stamped violently on the caravan floor, setting the whole structure shaking. A door was flung open sharply, then slammed with angry vigour. Dodo recognized Dalville's tread as he stalked away from the caravan. Her thoughts of rescue faded, replaced instantly by wilder fantasies.

Dalville would come crashing through the window, sword in hand, leaping to do battle with the murderous, lurching figure of Fantômas. Bressac would follow, seizing the censor's list, tearing it apart and flinging the shreds across the field to be destroyed by mud and rain. The Doctor would hobble in after them, banishing Larkspur and Howlglass with some handy gadget from the TARDIS. It would be that easy, she thought, that easy to put the world right.

The monotonous rain drummed on the walls of the caravan. Dejected, Dodo clasped her hands between her knees and squeezed them. She looked up when the door to the bunk room squealed open, half-expecting to see Dalville there, in silhouette, a sword balanced in his hand.

It was Fantômas, clutching a sheaf of sodden papers. He should have looked vast and impressive, shadowed against the new light. Instead it depressed him. His shoulders sagged and curved, his arms hung limp at his sides. He held his head crooked, arrogant, but this couldn't hide the softness of his eyes, or the way they leapt to avoid meeting Dodo's gaze. He sighed.

'What that man needs is a good mothering,' he pronounced coldly. His eyes fell and he sniffed. 'Who's eaten all my biscuits?'

Howlglass shuffled, brushing crumbs from his robe.

Fantômas smiled, though it didn't fit his face. 'Right. I thought it might be *her*.' He clapped one hand under Dodo's chin and twisted her face towards him. She stared back, struggling to hide her fear beneath a cover of pity. Fantômas pushed his face into hers and purred.

'Poor Dalville. He's in love, you can see it in his eyes.'

Again, Dodo spotted an odd splinter in the director's eyes. It was a guarded look of fear, or uncertainty. Dodo saw a weakness and snatched at it.

'You ought to be ashamed of yourself!' she squealed, realizing in an instant how stupid that sounded, then almost breaking into laughter at Fantômas's sombre reaction. 'We deserve better from you. Me, Dalville, the actors, and most of all, Bressac deserves better than you!'

The hand released her chin, the bearded face pulled back into shadow. Fantômas hurled the censor's list onto the floor and crossed to the desk, muttering half to Dodo, half to himself, as he went.

'What I say about Dalville is true, as far as truth goes

nowadays.' He pulled a manuscript from the desktop, holding it close enough for Dodo to see the scrawled handwriting and the blots of ink that stained the paper. 'As for Bressac, I'm a substitute for his unattainable desires. That's just one truth I don't want to hurt him with.' His gloves came off, revealing delicate, pale-white hands with smooth nails. They trembled as they held the script. 'And yes, everyone deserves better. Or if not better, then different.

'Look at this!' he barked, waving the wedge of manuscript paper in her face. 'This is the original copy of the play. I wrote every word by hand, staining every pure cream page with my pen, moulding these sentences from hot, sticky fluid. I was determined to capture the soul and the detail of Sade's text. I was *faithful!*'

He tore a strip from the front page, then another, then another and another, and another and another, another, another. He worked meticulously to destroy every page, scattering ribbons of cream paper across the floor, across Debord's list, a blizzard of censored words. Dodo wasn't sure whether to laugh or tremble. Fantômas smiled as he reached the end of the devastation.

'Finished. Obliterated. Like history. Now I have to write another version, a cleaner one that will make more sense to people like Citizen Debord, Citizen Minski and the rest.'

He turned back to his desk. He tugged open a drawer and produced another manuscript from within, perhaps a little thinner than the first, with the title page laid out in a blunt, mechanical type.

'Here's one I prepared earlier.'

At the heart of darkness is the machine. It ticks.

The machine is everywhere. It is a vast, pulsing, pumping chamber with walls of grey flesh. Veins and arteries riddle the wall-flesh, thin green lines that throb demurely, heavier white tubes that bloat with milky fluid. The flesh of the machine is soft and wet and supple, shuddering under its own weight. Only the bone structure supports the machine, black ribs lacing from the floor to the ceiling holding back the collapse. The machine slobbers to itself, overlapping voices whispering through the void.

The wall-flesh is pierced in a thousand places by metal pins that radiate from the shaft at the centre of the bone structure. The wounds bleed, sticky white liquid smearing down the walls. Some of the fluid is siphoned away in feeder tubes, tendrils that snake from the wounds to swollen lips on the surface of the bone-shaft. At the base of the shaft is a cage, its bars impaled into the seething floor-flesh.

An arm of flesh sprouts from one of the walls. A bulb forms on the end of the stalk, billows outwards and bursts, disgorging the Doctor into the machine. He is delivered out of the world. He steadies himself, tumbling out of the darkness onto his feet. He stands in shock, staring at his new surroundings. His eyes flicker in their sockets, swivelling rapidly in an effort to absorb everything. His hands rise briefly, as if to clutch his temples, then fall back, limp at his sides.

He is confused, not so much by the sights and sounds and smells of the machine, but by its timelessness. He is unused to stepping unprotected into the worlds outside time. Random thoughts flicker across his brain, a jumble of senses and observations. He begins to order them. It is a painstakingly slow process, an incredible one. He imposes a sense of linear time on the machine, seen through his eyes, through his mind. Satisfied, he gazes around himself, drawing in the sights. His nostrils flair, perhaps from disgust, perhaps from admiration. He is as much an enigma to the machine as the machine is to him.

He makes five minutes pass while he studies. He takes a tentative step, shifting through false time and illusory space towards the bone-shaft. At first he is pursued across the floor by ghost images of himself, echoes fragmented in time. His consciousness is shattered, the shards scattering in all directions, but he allows himself no fear. He masters movement gradually, regaining his identity as he grows more confident. He reaches the bars of the cage – they seem to him to be a mesh of vast, interlocking finger bones and he falters slightly, reminded of his own mortality. Then he steps through.

There are two things within the cage of the bone structure that demand the Doctor's attention. The first of these is the orrery suspended above his head. It is a model of a solar system – Earth's – trapped inside a vast glass sphere, a bulbous cancer at the base of the bone-shaft. The sun, the ten planets and their many satellites are contained by the glass, held on wire spines, rotating perfectly to the accompaniment of a clockwork motor. It is this noise that distracts the Doctor. Its size only impresses him.

The second thing appals him. Beneath the orrery is the heart of the machine, a mass of clockwork, of silent steel bones and churning grey flesh, of grinding industrial engines that cough and choke on their own steam. Everything in the machine chamber converges here – the veins and arteries, the feeder tendrils, metal pins jutting from the bone-shaft – breeding into a massive, incoherent engine. And at the heart of the engine, something lives, impaled on rods and spikes, sharp bones and burrowing flesh-tubes.

The Doctor pushes through a forest of dangling, throbbing tubes to get a clearer look at the machine's prisoner. It seems to be human shaped, though much of its body is hidden beneath a grey robe. Its misshapen head is exposed, jutting out of a bank of whirling, shrieking cogs. Its face is hidden, though the Doctor sees hints of features in the jumble of metal trinkets and shining glass that decorate its black mask. On its forehead is a colourful tattoo. It makes rasping breaths which grow more frantic as the Doctor grows nearer. It raises a hand, broken fingers swathed in grey cloth.

The Doctor stops and speaks uncertainly.

'Are you in pain?'

'Yes, my lord,' the creature replies. Its voice is resilient and thoughtful, only hinting at the pain. The hints are enough. 'That is your title, isn't it?'

'It most certainly is not,' the Doctor responds, indignantly.

'Are you sure?' the alien mumbles, unconvinced. 'Perhaps you were noble once but fell from grace? Perhaps it's a claim you chose to renounce?' It withers under the Doctor's hot glare. 'I'm sorry, I see less clearly than I have. Do you have a preferred name?'

'I am the Doctor.'

The being nods calmly, though its hand is shaking. 'Ah. Yes, I'm in pain, but you can't heal me. I'm cursed to this. The machines that kill me, also sustain my life.' From the Doctor, there is silence. Something on the alien's mask reminds him of a smile. 'You have a solid, obsidian face. All your strength's there. If there's anything real underneath it's wasted, or ghostly. I know how you must feel.'

'Who are you?' the Doctor snaps, impatient now. 'What are you doing?'

'I am Robin Goodfellow,' comes the reply, between harsh breaths, 'an artist–scientist of the Pageant, Masksmaster of Project Orbis Tertius.'

'Project?' the Doctor murmurs. 'What was the subject?'

'Planet D-zero-two-R-L in Mutter's Spiral. Earth.'

'Project objective?'

'To explore the relationship between individual psychology and the historical dynamic.' Goodfellow makes a spluttering sound that might be a cough. Part of his mask splits, releasing a trickle of grey mucus. 'This,' it adds, 'all of this, is our fault.'

The Doctor looks downwards, finding something fascinating about his shoes. His silence is uncertain and painful.

'Then you deserve my outrage,' he says finally. There is a weak anger in his voice, more than matched by the sympathy. Trapped in the machine, Goodfellow hangs his head as far as he is capable. 'What did you do?'

'I suspect you've guessed most of it.'

'Only parts,' the Doctor says. He reaches out and clasps the alien's hand between both palms, surprised at the warmth he finds, and the strength in his own, old fingers. 'Only minor details. I need to know the whole of it.'

'Briefly then,' Goodfellow replies. Something in the machine wrenches and he gasps, the fabric of his mask folding and fluttering. When he continues, his voice is strained. The Doctor realizes that he is forcing himself on.

'We identified a certain trend in human thought and history. We traced the trend to one symptomatic epoch, where its arguments and contradictions were enacted through human agency.'

'You mean the French Revolution?'

'Specifically, Revolutionary Year II, the Reign of Terror.'

'This is fascinating.' The Doctor chuckles. 'What was the trend?' He peers forward, eager and inquisitive.

'Reason.'

Goodfellow pauses, perhaps for breath. The Doctor blinks slowly and seriously, waiting for him to resume.

'We found a human, a man who would in later times be seen as a quirk of his era. We offered him a chance to remould future history. At the time he was rather depressed and accepted our offer.'

'Yes,' the Doctor interrupts, nodding, 'I believe I have met him.' He has a vivid recollection of a masked old man, squatting on the floor of a cell, babbling meaningful nonsense.

'We physically removed the Earth from normal space and reconfigured it inside this pocket universe, rebuilt entirely within a machine that would regulate and control the physical nature of the world. The mass-slaughter of

163

the Terror generated enough electromagnetic energy for that purpose.

'The world-machine would be run by a genetically engineered operator that would be programmed with an epistemic code based on our human's philosophies and ideals. The new history would be created through the operator, through the world-machine. We set it up and sat back to watch.' Sapped of his strength by the effort of talking, Goodfellow sinks back into the machinery, into the warm darkness.

The Doctor watches him, seeing no evil in him. He is still angered.

'There are laws against this sort of thing,' he says softly.

'Laws tend to serve the interests of their makers.'

'Most of the time, yes. Occasionally they exist to protect the weak.'

'You mean the humans,' Goodfellow's voice wavers from behind the shelter of the machines. 'The project wasn't designed to harm them. We just wanted to see what they would do if things were different . . . It went wrong.'

'What happened?' the Doctor asks. He is sympathetic again, finding it difficult to sustain his anger in the face of Goodfellow's pain.

'We hadn't realized. The human we used . . . his epistemic code corrupted the system. The system operator became perverted . . . developed independence . . . seized control of the machine. My tribe retreated to the edges of this world. As Masksmaster I remain, as a slave . . .'

The Doctor pauses, pinching the bridge of his nose as he unravels the implications of what he has heard.

'I see,' he tells Goodfellow darkly. 'I see.'

'I thought you would,' the voice comes from inside the machine, weak and disintegrating. The Doctor reaches forward to make contact, but the machinery snarls, biting at his hand. He withdraws it reluctantly, bitterness playing on his face. He tries to speak, to promise something, but there are no words.

Goodfellow's fragile breaths pursue him, haunt him, as he escapes from the machine.

'Can I go now?' Dodo asked, not hopefully.

Fantômas shrugged. For the past couple of hours he had been working solidly on the new manuscript, comparing it with Debord's notes and making minor corrections wherever he saw fit. He held his pen awkwardly, leaving his fingers stained with ink. Bored, Dodo had become fascinated watching the shape of the director's hands as he struggled with the pen.

'You'll still have to get your kit off,' Fantômas had said thoughtfully, the first time he had spoken for ages. 'It's in our contract. One decent nude scene per performance. I'm surprised Dalville hasn't kicked up a stink about it, though he is easily confused.'

'You're revolting,' Dodo had bleated, wishing that her voice was stronger and she could think of something pithier to blast him with.

'No,' he'd replied, so softly she barely heard, 'I'm rebelling.'

Larkspur and Howlglass took turns to guard her. She hoped that one of them would speak soon, so she could lose herself in the joy of their voices, but they remained obstinately silent. As the time dragged by, she began to feel left out. She began to fidget, reacting to imaginary itches and aches – a game she had learned as a girl, a game she played when she began to feel lonely at birthday parties, sometimes her own. Bored, she decided that Fantômas and his friends simply weren't interested in her. Somehow, that was worse than being a prisoner.

'Can I go now?' she asked playfully.

'No,' Fantômas replied.

'We should let her go,' Larkspur hummed, a low sound that gave Dodo a warm tingle in her toes and fingers. He spoke again, to her this time. 'You come from outside this enclosed, machine-bound world. You are beyond the control of our enemy. You should be our ally.'

Fantômas scowled. He scowled again as Howlglass nodded his agreement.

'Do you normally lock up your friends and ignore them for hours on end?'

'Yes,' Fantômas snapped.

'We're at a low ebb. We do foolish things.' Howlglass's voice was a rainbow of sounds, blending and colliding like a violent orchestral orgasm. 'We don't trust those we should.'

'OK, OK.' Dodo waved graciously. 'Apology accepted. So,' she leant forward to join a conspiratorial huddle with the aliens, reducing her voice to a dangerous whisper, 'what are you up to? Who's your enemy?'

Fantômas snorted. 'She's sending you up,' he called from the desk.

'Our enemy is the system operator of the world-machine,' Howlglass explained in hues of vibrant sound. 'You call him Citizen Minski.'

'That's not what *I* call him,' Fantômas whistled, grinning perversely.

Dodo gave him a sideways glare, feeling rather pleased with the way he'd been pushed out of the conversation. 'Why?' she asked.

'The story is long and somewhat convoluted,' Larkspur began. 'Needless to say, he is our responsibility and we must bring him to account.'

'Once we have done that,' Howlglass added, a waterfall of perfect, resonant words, 'we can restore the Earth's history to its original path.'

'You should talk to the Doctor,' Dodo murmured.

Howlglass nodded. 'He's beyond our reach in the Bastille, the heart of the operator's domain. But you're right, he would help us, in his own fashion.'

Dodo looked from Howlglass to Larkspur and back again, studying the lenses of their masks as though they were windows into the truth. They contained only murky darkness. Yet somehow she believed the aliens.

166

Their voices were too beautiful to contain lies, their tone too sincere. She wanted to trust them – she *needed* to trust them, to make sense of the world – but there was a nagging irritant at the back of her mind, something that didn't quite fit.

Yes, that was it.

'How's he involved? Why's Fantômas here?' she asked, jabbing an abrupt finger at Fantômas.

The director rose from behind the desk and bowed, gesturing elaborately as he went down. He bared his teeth in a vicious smile, his skin pinched back against his skull.

'Why is Fantômas here?' he asked slowly, his voice building in strength and vigour. 'He is here because he is conspicuous. People see his colour as he troops through the streets, they point to him and shout "Look! There's Fantômas, the travelling player". Seeing him, they gossip. They say he's a lunatic, a monster, a demon in fancy dress. But they never challenge him. He can go everywhere, but no one sees what he really is. If they could they would try to stop him.

'Fantômas is a clown, and a clown is his costume.'

He dropped to his knees in another elaborate bow, and began working at the buckles on his boots, shucking the boots off and hurling them into the corner. Dodo exchanged an odd glance with Howlglass and Larkspur, but the masks' expressions were inscrutably smug. She looked back to find Fantômas rising, no longer an imposing height. In fact, he seemed no taller than Dodo herself. She glanced indignantly at his discarded boots.

'You wear platforms?' she said, tasting mild rancour in her voice.

'And more besides,' the director replied. He shrugged off his coat, abandoning it to the floor. He was wearing a cream shirt beneath, his chest further buried beneath a series of tight leather straps. Dodo winced sympathetically. His tiny hands dangled from reed-thin arms that were decorated with criss-cross patterns of pale scars.

Fantômas spoke. Not in French, not in any human

language, just a single deranged syllable. His face shone, sun-bright, blistering with alien colours. Dodo flung an arm across her eyes against the light-burst. The burning face haunted her in the dark, glowing beneath her eyelids.

'Look,' Fantômas commanded.

Cautiously, she raised her head. Fantômas's face had melted. His hands went to his head, fingers sliding easily under the flesh and tearing it away. His beard and hair followed. His features were elongated and flattened, spread across the square of false skin stretched between his hands, but they continued to flicker with nuances, with transient and illusory emotions. There were tear-shaped hollows where his eyes had been. The face was powerless without them, a living mask.

Fantômas's hands lowered the remains of his face, revealing a new set of features, a woman's face. A pale, gaunt woman's face – thin skin pulled tight across high, fine bones, a tiny head, barely larger than a child's, crowned with a crop of short hair. The only echo of Fantômas was her eyes, the same eyes, subtly changed.

'Fantômas,' the woman said simply, placing the director's face neatly on the desk. Dodo gaped. 'He's a very unpleasant man. It's nice to talk without him around to spoil things. My name is Catherine Arouette.'

Dodo's head span. Something inside her skull clenched painfully, and she sank back onto the bed. Arouette shrugged wearily and knelt beside her. Her body was warm and her gaze was kind, sympathetic. She wasn't Fantômas, Dodo realized through mild delirium, she just lived inside his skin.

'That's a very good mask,' she said, giggling nervously despite herself.

'It's too good.' Arouette was unfastening the straps round her chest. She savoured her first breath, drinking it deeply. 'My friends here designed it.' She waved to Larkspur and Howlglass, who had been watching silently from the corner. They trembled slightly, as though accused of something embarrassing.

168

'Ours is a mask-based culture,' Howlglass hummed. (Colours exploded behind Dodo's eyes, as a shock leapt up her spine.) 'It makes liars of us.'

'And I'm a very good actor. It's not the first time a character has taken on a life of his own.' The player's feeble smile wore away, a darkness passing like an angel over her face. 'Poor Bressac. I've lied to him twice. I've deceived him by being Fantômas, and by not being Fantômas.'

'Why did you do it then?' Dodo asked. Her shock had faded, leaving hungry curiosity in its wake.

'For ease of movement: men can move effortlessly round Paris, but single women only draw attention and malicious gossip. To allay people's suspicions: Fantômas is colour without life. People don't try to dig deeper. For protection: Minski knows me. Sade knows my name.'

'How?' Dodo asked, burrowing closer to the truth.

'Sade killed my brother,' Arouette replied darkly.

'Is that why you're doing this? For revenge?'

'No. No. I want justice.' Her face was close, smothered with heavy shadows, so close they were almost touching. Dodo would have fallen back, if there was anywhere further to go. She snatched a glance at the robed aliens through the corner of her eye, drawing heart from their presence.

'At worst, I want to know why he did it,' Arouette drawled. She retreated slightly, the shadows on her eyes losing their menace. The pain was personal, trapped inside this woman, as she had been trapped in Fantômas.

'Tell me about it,' Dodo whispered.

'I didn't know my brother,' the woman began, gazing upwards at the ceiling. She spoke without feeling, as if reciting a story she had read as a child. 'He was the eldest of our family, fifteen years older than me. He left home when I was an infant, left to find his fortune in Paris. He found it,' she added wistfully. 'He was lucky. During the first twelve years of my life, he became rich and married. I knew about him only through his letters. He was a creature from legend or fable. My brother.

'On my thirteenth birthday, I came to Paris for the first time. It was arranged that I would stay with my brother, whom I had never seen, in his house, with his family. When I arrived in the city, it was like stepping into a city of magic, home to this imagined creature. My brother.

'He was everything I expected and more. I loved him, and he loved me. We had three months together, three months in which I learned everything, three perfect months. That's how I like to remember them. I lay awake one night, staring up at the sky through the bars of the attic window, wishing for something special, a sign, a miracle. And he allowed me to stay another three months in his home. Even his wife wanted me to stay. They insisted I write home telling my parents how much I was enjoying myself in Paris. So I wrote.'

She broke off to stare at her hands, disgust curling on her lips. The sleeves slid back from her matchstick arms. The map of meandering scars ran down to her elbow, thick chunks torn from her flesh.

'It could have gone on forever. It felt like that sometimes. But the Revolution came and disturbed our happiness. My brother and his wife fled Paris, afraid for their lives. In the chaos, I was left behind. I would have waited, I would have,' she insisted, 'but a mob came and ransacked the house. I had to flee. My brother had left me with a good idea of what men could do to a thirteen-year-old innocent.

'I stayed in Paris through the best and worst of it. I heard nothing of my brother until one day early in 1793. He had been arrested on charges of treason. I've no doubt he was innocent, of that at least. He was brought before a magistrate, before Citizen Sade. You know what happened?'

'Sade sentenced him to death,' Dodo suggested darkly.

Arouette giggled. 'No. He dismissed all the charges. He said there was no evidence and that it was a travesty of

170

justice to bring him to trial.' She giggled again, a bitter laugh without humour.

'But you said Sade killed him,' Dodo protested.

'Five years later, my brother was rearrested and brought before Sade to face the same charges on the same evidence. I wasn't there that time, but I heard that verdict and sentence were decided upon within a minute of the trial opening. Sade, without a pause, sent my brother to the guillotine, for the same reasons he had once freed him. And . . .' Her voice trailed away into nothing. Dodo leaned closer, eager to hear the rest.

'And . . . ?' she prompted.

'And I don't understand. I just don't understand.'

Dodo looked into Catherine Arouette's face, in a final effort to banish her confusion. She saw only mirrors and illusions, an annihilating void in the place of the director's flamboyance. She couldn't understand how Arouette had been there all the time, except maybe as a growth, an undisturbed embryo that had been nurtured in Fantômas's body, shedding it when it came of age. The woman was a tiny grey creature, almost shrivelled, almost mummified.

'You're two different people,' Dodo said softly. Arouette nodded slightly, dark shadows forming in the hollow sockets round her eyes. Dodo pulled her into a close hug.

One of them began to cry. Dodo wasn't certain which.

The black ships came low over the sea, setting the waves churning beneath them. They were living ships with scaly black skins, their stubby bodies buried beneath a mass of tentacles that dribbled in and out of existence. Quivering fat spiders, they hovered over the channel, dwarfing the mundane fleet of battleships and frigates that followed embarrassed in their wake across the surface of the water.

The Doctor adjusted the wetscreen controls, searching for the sound. He stumbled across it, and the laboratory was filled with the wail of the black ships. The banshee-screech was unbearable. The Doctor wrestled with the controls, restoring the silence.

'What are you doing?' Minski asked.

The Doctor had heard him come in, but feigned surprise. The child's lips twitched. From above – from the Doctor's viewpoint – he seemed rat like, black eyes burning resentfully from beneath the ridges of a rodent skull.

'I was playing with some of your toys,' the Doctor replied mischievously. 'I am afraid I became a little bored waiting for you.'

'My father's problems are deep rooted.' Minski smiled privately.

'I can imagine,' the Doctor agreed. He turned back to the screen, to the darkness swarming across the sea. 'I think you have problems of your own.'

Minski barely glanced at the screen.

'The combined forces of Britain and – hah! – Hell,' he said lightly. 'And one or two Americans for good measure. They'll land in Normandy in a few hours, while the demonships race on to hasten the fall of Paris.'

'You don't sound as though you care,' the Doctor said, surprised by Minski's indifference. In his experience, tyrants were possessive and paranoid, obsessed with fear of invasion and the erosion of their power. Paranoia wouldn't suit Minski. He was too . . . *banal*. That was the word.

'I don't. Paris means nothing to me. They can have it, for a while.'

'Ah.' The Doctor kept his voice calm, trying to tease the truth out of him. 'This is a trap. You will let them take the city then attack them from all sides.'

Child's eyes flashed, maybe recognizing the Doctor's game. 'My armies have been commanded to take up positions south of Paris, to await new orders.' The Doctor smiled, pleased with himself. Minski's next words knocked the smile from his face. 'There will be no

172

further orders. The demonships will destroy their positions before they can take the initiative. I've planned this very carefully.'

Minski gave him a gloating grin, a grin of victory offset by the grey blandness in his eyes. Baffled, the Doctor couldn't meet his stare for a moment. Minski seemed to tower over him from below.

'Did you see the soldiers in the tower this morning? Did you realize what they were doing?' Minski asked blandly.

The Doctor mouthed a quiet 'no'.

Minski bared his teeth. 'Nothing,' he said, so softly that it was nearly drowned by the hiss of the wetscreen. 'I have them running up and down my tower in order to keep them busy. It achieves nothing except their peace of mind.'

'How is that?' the Doctor rumbled, becoming vaguely interested.

'It's what they've always done. Imagine that you woke up one day and found you didn't need to breathe? Wouldn't you keep up the pretence of breathing, if only to comfort your lungs? I run an imaginary military, an illusory economy, a fictional bureaucracy. I've made them all redundant. My power is invisible.

'Yes, Paris is a trap, but my enemies won't be defeated by soldiers. It's the water and the whores that'll bring them down. The maggots of Paris will eat into their souls and make them mine.'

'What do you hope to gain from all this?' the Doctor barked, aware that in some sense this was still a game, but played now to Minski's rules.

'Control,' Minski said simply. 'I'm master of the machine, but the machine doesn't rule everything.'

'Really?' The Doctor faked a yawn. He was becoming impatient with Minski's half-answers and knowing stares.

'It's an incomplete power at present. You, for example, are outside my sphere. Your box –'

'It's reassuring to know that my yawns are my own,'

173

the Doctor responded, his impatience turning to anger. 'You are not master of the machine. You're a cog that has sprung loose and thinks it runs everything.'

If his outburst had stung Minski, it didn't show. He simply turned and pointed across the laboratory floor to the TARDIS, and the soldiers flanking it. Minski wore a plump, grotesque smile that was almost cherubic. There was no feeling in it, it was a gesture for its own sake.

'No,' the Doctor said, rage snapping in his voice.

'Doctor, if you don't give me your box, I will put you into my murder machine and you'll die. I will collect your companion and torture her. If she doesn't help me, I will give her to my father so he might further indulge his tastes. If she dies without giving me a key, I will have failed.' He reeled off each threat without feeling, reciting by rote. That was almost as frightening as the threats themselves. 'But at least I will have lost nothing,' the cherub's mouth added, in granite gargoyle tones. He tilted his head up to stare at the Doctor, the light from the ceiling obliterating his face.

The Doctor stood his ground, but offered a silent apology to Dodo, and a silent prayer to half-forgotten gods that she might escape Minski's plans.

'No,' he said. 'You will have lost everything.'

The child's head nodded, accepting his decision sullenly. He beckoned to his guards and they came forward, marching steadily towards the Doctor. He raised his arms and allowed them to take him away.

Dalville was asleep when Dodo returned to his caravan. He was coiled into a tense spring on his bed though his face was peaceful, radiating an innocence that he would have denied had he been awake. Dodo gazed down at him through tired eyes. She envied him. She would have climbed into her own bed and drifted to sleep if it wasn't for the certainty of nightmares.

Howlglass and Larkspur had showed her the world as it really was. They had peeled back the air and exposed the

174

workings of the universe for her to see. The sound of ticking had pursued her ever since. Inside, the lapping of the rain against the wooden walls helped dampen the noise. Outside, it buzzed around her like a swarm of clicking, mechanical insects. She'd been so frightened, she had run across the field between caravans. In her dreams, the clocks would have free reign.

She lowered herself onto the bed beside Dalville, gently so as not to wake him. He was naked from the waist up, and the light streaming through the shutters left an odd pattern dancing on his pallid chest. It brightened the undercooked flesh, picking out each feeble hair in detail. His ribs were starkly visible, pushing at the underside of his skin. Dodo's fingertips shook as she lowered them onto his chest, tracing the pattern of light and bone across his stomach. Something kicked in her stomach – a cold, churning, excited thing.

His skin rippled. Scorched, her hand snapped back.

He sat up, blinking the sleep out of his eyes. Dodo shuffled back on the bed, suddenly afraid of his proximity.

'Sorry,' he said. 'This always happens. I lie down for a minute at breakfast and next thing I know it's dinner. Where've you been today?'

'Round and about,' she fudged, hoping to avoid awkward explanations. 'Thinking. This and that.' She shrugged.

'Are you still upset?'

She thought about this. Then she shook her head vigorously and shuffled a little closer back towards him. They gazed at each other, still and silent for a long, dry minute.

'I just saw Fantômas,' Dodo said smoothly. 'He said we'll have to go to the Bastille tomorrow, to begin rehearsals.' That was true enough. It had been Fantômas who had told her. He'd replaced his mask and his boots, and had unspoken the word that made him Arouette. He had been arrogant and colourfully hurtful. Every trace of

175

the woman was gone, buried silently inside him.

'We don't have a script,' Dalville protested.

'He's finished the revised version. He'll have copies for us.'

'That was quick.' Dalville's eyebrows arched in surprise. 'Still, the play's the thing, isn't it?'

No. The play's an elaborate camouflage, designed to get Arouette into Minski's domain so she can shut down the world machine. The play's gone, overwritten by another set of words, different words imposed by blind, timid officials. It doesn't matter. It's just words. In the long run, it's waste paper.

'I suppose so,' Dodo replied, making herself sound certain.

'Bressac's been cut. He's very upset,' Dalville told her softly, pushing his face closer to hers. Dodo nodded and their cheeks brushed. She grimaced, hating the excitement she felt, the pleasure that sparked off his skin. She raised her hand to his chest, trying to recapture the feeling.

'I saw him just before I came in. He looked happy.'

Bressac had been smiling when she saw him. It was a fixed grin, his mouth jammed open and his teeth shining automatically. The light in his eyes was relieved not upset, serene rather than angered. There had been no cracks in his defence. All the bitterness and the disappointment was bottled away inside him. Outside was a husk, a Bressac-impersonator. It didn't seem right.

'He never looks happy,' Dalville murmured, reflecting Dodo's feelings exactly. She almost shrank back from him, wary of their intimacy. Dalville put his hands to her face, letting his fingers burn against her forehead. He pushed the hair out of her eyes, glimpsing her full, naked face. He frowned.

'Dodo, what's wrong?'

'It's nothing. Just something Fantômas said. No, nothing horrible,' she added quickly. 'It was just something he said.'

No. Arouette had said it, just before she'd pulled on

Fantômas's face and clothes, sealing herself away inside him.

If our plan succeeds, the past ten years of history will be erased. Minski will never have existed. I'd be happy to see that, but . . . We're doing this because this history is wrong. I don't know if this world is any better or worse than the real one.

Everything will change. We have the chance to start anew, but nothing of this world will remain. We won't be remembered, or commemorated. But you . . . You're not from this time or place. If we succeed, you will be able to escape the change. Please, keep the difference alive. Remember us. Take something with you, no matter how small.

Dalville sat on the bed before her, cross-legged and stripped to the waist, unimaginably distant yet so close the air between them ached, non-existent and vividly real, more alien than Larkspur and Howlglass. He was the difference, wrapped in solid, electrifying flesh. Her fingers tumbled down his chest and stomach, tickling the alien. Alien, she thought, alien body, male body, unique anyway, Dalville anyway.

She pushed forward, almost knocking him back with her momentum. She kissed him feebly then laid her head alongside her hands, flat on his chest. Her fear of his closeness crawled away, fatally wounded. Vaguely she felt his fingers picking at her back, tripping the pins that fastened her gown, nuzzling down her spine. They clung together in the stifling darkness, listening to the rain hissing against the caravan walls. It was the second perfect, infinite moment of the day.

'I want to rehearse,' she told him, bursting the moment.

'We haven't got the new scripts.'

'I know, I know,' she replied, peeling the gown away from herself with lazy anticipation, like a long-awaited present. Dalville leaned forward, planting his warm mouth on her neck. 'I want to rehearse the scenes they're going to cut.'

7

If God Really Existed, It Would be Necessary to Abolish Him

The Doctor hummed 'Jerusalem' in the dark, in the murder machine. He was comfortable here, surrounded by gloom and silence and sudden death. They stripped away all his burdens, the pain in his bones, the dimness of his eyes and the dullness of his hearing. His mind was free, his intellect fortified by this lethal, self-contained world.

The traitor's head had explained the murder machine to him. She had second-hand experience of it, frozen in her dead brain. She had taken him through her ordeal, from the moment of confinement to the moment of her death. The murder machine occupied one whole level beneath the Bastille. It was a maze of death, loaded with traps designed to maim and kill, built to Minski's design. It was inescapable, the doors sealed from the outside. It was the borderland between life and death.

It puzzled the Doctor. The murder machine was too melodramatic for Minski. If he needed to kill he would do it simply, silently, with minimal effort. This was too elaborate, and he couldn't imagine Minski deriving any pleasure from it. Sade might, but not his sterile, joyless son. It had to serve another purpose.

Control, he realized. It was Minski's obsession. In the murder machine, everything was determined and inevitable. There was no freedom for its prisoners, save inexorable death. It was a model of the world Minski wanted to build, a machine which he ruled, a maze with no escape.

The Doctor sat motionless in the darkness. The

darkness was everything. The darkness was death. He defied it. His best chance, he decided, was to keep still, close to the entrance through which he had been forced. He had no means of finding, or opening the door, but he guessed it would be used again, when another prisoner was offered to the machine, or if they came to recover his corpse. In the meantime, he would wait.

A light shone over his head, a light with a fine, hard edge. He gazed at it for a moment, the moment before it fell.

A solid lunged out of the gloom, seized his shoulder and pulled him aside. The blade nicked the air to the side of his head before slicing into the ground at his side, sending a vibrant *clang* echoing through the cold passages. The Doctor fell back, struggling to catch his breath. From the sound of it, his rescuer had the same problem. His breaths rasped weakly out of the gloom, close but not close enough for the Doctor to make out his shape.

'Thank you,' the Doctor called, hopefully in his direction. 'Your timing is excellent.'

'I know, and it worries me,' came the voice of Monsieur le 6. 'Don't you think it's strange?'

Tongues of fire leapt into the night sky, stroking and scorching the darkness. The rain lashed at the flames, only to sizzle into steam against the heat of the camp fires. Bressac looked out across the site, from a dark corner of his caravan, contemplating the grey sky and the orange-tinted earth.

The persistent rain hammered his face, fouling his clothes and his hair. He smiled bitterly. He had come out because he thought a walk in the evening drizzle would be refreshing, and might lift him out of his depression. The smile faded gradually, eroded by the downpour. It had not been a good day.

He had brought a bottle of wine from the caravan. He couldn't bring himself to drink from it, and so he spent his time looking into the glass. His wispy reflection stared back at him, stretched out of shape by the curve of the bottle. He turned the bottle in his hands and his face was suddenly cut in two by a flaw in the glass surface. He clicked his tongue, unimpressed with what he could see. He raised the neck of the bottle to his lips and sipped. A bead of wine rolled on his tongue, pausing before dropping down into the darkness.

'Bressac', an odd name – familiar, but with no real meaning for him. He would keep it for the moment. He would remain 'Bressac' until the play was done.

The wine hit his stomach, sending calm ripples through his body. He relaxed and leaned against the caravan wall, remembering what he had seen. He had returned to the caravan to find Dalville and Dodo wrapped asleep together on Dalville's bunk. Dodo had woken and stared back at him, giving him a dreamy smile that took up the whole of her face. She'd tugged some of the cover away from Dalville, pulling it protectively across her delicate, exposed chest. She had mumbled something and slipped back to sleep. And Bressac had simply stared.

He couldn't put a name to the sum of his feelings. It was a cold brew of sensations. There had been some guilt and perhaps some disappointment, though whether with Dodo or Dalville he wasn't sure. There had been a cool unease at the sight of Dodo's alien body. There had been a tremendous sense of joy for the sleeping duo. There had been a splintering pain as he realized he was now, forever, excluded from some part of their lives. There was an intense, unspeakable frustration, married to intense, unspeakable excitement.

There was hate. Clear, burning in his head. He hated Fantômas.

He had left the caravan quietly, so as not to disturb the sleepers. Once outside, the streaming rain had hidden his blistering tears. Dizzy and delirious, he'd slipped into a waking nightmare. Dodo was there, nude but indeterminate, flat chested and sexless. She had a boy's haircut, the heavy fringe straggling over deep eyes. She beckoned to him with her index finger. Behind her, Fantômas moaned, nailed erect onto a swaying wooden cross, the blood spilling from his wrists and the wounds in his forehead. Everyone was there, the whole cast in the crowd, chanting as the director died for their sins. Even Dodo's friend, even the Doctor was there, a white-haired skeleton in a night-shroud. Despite this, Bressac had the intense feeling that someone was missing. He couldn't think of the name, but there was a vivid absence. He panicked as Dodo took him by the arm, pulling him away. He panicked as Fantômas's moans rose into a chilling death-bleat. He panicked, and the panic had jolted him back into the waking world.

He had slumped against the caravan wall then, thrown his head to the ground and retched and retched until he was sick. After that he had lost track of time. The rain helped. Foul though it was, it put him at his ease.

He gazed longingly at the crowds of strangers who accumulated on the field by night. They were anonymous people, he realized, nameless spear-carriers and faceless walk-ons, with no big speeches or decisive moments to their credit. They were the tides of history. Bressac envied them.

He tucked the bottle under his arm and set out to join them.

Garce could see his destiny in the fire, flickering among the tongues of red and gold. He had the sudden, wild impulse to thrust his hand into the heart of the flames and watch it burn. His flesh would shrivel and blacken, crumbling into ash to reveal the cold white bone beneath. Hellfire.

The rain, on the other hand, reminded him of England.

People flickered round him, like shadows cast on the caravan walls. The air was thick with the babble of their voices, a jumble of French words and phrases that left

181

Garce's ears numb. Most of what he heard was so vague and so fast that it held little sense for him, but he was enjoying himself. He imagined that the old Hellfire Club was like this, before it became serious and turned to governing. The rest of Paris slept its enforced sleep, dreaming imposed dreams, but in this little island of the night everyone was free to pursue their own pleasure.

Garce had his own desires. They moved through the crowd in clothes both gaudy and drab, rich and humble, elaborate and revealing. Garce's taste was for younger girls with streaming dark hair, haunted eyes and innocent, dusty faces. Tonight, he abstained from them. He had a task to perform, one final service before fleeing Paris. He'd find a woman later and get her out of the city before daybreak.

The black ships were in the air. Paris would burn tomorrow.

Randolph loomed out of the darkness, pushing his way through the crowd towards the fire. His shattered face seemed even more sour than usual. He eyed the bustle of people with unconcealed distaste. There was no sign of his foppish façade, just dark and brutal energy. He moved violently, shoving a path between kissing lovers. He spat on the ground at Garce's feet.

'Decadence,' he pronounced, lips curling, eyes growling at the world.

'I thought we liked that,' Garce prompted, without pleasure. He didn't want to antagonize Randolph while he was in this vicious mood.

'Not this,' came the reply. 'This is too French. It's wasted on harlots, crooks and actors — on scum. They don't have genuine blood.'

Garce fingered the pistols under his coat, suspecting that his colleague was about to be proved wrong.

Randolph saw his gesture and offered him a slight smile. 'I've found our demons, m'dear,' he said. 'It looks as though they're preparing to leave. Hell's locked to them now, but I'd prefer to strike before they discover that.'

Garce nodded soundlessly and they set off together across the wasteland, between the fires, vans and scattered bodies towards their prey.

'They're fallen demons now, I suppose,' Garce muttered, almost to himself, to relieve his tense fear. 'Do you think they're really going to betray our plans to Minski?'

Randolph laughed, like rank water spilling slowly from a gutter. 'No. Howlglass and his friend are embarrassments, no more.'

'What is it they've done?'

'They've conspired with lower creatures.'

'The French?' Garce hazarded a guess.

'Women,' Randolph croaked. 'That's if you can call Arouette a woman. I've heard the scars go right up her legs.'

The back of Randolph's hand struck Garce's stomach suddenly, bringing Garce to a halt. His fingers stabbed out, drawing Garce's attention to the three deceptive shapes clustered round the door of a caravan. Garce recognized the two hunched, robed shapes without hesitation. Tyll Howlglass and Larkspur – devils in disguise. His fingers went to his flintlocks again, hard edges poking out beneath the cloth of his coat. Their weight was reassuring, though he knew they would be next to useless on the demons. The cold metal reminded him only of death, waiting for him on some unsuspecting future road. The third figure was a tall, bearded man, dressed extravagantly. Another disguise, Garce realized, one he would not have suspected if he hadn't known otherwise. He regarded the bearded Arouette coldly, as another symptom of decadence. This city contaminated everyone – Garce was glad to be getting out.

'I'll have to kill all of them,' Randolph whispered, close to his ear. 'You deal with anyone who gets too close.' He held the deathmask in the palm of his hands, cradling it as though it were precious and fragile. Garce watched sullenly as Randolph raised it to his head, stretching it over his face. His poker eyes glared out of the slits in the mask, like glints of light on still, black water. He said nothing, remaining silent and terrifying, but set out towards the group by the caravan. Garce watched nervously, one hand hovering over the butt of his pistols. Randolph was better equipped to kill the devil. He had Hell and Hell's weapons on his side.

The man, the woman, the *whatever*, saw the danger first. Her head swung round and her mouth twitched into a warning scream. It was drowned by the first explosion, the burst of fire from the deathmask that took off Howlglass's head. The second explosion carved a hole in Larkspur's stomach, large enough for Garce's fist.

The attack was quick and left none of the mess that Garce had feared. The demons had no blood, no viscera, no brains. Their bodies burst into fragments of dry, grey dust that was pummelled to the ground by the rain. They screamed as they died. They screamed and their voices woke old, bad memories.

Children screamed as Garce burned their house in Ireland. He had seen their grimy faces staring at him from the window of the upper storey. He learned later that some had burned to death, before the smoke could kill them. They were still screaming. He could hear them now.

The demons' bodies collapsed, crumbling into themselves. Searing light blazed through the holes in their decaying shells. The light − Garce realized, watching ghoulishly − the light was screaming.

There was a girl he had raped once, or twice, or thrice. It had been a cold night, and he'd lit a fire in her hearth before setting to her. She hadn't screamed once, but met his efforts with a defiant, hateful silence. She screamed now. He could hear her.

The light burst out of the shells of the demons, scattering more dust across the field. Two radiant lights hovered in the air above their corpses, then leapt into the air, spiralling endlessly towards Heaven. Their voices still sang, still screamed.

Two nights ago, he had murdered a woman and stolen her blood. She had screamed.

He blinked, noticing that the demon voices were gone, that the demon bodies were reduced to mounds of fine dust. There was a commotion in the background, the shocked murmurs of the first few to notice Randolph's attack. He was still moving, stalking his final target. Though he still wore the deathmask, he had pulled his pistol from his belt, raising it to Arouette's head. The player stood her ground, perhaps shocked by the sudden attack on her allies, perhaps trying to face Randolph down.

That wouldn't work. Randolph no longer had a face.

Someone screamed on the edge of the crowd. A man's voice, calling out a name. It took Garce a moment before he realized that it wasn't another bad memory. A man shoved past him, knocking him aside in his flight. By the time Garce regained his balance the man was bearing down on Randolph, swinging a bottle towards his head. Garce opened his mouth to shout a warning, but his partner's name died unspoken on his lips. Randolph wouldn't hear. The mask would, but the mask was not Randolph.

Randolph sensed the danger anyway, and swung round to confront it. The bottle shattered against his face, his mask, sending glass and red wine and blood in a shower across the field. The pistol exploded in Randolph's hand, sending his assailant sprawling backwards, a red wound opening on his chest. He struck the earth with a delicious thud.

He was screaming. His voice pierced Garce, like a cold silver needle through the heart. On an impulse, he pulled out his own pistol and put a ball through the back of Randolph's skull. It should have killed him, but he stood for a moment, as if contemplating what had happened and trying to make sense of it. Then he fell, silently, not screaming.

Garce threw down his pistols and ran from the camp

site into the dark of the silent city. The screams pursued him.

Bressac could hear the blood rushing through his ears, carrying the sound of his heartbeat with it. It was a painful throb, stumbling and growing ever slower. He was lying awkwardly on the ground, his back and his hair plastered with wet earth. Shards of glass were crushed into the palm of his right hand, and his ribs felt shattered and soft and wet. They were twinges, not real pain.

In the night he would lie awake listening to his heart. Sometimes a second would pass without a beat and he would sit up shivering, afraid of death. He tried to move now, but his body was cold. This was the moment he'd been waiting for, during those long, lonely nights. This was the moment he'd secretly hoped would never come. He had often wondered what it would be like, and what he would think in the final moments.

It isn't fair. I don't deserve this.

A voice in the corner of his mind was babbling, begging for more time, or at least a sign from Heaven that there was another time to come. He hoped it wasn't his real voice. He didn't want to beg on his deathbed. Death-mud. Whatever.

His heartbeat grew slower. He had a few seconds probably. His fear was balanced by a sense of calm, peaceful resignation. He hadn't expected that. There was a bustle of people around him, vast figures stretching into the night sky over him. He didn't recognize any faces. Rough hands clamped round his shoulders and tried to lift him. He muttered his protest – he didn't want to die while being dragged out of the earth by strangers.

It was strange. He'd always wanted to drown. In the days before Minski, they would execute lovers by drowning – binding them naked together, weighing them down and dropping them into the river. It seemed such a romantic way to go. He sweated, trying to imagine the sensation of Seine-water flooding his lungs, the face of his lover struggling and dying before him, in his arms. His imagination failed him. There was no face.

He thought of Dodo and Dalville sinking together. It didn't help.

A woman screamed on the edge of the crowd. Dodo, he guessed. The shrill note was joined by Dalville's tones, calling out his name, calling out his character's name, the name of Bressac. That was reassuring. It wasn't he who was dying, but Bressac – a collection of speeches and immoral acts, now erased. He smiled as he saw Dalville and Dodo push through the crowds towards him. He tried to wave to them, but his hand was no longer there.

'What happened?' Dodo shrieked. She repeated it, again and again, until it no longer seemed a proper question, but the only thing she could say. She dropped to her knees beside him and grabbed his hand.

'Where's Fantômas?' Dalville was yelling. His eyes, heavy with tears, were casting round the crowd, as if he couldn't bring himself to look down. 'Where the hell is Fantômas?'

Bressac guessed they had been disturbed by the commotion and come running. It looked as though they had flung on the first thing that came to hand to cover themselves. Dalville was naked to the waist and the firelight set glowing tiger-patterns dancing across his chest.

Terrifying.

'I'm scared,' he said, forcing the last of his life into his lips. Dodo's mouth wrinkled and she burst into tears, burying her face on his chest.

Beautiful.

Dodo screamed.

Garce stumbled and fell against a wall. His shoulder crunched on impact and went numb. He collapsed to his knees, sinking into the heavy puddles that had collected on the ground. The rain lashed at his back and his head and he pulled his face lower to protect his skin. He had to fight to catch breaths from the howling winds, his lungs wheezing and fraying after the effort of the chase. The screams reverberated in his head, a symphony of pain and guilt.

Footsteps splashed through the puddles behind him, kicking and splashing as they went. Garce rolled onto his back to see, afraid it might be a soldier. The last thing he needed was to be arrested, to be trapped in Paris on the eve of its destruction. His pistols, he reached for his pistols . . .

They were gone. He'd hurled them away in his flight.

It wasn't a soldier. It was a hollow-cheeked woman, whose cropped hair had been slicked back against her head by the rain, a skull-faced woman with paper-thick skin. Her eyes were unquiet, lightless, devoid of pleasure. An intrigued warmth crept up Garce's body. Here was something he could salvage from Paris. He struggled to stand, to make himself presentable.

Her clothes were familiar, as were the dark, bloody marks that stained them. By the time he recognized them, it was too late to run or hide or plead. She was already raising the deathmask to her face. One of her eyes shone naked through the hole torn by Garce's own pistol-ball, the other merged into the black skin of the mask. Both watched him impassively.

'You abused this mask,' whispered Catherine Arouette. 'Your attack was crude and clumsy, full of sound and fury. You didn't appreciate how subtle your power was. One thought, that's all it takes. One tiny, silent thought.' She held up a trembling hand, stripped of its glove and exposed to the rain. Her forefinger and thumb made a broken, imperfect circle. They twitched and the circle closed. Beneath his ribs, Garce's heart stopped pumping. He pitched face-forward into the puddles.

There was a moment of perfect silence.

Then.

In the darkness, the Doctor imagined *shapes*. Sightless, he gave form to the things he could feel and hear. Monsieur le 6's voice was a thin, snaking line and his rough breaths were jagged and blue. The cool breeze that whispered through the stone passages was a circle, a hungry mouth gaping and screaming. The hidden walls were grey plains, stretching endlessly under the earth. The traps he had sprung were fine points, dripping red.

The Doctor had triggered a handful of traps by accident, though le 6 had always been on hand to pull him clear. He had an astonishing grasp of the twists and dangers waiting in the dark, though he didn't understand how. He saw them intuitively, without eyes. He had survived a day in the murder machine. With his help, the Doctor had managed half that.

'I believe I know how you are doing this,' the Doctor said at length. He had toyed with the idea for a while and there seemed little point in holding his speculation back.

'Enlighten me,' le 6 rumbled. His voice came from the gloom, from behind a new, dark mask.

'I believe this world came into being because of you,' the Doctor said, softening his tone so as not to sound accusing. 'Ten years ago, alien creatures came to this world, and offered to create a new future, based on your ideals and philosophies. Am I right?'

Le 6 purred in the night, as if considering or remembering. The Doctor wished he could see his face, the reactions and emotions written there.

'Yes,' le 6 said finally, decisively. 'I . . . I had . . . I think I had some authority at the time. I was . . . I hope I was a liberal voice. But I couldn't stop the bloodlust, the offerings to the guillotine.

'You know,' he snapped, yellow hysteria lining his zig-zag voice, 'the guillotine was designed as a rational means of execution. Guillotin wanted to end torture by removing the human element from executions. He never questioned whether murder was reasonable. Poor Doctor Guillotin was too human. Minski sacrificed him to his own machine.

'It was all the *blood*.' His voice wavered, plaintive and

189

small in the vast blackscape. 'I believed in liberty and reason, but in the days of the Terror, I lost sight of them. All the blood! All the death! It destroyed my faith in everything.

'They came to me in my despair. Creatures like men, but not men, glowing angels in dirty robes. Outcasts, they called themselves, and exiles, but I thought they were messengers from my forsaken God. They offered me the entire world! And in my despair, I accepted.'

The Doctor put an arm out in search of le 6's shoulder. 'I know,' he said softly, trying to calm him. 'This world has come about because your ideals corrupted the aliens' system operator. It became Minski. He is your creature. This machine was of his devising. It is his madness given a design. You can sense the design, because his madness comes from you.'

The air near le 6 rustled. It sounded as though he was nodding. 'That's very persuasive,' he said, between heavy breaths. 'Most things in Heaven and Earth are dreamt of in my philosophy. Yes, that would explain a lot. Unfortunately, it doesn't get us anywhere.'

'I was hoping you might think your way to an exit,' the Doctor suggested.

A curt laugh echoed from le 6's direction. 'You think I haven't tried that. All the entrances are barred from the outside. I'm sorry.'

The Doctor fell back against the nearest wall and groaned. He had spent most of the day brooding on possible escape routes, exhausting himself in the process. Minski's dark design crowded round him, offering only a quick death of light and steel, or a lingering one of thirst and starvation.

'Really,' le 6 called sheepishly. 'I'm sorry. I didn't want the world to turn out like this. I just have a nasty mind.'

The Doctor sighed. An idea popped into his mind, the child of desperation. He spoke quickly, before it escaped him. 'There is a way out.'

'How?' The air rippled as le 6 leaned forward.

The Doctor smiled. 'There are gaps in the air,' he said.

The cells seemed empty without Monsieur le 6.

Citizen Cameo smiled grimly at the irony. The cells had become more crowded since his escape. Condemned cell 6 was full now. It had accumulated skeletal, empty-eyed prisoners across the course of the day. It was no longer a special place.

The lustre had drained out of her job since the escape. It was as if her interest in le 6 had been a barrier between herself and the world. There had never been any pleasure in preparing the execution lists, but now the satisfaction of doing the job properly was gone. Her walks through her territory were soured, as if she were soaking up all the misery she had overlooked in the past. She was a gaoler who had ceased to believe in bars.

When Cameo looked through the cell windows at the condemned, she still saw the dead. She realized now that she had always been one of them.

She was strolling through one of the deeper corridors, pondering on how best to act on her new-found feelings, when a fracture opened in the wall ahead of her. It was a thin black fault line that tore open, ripping through the stone as though it were paper or cloth. It spat out two dishevelled and familiar figures before sealing itself imperceptibly.

She blinked and looked again. The wall was stone-solid, but there were also two old men in the passageway who had not been here moments before. She decided to accept both as given truths, to forget anything else. It would make life simpler. She reached for her pistol, putting her fingers against the butt but stopping short of drawing it.

The Doctor was on his feet first, but paused to help le 6 before addressing the gaoler. Cameo waited patiently. She would be required to report at the guard-house in an hour, but that no longer seemed important. She wanted to see le 6 one last time, to see what effect a day's freedom had had on him.

'We seem to have company,' the Doctor murmured.

Le 6 looked up and grimaced. Physically he was little changed – maybe he moved a little easier than last she saw, and held himself with a little more dignity. He shrugged. 'Bad luck,' he said.

'Possibly,' the Doctor hissed. That one had an infuriating, arrogant voice, and his strangled whisper carried for miles. 'There is a secret thread that binds this world together. I don't believe luck is an issue.'

Le 6 gave her a cool, ambivalent stare. His eyes were familiar, the only part of his face she had learned while he was her prisoner. They were the eyes that had glared from behind the mask while she tormented him. He had always resented her, but he had never rejected her. He had collaborated with her schemes. That had been part of the fascination, part of the fun.

She matched his eyes with her own.

'What do you want me to do?' she asked.

The Doctor snorted and folded his arms defiantly. Le 6 ignored him and stepped forward, his arms held wide.

'We need somewhere to hide and rest tonight.'

'I can't get you out of the Bastille,' Cameo warned.

Le 6 shook his head. 'Somewhere inside the tower, somewhere we will not be disturbed but from which we can escape easily should the need arise.'

Cameo thought, then nodded. The Doctor stepped back in surprise. Le 6 smiled and the gaoler joined him, sharing in their secret.

'There's a perfect place on the next floor up. I'll show you.' She paused, then added, 'Then I'll leave the Bastille, throw off this uniform and its badge. I'll be a better traitor than I've ever been a gaoler – I'll be a good traitor!' Even the grim, cadaverous Doctor managed to smile at that one. Heartened, Cameo slammed her hands together in a decisive clap.

'Now citizens, if you'd care to follow me, I'll show

you to your rooms. I hope you're both keen on the theatre.'

Dodo was still awake when Dalville returned to the caravan. He knew it before he saw her. The edges of the inner door glowed with the lamp-light, and her voice hummed faintly, muffled by the thin partition. He didn't want to go in. He doubted whether he could face her, or if she could face him.

He pulled the outer door closed softly, and locked it after him, locked himself in for the first time in years. Up until now, he had nothing worth stealing. He wasted some more time by brushing the rainwater from his cloak before hanging it over the back of the chair. Then, because he still wasn't ready, he stood in the darkness and allowed the pain to twist his face. No sound, no tears, simply the tortured flexing of flesh and muscles. He mouthed a soundless parody of a scream. He waited until the waiting became unbearable, until the sweat glued his clothes to his skin and the gloom stung his eyes.

He could still hear her, singing to herself next door. He would have to see her sooner or later. It hurt him to walk to the door, to open it and step through, but he did. It hurt even more to stand before her, undeservedly alive. Her voice died as he came in. He heard her sit up, the bedclothes rustling as she moved, but he didn't look.

Then he did.

Dodo was sitting on his bunk, dangling her legs over the edge, kicking the air in a senseless, random rhythm. Her face seemed small and shocked, her cheeks darkened by smeared tears. The oily light gave her skin a warm yellow glow, but it couldn't quite hide the ash-colour of her face or the cold white of her shoulders and back, pocked with teenage spots. She was blissfully naked, too innocent to know shame. Dalville's heartbeats were pincer stabs through his ribs. He stepped into the shadows to peel off his own, dripping clothes, out of her beady-eyed gaze.

'What's happened?' Dodo asked in a wavering, faraway voice.

She still didn't quite believe. She still harboured a foolish hope that Bressac's death wasn't true, that no one had died, that somehow a mistake had been made. It was numb grief – the feeling would come later. They had both seen Bressac's undeniable, empty corpse. They had seen the bloody hole punched into his chest. Dodo had shrieked hysterically, and Dalville had watched paralysed as he died. And still, part of him was unbelieving.

'Fantômas says that he's spoken to the authorities and they've arranged the burial for tomorrow morning,' he reported, bland voiced.

'I don't like funerals.'

'Neither do I,' he answered feebly. He worried about that, he didn't want to sound weak. It made him feel disadvantaged. Dodo nodded sullenly. Dalville found himself staring at her, desiring her. She noticed his gaze and shrugged. Her arms fleetingly folded over her chest before falling away to her sides.

'What about the play?' she asked.

'It goes on as scheduled. It won't be affected, not really. After all, it's not as if . . . as if . . . he was in it . . .' He gave up at last, the tears guttering from his eyes. He raised his hands to cover his face, grateful for the darkness. Dodo slipped off the bunk, not quite silently, and snuggled against him, her palms resting flat on his chest. He clutched her back, holding it as though it were porcelain. Gradually she began to sob with him, rubbing her face against his shoulders. The tears ran till they dried.

Dodo was beautiful, despite what Debord thought, or she protested. She *felt* beautiful, holding him as much as he held her. His body seethed in contact with her. He was afraid of death. He wanted to live so badly. He wanted *her* to live. He wanted to make her immortal.

She kissed him painlessly, on his mouth first, then his throat. He lowered a hand onto her body, onto her frail flesh. It was dying even as he touched. Shapeless and soft

194

under his palm, it was less exciting than the gasp of breath at his shoulder. He folded her skin between his forefinger and thumb and pinched viciously. Dodo gave a slight shriek and pulled away.

'That hurt,' she said. She brought her arms up to her chest, suddenly bitter, suddenly aware of herself. She slumped back on the nearest bunk, on Bressac's bunk. Her face curdled, bulbs of water forming on her eyelids. Guilty and afraid, Dalville gritted his teeth and endured the silence.

'I don't want to go,' Dodo said at last. She leaned back on the bed, relieved by the admission. 'The funeral. I don't want to go.'

'You're going to have to,' Dalville told her.

'I know. But I still don't want to. Do you still want to corrupt me?' she asked.

He shook his head. 'Bressac's dead,' he said, spilling his thoughts so quickly he had no time to falter. 'No, I don't want to corrupt you. You're innocent. Everything innocent is precious.'

'You're too late,' she said sadly. 'I lost that ages ago.'

Her face cracked again, salt tears easing between the gaps. She twisted her head away, burying it in the comfortable dark of Bressac's pillow. Dalville reached for the lamp, extinguishing it with a gesture. The light drained from the room, leaving a hot bristling gloom in its place. Dodo became a pale white blur in the dark, twisting on the bed. Dalville lay quietly beside her, a protective arm snaking over her shoulder. Her skin burned on his.

'Can't keep your hands off?' she quipped drably. 'It's not as if we're going to sleep much anyway.'

Hidden in the dark, he blushed. He thanked God she couldn't see him.

'Sorry. I've been . . . like *this* all night. Can't keep you out of my mind. I'm sick.'

'No. I know. I know exactly how you feel.' The voice and the body came out of the dark, cuddling up against him. He eased alongside her, wrapping and twining their separate skins together. They held each other and mourned silently in the baking dark.

'Bressac's dead,' someone said. Dalville wasn't sure who.

At the first sign of sound and movement – of shadowed bodies stirring and stroking, of lips mumbling senseless nothings – Fantômas decided that his time was up. He stepped back from Dalville's window and made across the field to his own door. The rain beat him, he welcomed its blows.

He cast around him, searching for other faces. There were none. The field had never been so empty, nor so desolate. He bared his teeth, hissing with lonely pleasure.

'*Now*,' he began with a whip-crack voice, 'let's pull a discreet veil 'cross this sordid scene. Whining like animals, they wash away the taste of death with the taste of flesh, their nauseous fear given shape in sweat and lust. They deserve more, we think, than our prying shallow eyes sharp'ning their fear and blunting their pleasure. We should hate not them, but despise instead ourselves.'

I hope that's not meant to be pentameter, said the creature within him. He shook his head. He reached the door to his caravan, pausing for a moment.

'*Now*, a quick reminder of what we're happy to forget.'

Bressac was waiting for him, stretched out on a table. There was a cloth draped across his body, obscuring the hole in his chest. It couldn't hide the pallor of his skin or the red blossom that had swelled on his lips. Fantômas (or possibly Arouette, such things were never certain) leant over and kissed him.

'In memory of the resurrection,' he (she) said. He'd (she'd) taken the blood-bead from his lips. He (she) swallowed it bitterly. That settled it. It was *she*. Things that happened on the inside were always *she*.

She took Bressac's dead hand and squeezed. It was cold

and hard, a slab of meat from the butcher's block. For the first time in years, Catherine Arouette found she was able to cry.

'I'm sorry,' she said in Fantômas's voice, clutching the cool hand. 'You will live again, I promise. You *will* live again.'

8

All the World and All the Men and Women

In the morning, they buried another man. His name was Jean-Louis Pelot, a name he had been given at birth. Dodo attended the stranger's funeral, feeling oddly relaxed. It didn't feel as though they were burying Bressac. It was almost as though he wasn't dead.

The rain held off for the occasion, but traces of the downpour remained. The burial plot was scarred with water-filled craters. The harsh glare of the sun reflected in the surface of the puddles, dazzling the small crowd of mourners, a radiant white among the sea of grieving black.

Citizen Debord was in the crowd. Dodo had jostled against him unawares as he moved through the field, and their eyes met. He bowed slightly, setting the bones cracking in his back and his neck, and when he looked up there was a sad damp in his eyes. Dodo said nothing, but let him pass. He glided away like a black-clad ghost haunting the burial plot. His clothes were the right colour, but they seemed too muted, too sterile for the occasion.

Dalville stood beside Dodo, one hand permanently squeezing her shoulder. He had come in a shabby, vivid black, too elaborate for mourning. Dodo herself had found in the company's wardrobe a dark coat and skirt that verged on the appropriate. Beneath these she wore her outfit from the TARDIS, twentieth-century clothes which had not yet been made, and so were hardly disrespectful. They were both too tired to cry. Dodo stifled more than one yawn, hating the urge and exhaustion that made it.

Funerals, funerals. They were the only events in her life when her clothes really mattered, when they were more than a decoration. No one here was more than the sum of the clothes. Everyone was midnight black.

The priest was embarrassed by the whole thing. He went through the motions, stammering his way through something that sounded vaguely right but never appropriate, not for Bressac. A small group of revolutionary labourers, distinguished by their tawdry sashes, raised the coffin onto their shoulders and carried it into the distance, to the edge of the grave. Squinting, Dodo saw them tip the coffin over the edge. A heavy grey sack tumbled through a panel in one end, then the pallbearers returned, carrying the reusable box with much less effort. They were dressed in everyday clothes – working clothes – their sleeves rolled up to reveal tanned, hairy forearms. No respect, Dodo thought, hating them vaguely.

The crowd began to drift away, returning to their lives as though nothing had happened here. Dalville remained, clutching Dodo, to the last. A few tears welled in the corner of her eyes, but nothing developed, nothing came.

'Most of the others are going straight to the Bastille,' Dalville hmmed, kissing her under one ear. 'There's something I want to do first, though. Something I promised Bressac.'

It was the first time she'd heard the name today. She nodded grimly.

They left the field arm in arm, though they weren't the last to leave. A woman was on her knees, praying in the mud. She had hollow eyes, a pinched face and hair stripped almost down to her scalp. She didn't look up as the actors went past, nor did Dodo bother to look down at her.

'All our flesh,' she was muttering, her hands clasped, 'is shadow.'

Dalville left Dodo on a footpath along the Seine, while

he disappeared onto a bridge, clutching a cloth-wrapped bundle he had brought to the funeral from the caravan. Dodo watched through eyes cold with melancholy, as he paused at one side of the bridge and gazed dizzily over the edge, into the foul yellow waters below. He dropped the bundle into the river. It hit the surface with a depressing *plop* and sank out of sight.

There seemed to be so much rubbish in the river – one more piece would make no difference. Dodo imagined seeing a raft of corpses floating along the course of the river, though a closer look revealed many to be bundles of rubbish clustering together to form suggestive shapes. Others were further away, and Dodo couldn't account for them. They might have been bodies. Her eyes flicked down the length of the river, spotting the stacks of chimneys and cooling towers on the horizon.

Battersea power station, she thought nostalgically. Ten million years and this will all be gone.

Dalville had returned from the bridge and patted her on the rear to draw her attention. She thought back to the exhausting, passionless night before and felt overwhelmed by banal guilt. Gloomy clouds were already gathering on the city skyline, and spots of rain danced through the air, splashing harmlessly against her skin. The storm broke before they reached the Bastille. Lightning struck the city, though never near Dodo, confirming her worst suspicions.

The Doctor had enjoyed a night's relaxation on a comfortable bench backstage at the Bastille theatre. By the morning he was invigorated, welcoming the chance to take on Minski again. *Things* would have to be done today, and those things would have to be done urgently. What he had seen in Minski's laboratory the previous day convinced him that events were moving towards a determined conclusion. If only he hadn't wasted so much time in the labyrinth.

Le 6, on the other hand, didn't seem to have slept at

all. The Doctor found him wandering aimlessly round the auditorium, pausing on the stage and trying to speak, to declaim at row upon row of empty seats, but finding nothing to say. His surroundings were haunting him.

The Doctor decided to leave him in peace. There must be something in the theatre that spoke to the old man, that reminded him of what he had once been. It would be better to let him remember on his own. He no longer looked like a victim, like a defeated and half-insane prisoner. There was several days' worth of white stubble bristling on his chin that lent his face a new gravity, and squeezed out the defeat from it. The Doctor waved across the theatre to him before he left, but said nothing. Le 6 simply bowed.

He made his way down the levels of the Bastille, adopting a strutting walk through the corridors that ensured he wasn't challenged or even approached by the bustle of bureaucrats and soldiers who filled the passages. They were all engaged on their own self-important, meaningless work, dancing on the end of Minski's puppet-strings, too busy to stop and question him. The Doctor found it easy enough to hide the sadness in his eyes.

He almost collided with Minski and Sade, during one daring moment when he braved a busy thoroughfare, but he saw them first and darted into a side passage. He was tempted to leap out behind them and confront the First Deputy, just to see what his reaction would be. It was a frivolous thought though, and he was determined to be single-minded. He let them pass, certain at least that they wouldn't be waiting for him in the laboratory.

The traitor's head was there. It turned on its spike, its eyes boring across the cluttered floor to meet him as he entered. He made straight for it, ignoring the deeper voices that called out for the sanctuary of the TARDIS. The head of the traitor was what he needed, the head and the dead knowledge frozen within.

'I need to know,' he said sharply, 'what Minski is planning.'

'What makes you think he's planning anything?' the head replied. 'He's a straightforward tyrant. He rules for the sake of ruling.'

The Doctor found himself nodding in agreement. 'There must be more to it though,' he said. 'He wants to consolidate his power. Every time he speaks, he hints at it. And this business with the invasion. I cannot believe he would risk everything for the sake of an elaborate trap. He doesn't act like a gambler.'

The head jostled on its spike – another feeble, poignant effort to nod. 'What do you want me to tell you?'

'You were a woman once. You have her dead memories. I want to know what it was that brought you into contact with Minski, what he wanted from you.'

The head frowned, creases rippling on her chalk-white forehead. Dry eyes twitched in their sockets. Light blue lips curled in disgust.

'I was one of his experiments,' she said, after a drawn-out pause. 'I was one of the volunteers – it was a way of getting close to him, of lowering his guard. At first he gave us treated food and water, but that made everyone sick. Then he operated on us directly. It worked on the others, but it almost killed me. I was his failure, and he killed me as much for that as for my treachery.'

The Doctor gazed at his hands, studying them in painful detail. The veins poked out through his flesh, twitching with slow, forced heartbeats. A slow second passed before he could bring himself to meet the head's corpse gaze.

'What kind of operation was it?' he asked in a sad, small voice.

'He sewed black worms into our flesh, to eat at us from the inside.'

'*Worms?*' The Doctor nearly exploded with incredulity.

'Maggots,' the dead voice slurred, correcting itself. 'There are still some here, in the containers. He must have been breeding them.'

The Doctor glanced over his shoulder at the tubs he had seen the previous day, at the host of churning black grubs that writhed mindlessly inside them.

'You weren't the only one! Who else was this done to?' he barked.

'Volunteers at first, soldiers like myself,' came the reply. 'Later he started to take people from the streets, prostitutes mainly. He doesn't need to hide what he's doing. When you hear that Minski is seeing women and men of ill repute at the Bastille, people invent their own ready explanations. He'd drug them, so they wouldn't remember the surgery.

'I think,' the head added, 'they must be a plague he's grown and nurtured. I think he means to infect the lower orders with it, let it rot them from within. Minski's trying to kill off the most despised profession in Paris, and their clients with them. It's a moral crusade.'

The Doctor frowned, briefly assessing the head's theory, finding it unsatisfying. He knelt by the nearest tub and stared in. The maggots within began to writhe hard, straining up to latch onto his flesh. Hungry little things.

'The whores and the water of Paris,' he murmured, remembering what Minski had said. 'He has obviously perfected a version that's soluble, that can be consumed orally. I imagine he only began implanting them surgically because the early oral variants didn't work.'

'What do you mean?' the head's voice echoed from above him.

He looked up and addressed it sharply. 'France has been blockaded during Minski's reign, has it not?' he asked, ploughing on before he could hear the answer. 'You were right about these maggots. They are a disease – a genetically engineered virus that can be transmitted through personal contact.

'Very soon the British army and its allies will take Paris. While they are based in the city they will drink its contaminated water, sleep with its contaminated people, eat its contaminated food. They will return to Britain, and to the rest of the Empire, and to America and Europe, and they will spread the virus across the globe.'

'And kill everyone?' the corpse-voice prompted from above.

The Doctor shook his head, staring once again into the box beside him. He'd have to analyse one of the maggots. Fortunately he had an entire laboratory to hand.

'I wonder what they *do*?' he hissed, as he tore the seal away from the uppermost box. The grubs seethed, leaping fruitlessly at the opening and the Doctor's hand. He shuddered.

There was a mob waiting at the gates of the Bastille, a sea of mute features and drab brown clothing standing in the tower's raw shadow. Soldiers moved through the crowd, muskets held warily in the crooks of their arms, their blue, white and red plumage adding a splash of colour to the scene. A staccato drumbeat played across the crowd. If anyone had spoken, they would have drowned it out, but there was only silence.

Dodo tramped across grey flagstones towards the edge of the mob, growing more apprehensive with each step. Beside her, Dalville felt tense and coiled, his hand tight on her elbow. The glum silence was uncomfortable, but it became worse – *oppressive* – when she realized that she and Dalville were the only people in the square who were not part of the mob. She felt as though she were disturbing their sacred ground, and that their hungry eyes were watching them, calculating when to pounce.

She resisted them. She walked straight on. Towards the mob.

Dalville put a reassuring arm round her shoulder and tried to pull her free of her path, but she fought him. She brought her jaws together, gritting awkward and mis-shapen teeth against each other.

'I don't want you to see this,' Dalville whispered, almost loud enough to kill the drumming.

The ranks of the mob opened to let them in. They entered, merging with it, pushing their way through. And, at last, Dodo saw what lay at the crowd's heart.

A stage, wooden, flanked by musketeers. Grey figures, dead-eyed men and women escorted by soldiers, mounting the stage – rag and bone shapes without dignity or hope. The drummer on the stage, dressed in a ragged, piecemeal uniform, or one contrived to appear that way. She drummed out the tattoo repeatedly, mindlessly, like the vacuum in her eyes.

At the heart of the stage, the machine. Its shadow seemed longer and deeper than that cast by the Bastille. Dodo recognized the oak frame, and the edge of steel that was held within it. Not the engine, not the grey box throbbing and hissing with power, not the chimney that poked out of the side belching black smoke across the crowd. That was new to her.

The first of the grey men was led to the machine, given to it, his head placed in the block at the foot of the wooden frame.

'Dodo, please,' Dalville hissed.

She turned slowly to look at him. 'Do you think I haven't seen anyone killed before?' she replied, surprising herself with the cold anger in her voice.

The prisoner was secured, looking upwards towards the blade, the lump on his throat naked and open to it. The engine began to judder and shake, steam escaping through loose folds in the metal. The drummer reached a climax, then fell silent.

'Once, I almost killed the entire human race,' she said, but her voice was flattened by a grunt of constipated effort from the machine. The blade fell. A ragged cheer broke out among the mob.

Dodo watched. She remained watching, her eyes

locked on the stage until its engine began to make jolly chugging noises and raised the blade in short bursts back to its starting place. Then she looked away, glancing disgustedly at the crowd around her. If it weren't for their clothes and their one moment of shared excitement, they might have come from the funeral.

'Let's go,' she said. Dalville took her by the hand and led her through the crowd towards the tower.

Fantômas was waiting for them inside. There was a smug smile parked on his lips, and he gave another of his curious, empty bows as he saw them. Dodo felt Dalville tense at her side, and was for a moment scared that he was going to spring forward and attack the director. She thought she even saw a glint of disappointment in Fantômas's eyes when he didn't.

'You couldn't have been there, could you?' Dalville accused.

Fantômas shook his head and spoke lightly, with an edge of sadness.

'I said my farewells in my own way.' He coughed. 'Citizen Minski has kindly laid on a meal for the troupe. The others have started, but I thought I'd better wait for you.'

'Thank you,' Dalville said, contempt lining his voice. Fantômas ignored the barb and nodded graciously. He escorted them to the dining hall, where the rest of the cast were assembled, eating and drinking vigorously while a handful of soldiers held a jealous, unenthusiastic vigil. The director led them to their seats, and then took a small amount of pleasure by sitting in the spare seat alongside them. Dalville mumbled something harsh under his breath. Dodo wriggled uncomfortably on her chair, feeling drowned by the crowd and the activity around her.

'Red?' Dalville asked suddenly, waving a wine bottle in front of her. She mumbled a 'yes'. He poured a healthy amount into her glass and passed it to her. The bowl felt heavy between her fingers and a ghost of her face stared up at her from the surface of the drink. She didn't feel thirsty.

'Red, Fantômas?' Dalville asked curtly.

'Apparently,' Fantômas was whittering close to Dodo's ear, 'we'll be performing in a private theatre in the tower. Minski included it in the design for his father to stage productions.'

Dodo shuddered, imagining standing on a real stage, in front of real people in real seats. That would be better than a cleared-out school gym, in front of teachers and pupils, parents and aunts. The idea terrified her.

'I'll take that as a no,' Dalville responded, raising the bottle instead to his lips and taking a swig. Dodo felt even less thirsty than before. A series of waiters with remarkably clean fingernails had emerged to lay plates before them. Dodo stared at the mix of thin meat and strained vegetables and discovered she had no appetite either. To her left, Dalville was tucking in regardless. Dodo eased a hand under the table and found his thigh. She squeezed it gently, setting him giggling.

To her right, Fantômas began to choke. Dodo swung round irritated to see the director's face bulging, eyes and cheeks billowing out under pressure. He was valiantly trying to contain a mouthful of food, his lips defiantly pursed. He was forcing himself to swallow, his throat throbbing as he worked each bite down. When his skin began to turn grey, Dodo lost any hope of starting on her own meal.

Eventually it became too much. The director rose from his chair and bolted from the room. From the far side of the hall, the soldiers and waiters jeered at his rapidly retreating back. Dodo wasn't sure that some of the more distant players hadn't joined in as well.

He must feel awful. He must feel so humiliated.

'Someone's tried to poison him at last,' Dalville suggested. Dodo ignored him, pushing herself out of her chair to her feet. Dalville tugged her sleeve.

'Don't go,' he pleaded. 'He's not worth it.'

'I'm sorry.' Dodo pulled away and ran out of the room in pursuit of the director. She found him gagging in an annexe at the end of the nearest passage. As she watched, he vomited most of the meal onto the floor.

She hadn't eaten for almost a day. She felt grateful.

'Fantômas, are you all right?' She felt stupid for asking. He looked up at her, fixing on her through nauseous, bleary eyes.

'I'm fine,' he slurred. 'It's *Catherine*. She hasn't been this ill since the last time she was here.'

'You've been to the Bastille before?' Dodo asked. Another silly question.

'Of course not,' the director's voice boomed. 'But *she* has.'

Whoever it was – Catherine or Fantômas – they turned and threw up again, emptying their shared stomach through their shared mouth.

The smell reminded Dodo of long car journeys and of childhood days out at the beach. She'd never enjoyed either. 'Well,' she said, flapping her arms at her side. 'Let's clean you up.'

It took almost half an hour to find a bathroom, and someone who could authorize the use of the bathroom. Dodo stuck close to him, but he insisted she stay outside while he cleaned himself. She sat on the floor and tried to catch up with her sleep. It didn't work – she was too frightened of what might be hiding behind her eyelids. When Fantômas emerged – cleaned, dry and immaculate as ever – she was crouched in a corner, staring aimlessly down the length of the corridor with aching, dusty eyes. The player offered her his hand, and she took it, finding it tiny and fragile despite his thick gloves. He pulled her to her feet with a silent but tangible effort.

They returned to the dining hall to find the meal over and done with, and the players gathered around two improbable newcomers at the heart of the hall. If it wasn't for the earnest way the soldiers clustered round the pair, Dodo might have mistaken them for another two actors.

The first she mistook for a child, a blonde little boy with haunting black eyes and features that wavered between bone-thin and slightly chubby, but were always cruel. He was the sort of boy she might have fallen in love with, in the first year at school when love seemed like nothing more than a grown-up game. She could imagine him as a choir boy, or one of the ineffectual kinds of bully who could threaten but never deliver.

Then he spoke, and everything changed. His was a hollow, adult voice like fingernails scratching against a slate.

'Ah, and this must be the notorious Citizen Fantômas,' he called, waving to the director.

Fantômas nodded and made a generous bow, a bow with none of his normal mockery or contempt. 'I am Fantômas, no more,' he declaimed. 'I am a delusion, and thus no citizen, but even this ghost delights in *your* presence, Citizen Minski.'

Everything changed again. Dodo looked at the child again, wary that there might be more surprises to come. The boy's face lit up, evidently amused by the player's sycophancy. Fantômas by now had turned to Minski's companion. He was a vast man with a heavy hawk-skull and a barrel-chest that threatened to burst out of his shirt. His expression seemed fixed in a permanent ugly smile.

'I am Citizen Donatien Alphonse François de Sade,' he said, his voice resonant and impressive, 'and I'm looking forward to the play.'

Fantômas faltered, then bowed simply. When he spoke again, something had broken in his voice. For an instant he sounded uncertain, then genuine.

'I'm sorry, citizen, I didn't recognize you,' he said. 'You weren't at all what I was expecting.' He coughed, then began again. 'May I assure you that I have taken no liberties with your text. Alas, I cannot say the same of the Office of Public Safety . . .'

'No.' Sade raised a massive hand, silencing even

Fantômas. 'The Office exists to protect us all. I will be happy with whatever they recommend.'

'Thank you.' Fantômas nodded graciously. There was still a slight note of puzzlement in his voice. 'If it's not an imposition, we would like to see the venue and hold a reading of the new text during the course of the day.'

Minski nodded agitatedly. 'I'll attend if you don't mind. My father is rather traditional in this respect and will wait for the first performance, but I'd like to be there as your drama unfolds.'

Fantômas nodded, still flustered, still perplexed. Dodo watched him from the crowd, wondering what had unsettled him. It was his eyes that were wrong, his eyes more than his voice.

'I am disappointed,' Minski continued, 'that my censors have seen fit to make so many cuts. There will be *some* sex and violence left, won't there?'

Fantômas shrugged. 'Not so much in the script,' he replied. 'But I'm sure we can improvise.'

The man who had once been Monsieur le 6 reclined on a bench in a dressing room behind the theatre, staring at the ceiling and soaking up the atmosphere. There was not much to tell for either, he reflected. The room was dark and its roof was a distant, pale shadow. There was no atmosphere either, except the ghosts of past performances. There had been few of those, he guessed. A theatre should be filled with energy and life. It should buzz with possible plays and anticipate the coming of the crowds. Not this place.

It was like cell 6. It was like being in prison once again.

He lay still, searching the ceiling again. This time he saw the spider building its web in the corner, slicing up the darkness with its pale thread. Le 6 let his eyes follow the pattern of the web, not searching for any sense but simply admiring its intricacy and its beauty.

It was a beautiful, elaborate trap.

'Monsieur le 6,' he said, rolling the words on his tongue. Another trap. Monsieur le 6. Monsieur le 6. Monsieur le 6.

'I am not a number,' he said decisively. 'I wish I knew what I was.'

The spider quivered on its web, waiting for hapless prey to stumble into its design. It wasn't an active hunter, but a schemer. If it hadn't spent so much time planning and building its web, it might seem lazy.

As time drew on, Monsieur le 6 began to hear voices. At first, he convinced himself they were in his mind — phantom fragments constructed from long forgotten experience — but gradually he realized that a crowd had gathered nearby, probably in the auditorium itself. They weren't an audience — their chatter seemed too relaxed and enthusiastic for that. There was a hushed note in most of the voices which le 6 recognized but couldn't name. He couldn't tell what they were saying. He didn't want to. He just wanted to be left alone, to think and to remember.

The spider clacked round the outer edge of the web, waiting.

'Hungwy widdle spider,' le 6 chirped sadly. 'Poor widdle fing.'

A couple of voices detached themselves from the group and drew closer. Le 6 grimaced, realizing they were heading his way. He lay still, uncaring.

The door at the far end of the room was flung open and a young couple tumbled in. The man was shabby but arrogantly attractive. He towered over the child in his arms, the little girl with the severe adult's face. They rolled into the room together, their bodies held close and tight.

Le 6 rolled his eyes in despair.

'Are you ready for the fate worse than death?' the man asked coyly, his eyebrows dancing.

The woman burned him with a glare. 'It's only a read-through. I won't have to do it until dress rehearsals.'

'Or lack-of-dress rehearsals,' the man responded. She punched him playfully. Le 6 felt the bile rising at the back of his throat.

Actors, le 6 guessed. He shook his head sadly.

'You know, you're the one with the problem. You really, really want to see me, like, on stage, like, ah . . .'

'Naked,' the male voice pronounced, rolling the succulent sound along his tongue.

'Yes,' the girl replied emphatically. 'But you can't stand the idea of other people watching,' she finished haughtily.

The man shook his head defiantly. Le 6 gritted his teeth, afraid that he was going to give in to his worse nature and start picking sides.

'Ah, but there's a difference,' the man responded. 'If you do that in front of a bunch of impotent old men, they only see you, they don't even get close to you. They won't ever know about the little sounds you make. They'll never see what happens to your eyes when you make love in the dark. They –'

'Excuse me,' Monsieur le 6 protested, 'but I am a prude.'

The woman jumped and made a slight, startled squeak. The man raised his hand and gave him a puzzled smile. Le 6 lay unmoved on the bench.

'Hi,' the man said. 'Are you one of us?'

'Yes,' le 6 lied easily. It was simpler than truth.

The actor nodded thoughtfully and began to create his own story around that first falsehood, like the spider weaving its web. 'You're an extra?'

'A spear-carrier. New to the role,' he said, by way of embroidery. 'So new, I don't know what it is.'

'Oh Christ, you must be one of the jolly friars. You *can* sing?'

'Like an angel' – Le 6 found himself nodding despite himself – 'sitting on a spike.'

Silence from the actors. The young girl's face was ashen, the man's arm rested protectively round her shoulder. There was pain there – a smoothed-over, voiceless pain – but pain nonetheless. Briefly le 6 considered apologizing and admitting to the truth, but the man spoke again, saving him the ordeal.

'Right, um, sorry, you've caught us at a bad time. I'm Dalville, this is Sophie. The rest of us are in the theatre.'

'I'll be out in a while,' le 6 said, folding his hands across his chest.

The woman, Sophie, stepped forward tentatively, as though afraid of catching something from him. She shoved a wad of paper onto the bench then pulled back, falling into Dalville's arms.

'It's the new script,' she said. 'I can, er, share with Dalville.'

'As she does.' Dalville brought his hands together into a thunderclap. 'Right, then. We'll leave you to it. Busy, busy.'

He took Sophie by the shoulder and eased her through the door and away.

'A star is born,' he mumbled, though le 6 caught it clearly.

'What do you mean about my eyes?' he heard Sophie ask, but the reply was lost to him. He chuckled, enjoying the effect he could still have on people.

Bored with the spider, he pulled the script from the bench, just to see the title, just to see the author's name.

'*Les Infortunes de la Vertu* – le Marquis de Sade.'

He sat up sharply, remembering.

He remembered shooting at a man in the tunnels, a man with a parody for a face, a nameless man he had for a brief instant hated with a passion close to love. It had been an anonymous, senseless rage – forged around a second's fiery intuition.

Here, now, on the page before him, was the name he needed, the name he had been searching for. It had come to him by accident, like a fly stumbling into a spider's web, lending it meaning. All of a sudden, the world made sense.

213

He flipped through the script, searching the unfamiliar pages for more clues. Above his head, a fat bluebottle had been snared by the web. It buzzed frantically, struggling to pull free from the thin strands, its cries becoming louder and shriller as the spider descended towards it. Monsieur le 6 did his best to ignore the fly's shriek — though it haunted him — and read on.

9

Frenchmen! A Further Effort,
If You Truly Want to be Republicans

The black ships descended. They blurred out of nothing across the horizon of Paris, their skins hardening and darkening as they fell. As they fell, they screamed. A single, harsh note burst across the Paris streets, warning the dead citizens.

As one they looked, the soldiers and the children, the merchants and the prostitutes, the lovers and the poets, the destitute and the insane. They saw the black ships hanging over their dead city, half-invisible against the storm clouds. All who saw them trembled. Those who didn't understand panicked, retreating into their homes or the homes of others, desperate for sanctuary.

A few who saw the black ships remained still, their heads craned towards the sky, watching. They sensed what the ships represented, and knew there was no point in running or hiding. The ships were vultures squabbling over a dying body, ready to descend. The few remained in the streets, waiting to die in the early onslaughts.

The few who waited *knew*.

They were already lost.

The Doctor knew. His heart screamed inside his ribs, pounding furiously until it seemed it was going to burst. His hand formed a claw, squeezing at his chest, almost prepared to tear it open to ease the pain. He shrieked.

The pain stopped, his heart with it. He fell. He struck the floor.

The first Change was coming. He'd felt the storm

brewing months ago. He'd fought against it, but his efforts only seemed to strengthen it and darken its edges. The tide would pass across him, scouring his landscape, leaving scattered devastation in its wake. The clouds swirled, darting round him ready to swallow and consume his self. He felt the tears bulging on his eyelids, dribbling down a distant, detached face. The Change was more frightening than death. The Change would destroy part of his self forever. He'd know that for the rest of his lives, and the knowledge would torment him.

One heart, he thought blissfully. One heart, soon to meet its twin.

The one heart pulsed feebly. The pain seared through the Doctor's body, jolting him awake. He screamed, unstoppable tears bursting from the edges of his eyes. The beat of his heart grew, faltering at first, then slowly stronger. Each new surge of blood burned in his arteries.

He lived, and, for the moment, he was himself.

He climbed painfully to his feet, glancing nervously around the lab. Only the woman's head was there to glance back at him. Her cold flesh lips smiled with painful sympathy. The Doctor felt a little relieved that his outburst hadn't had a wider or more hostile audience.

'Are you all right?' the head asked. 'It looked like you were having a heart attack.'

The Doctor shook his head bullishly.

'I had a heart attack once,' the head mused. 'Not for long though – '

'Yes, yes,' the Doctor blustered. 'Now, what was I doing?'

'You were talking about the maggots,' the head prompted.

'The maggots, yes. I examined them, and – '

He broke off, glancing down at the remaining packages of surging, clamouring grubs. They responded to his interest by clambering on top of each other, forming piles that surged ever upwards. If it wasn't for the seal on the container, and the brutal competition between

216

the contents, they might have been able to reach him.

'Minski talks a great deal about control, about *mastery*. He also says much about the limits of his power. I was selfish enough to think he meant me, or the TARDIS. No. A mistake. He meant you – all of you!

'Minski has direct control over the physical aspects of this world, but not the creatures within it. It is true he can force people to act through circumstances. He can deceive people, but,' the Doctor paused, adding weight to his next few words, 'he can't make you jump if you don't want to.

'Can you imagine how galling that must be for the master of the machine? These creatures,' he tapped the top of the container, 'are his solution.'

The maggots gathered round his finger, their mouths yawning hungrily, snapping at it but biting frustratingly on transparent plastic. The Doctor felt a moment's pity for them. They existed solely to be used. They were probably happy, in their own way.

'They're not alive in any meaningful sense. They are engineered machines with organic components. They are programmed to eat, and to secrete.'

'They eat human flesh,' the head mused.

Again the Doctor shook his head. 'They feed on nervous tissue and on cerebral material,' he said. 'Once inside the body they latch onto the closest nerve and follow it to the central system and from there to the brain, consuming as they go. It's the start of their life cycle. By the time they are fed, all the important parts of the victim's nervous system are seeded with their secretions. They die after a few hours, but they leave traces of their engineered DNA . . . how to explain . . . uh, their life-essence, and fragments of machinery behind. It can be passed through human contact, and between generations. It would not kill you, but it would alter you. You would become susceptible to his control.'

He brought his hands together, casting his eyes arrogantly towards the ceiling. It was a favourite gesture of his, but he only now realized how close it seemed to prayer.

'It is a perversion! It passes through people unawares, leaving invisible chains behind. Once infected, you cannot be sure whether your actions are of your own free will or directed by him! It will take years to spread but, by the end of that time, Minski will be master of a world of puppets.'

The head swivelled, its lips trembling with disgust.

'You don't need to do that,' the Doctor said softly.

'I can't feel disgust, old man, but I can *remember* it. Minski cut me open and put those maggots into me. He let them feed on me.'

'You were lucky,' the Doctor reminded her. 'Your body rejected them.'

'And so I died instead.'

The Doctor nodded thoughtfully, weary from the explanations and the lingering pain from his collapse. He sighed, clambering onto the nearest operating table and lying back peacefully.

'I suspect he will wait for a few years before activating the process. He will have a sizeable part of the global population to work with by then. At the moment, who can tell? Everyone in the Bastille could be infected.'

'Except us,' the head chimed.

'Except us,' the Doctor agreed. He raised a hand to his temple, swallowing hard. The taste was dry and unpleasant. 'I had breakfast with him yesterday. I didn't eat or drink anything.' He glanced across at the TARDIS, realizing how easily Minski could have taken her. He wondered why Minski hadn't tried to infect him directly, by force-feeding. Possibly it hadn't occurred to him.

Unless, he realized, he *was* contaminated, and the First Deputy was simply drawing him through a devious, humiliating game. No, that didn't seem likely. An older kind of tyrant would, but not Minski.

He lay back on the couch, heavy lids falling across his

eyes. He needed time to think, to decide the best course of action. It would be so easy to get sidetracked into trying to put an end to Minski's plans and to the suffering he saw. The true problem lay in the existence of Minski's false world. The suffering would end if that was resolved.

Then the real suffering could begin, the suffering history recorded. It hardly seemed worth the effort. The Doctor began to understand what had led Minski to build the labyrinth of traps – the blind, deadly murder machine. It was an offering to the universe – a homage, perhaps a parody, perhaps an imitation, of life itself.

'Doctor!' the head shrieked. He looked up in time to see its forehead crack open, fragile flesh and bone tumbling to the floor like fragments of eggshell. A larger hole burst at the back of the head. This time there was some congealed blood and a smattering of cold brain. Her mouth hung open, the Doctor's name slurring on the now irrevocably dead lips.

The Doctor followed the shot back to its source, to the door. He found Citizen Sade, broad frame squeezing out the light from the doorway. The pistol was wedged between the heavy fingers of one hand. It was – the Doctor noted – his bad hand on the arm that had been wounded the previous day. There was no sign of his injury now. He held the gun stiffly but well.

'She talked too much,' Sade said simply, jabbing his pistol at the direction of the head.

'She could do little else,' the Doctor muttered. Sade shrugged, his mouth creasing to form his usual sardonic smile. The Doctor turned away, gazing sadly at the remains of his ally, his confidante. She stared back, open mouthed, a stupid totem on the altar of a primitive god. His title still blurred on her lips, and he made a silent promise to her to put an end to this universe. The real world was a poor alternative, but it could promise her no worse a death.

'Now,' a voice said at his back, 'melodrama.'

Sade sneaked up behind him and prodded his back with a pistol muzzle. This one was cold, fresh and loaded, but the Doctor ignored it, wheeling round to face his attacker. It would be good, at last, to have a target for his rage, a totem of everything rotten that could be torn down and defaced. Sade was the perfect symbol for this world.

'Do you know,' he said, danger seething under his tone, 'that when I saw you with Minski yesterday, I sympathized with you. I thought you were a much better person than your son. I was a fool! Perhaps I was compensating for everything I have seen or heard said about the Marquis de Sade. I couldn't believe that anyone could be such a monster. You had to have some redeeming quality, but I searched too long and too hard for it!'

Sade's heavy features twitched, but his smile remained unchanged. He was enjoying the outburst, the indictment. It pleased him.

The Doctor, irritated, blustered on. 'Do you want to know how posterity will remember you?' he asked. 'Your legacy will consist of one word – *sadism*, the enjoyment of pain inflicted on others. You will go down in history as one of the most evil men who ever lived, as a practitioner of obscene arts, as a hedonist who sought gratification in depravity!'

He paused for breath and realized that Sade was still smiling. It was a perfect, understated line across his lips, the same grin that the Doctor had seen so many times.

Exactly the same. So many times.

'After all I have said, I don't know how you have the nerve to smile like . . .'

The same. So many.

The Doctor lapsed into silence, his eyes fixed on the familiar crack between Sade's lips. A hushed realization blossomed.

'No,' he said softly. 'I am lying. You will have no legacy. You will be forgotten, because in the history I know, you never existed.' He could feel his voice, low and calm but shaking through his frame. It had a similar effect on Sade, knocking the smile from his lips. Without the smile, there was nothing there, not even hatred.

Sade's finger trembled on the trigger of his gun. The Doctor gazed into the barrel, into the heart of Sade's power, into the moment of his death. It lasted for an unreal, stretched second. It was more like a dying memory at the back of his mind – or a faded photograph – than a real, lived experience.

At the end of the moment, he reached out and seized Sade's wrist, pulling it aside. The pistol spoke to one side of his face, skimming past his flesh and flattening itself into the closest wall. The heat and the flash of the shot seared his eyes, blinding him. Afraid of losing the initiative, he wrenched hard on Sade's arm.

Something gave. Sade yelled, at first from pure agony, then pure fear. He was still screaming when the hot scar faded from the Doctor's eyes. He was gazing in horror at his arm, the arm which dangled in the Doctor's wrist, pulled loose from its socket. There was no blood. It was a clean break.

The Doctor dropped the arm in shock. It struck the floor with a reassuringly fleshy sound which failed to mask the clatter of metal within. The shoulder-joint burst open, a long taut spring leaping outwards, snaking freely across the laboratory floor. It was pursued by a gang of cogs and gears and metal pins. They formed outcrops and islands of metal round the continent of the arm.

Sade's screams grew harder and higher.

The black ships hovered, raw and jagged over the city. For an hour they had hung silently, perhaps quivering slightly as the storm buffeted them. Below them, Paris held its breath, pregnant with anticipation. They had become an ominous marvel. Some of the braver citizens had ventured onto the streets to watch and stare. They joined the despairing few, whose necks already ached with the effort of watching, and whose eyes had been wrung dry.

For Citizen Edith Cameo, the black ships were just another thing to fear. She had fled the Bastille for the outskirts of the city the previous night and was certain that trained assassins were close on her heels. She felt naked without her gaoler's uniform and tricolour sashes — naked and renewed. She'd burned the trappings of her Revolution on a bonfire during the morning, watching the hollow symbols blacken into ash. It had been a potent moment.

Citizen Debord's offices were situated directly underneath one of the black ships. Its scream hummed through the structure of the building and rattled the windows. Unable to concentrate on his work, the censor descended to the cellar of the building and huddled in the shade of the printing presses, sobbing gently to himself. The scream was muted down here, among the massive engines, between their iron spars and gears. He had killed a man with his pen, and the voices of the ships rang with cries of guilt and accusation.

A soldier stood on high ground to the south of the city, inspecting the black ships through a bino-telescope. He shook his head in despair, recalling with disbelief the order to stay put, and the silence that had greeted all the queries he had waxed to the Bastille. The soldier — still a young man — held a high rank in Minski's army. Despite this he felt disillusioned, old before his time, as though greatness had passed him by. He returned to the dark privacy of his tent, retrieved his pistol and slipped the barrel into his mouth. His tongue touched cold metal, tracing its outline as he waited.

At noon, the scream of the black ships stopped. They dropped silently towards the city. Beams of purple fire spat from the underside of each of the craft, lashing at public buildings, at populous areas, at the power stations along the banks of the Seine. One beam scythed through the Bastille, slicing it through halfway up its length. One of the ships set itself down on the forecourt at the front of the Bastille, appearing just large enough not to be dwarfed by the tower. Folds opened on the smooth black skin of the ship, disgorging lines of men with vicious red uniforms and muskets tipped with shining white steel. They too carried emblems of blue, white and red, different symbols of a different order.

Their flags flew at the gates of the Bastille while around them, the city burned.

Hellfire.

A rumble of thunder rolled through the Bastille, setting the auditorium shaking. Dodo was squatting on the floor when it struck and was almost knocked over. Most of the other players were seated or lounging and weathered the blast. Only on stage, where a gathering of comic friars were practising their singing, were there any untoward effects. It knocked the wind and the song out of the assembly and one stumbled over, tumbling into his closest fellows and sending them sprawling across the stage.

The rumble drowned out the music, which was something of a blessing.

'From the top please,' Fantômas called once the noise had died away. He seemed typically unruffled. Dodo gazed across the chamber to see Minski, sitting alone among the seats, feigning an interest in the proceedings. The friars regained their breath and burst into song once again, their voices jumbling awkwardly together, failing to merge into a chorus. Dodo hid a giggle behind her hand, where Fantômas couldn't see it.

'Enough,' the director screamed, mercifully killing the din. He waved dismissively and strolled away from the stage. Dodo leaned back uneasily as she realized he was approaching her.

'Where's Dalville?' he asked brusquely. Dodo shrugged.

'Miserable weather isn't it?' Fantômas continued, leaning forward slightly so that Dodo could see his eyes. Her eyes, all Catherine's.

'It isn't?' Dodo responded, recognizing the hint.

Catherine shook Fantômas's head and whispered.

'The Pageant have begun the attack on Paris. Their ships, an assault force of British soldiers . . . the Bastille will probably hold out for a couple of hours, three at best.' Her eyes were dark and terrible.

'Surely that's a good thing.'

'Hardly. Minski will have time to seal off access to the world-machine. He'll hide outside time and space and lock us out until he's ready. Our only chance is to expose him now.'

Dodo shivered and hugged herself. She had just realized that she had no idea what Arouette wanted her to do. The woman smiled from behind her beard, her eyes twinkling with sympathy.

'Just lie back and relax,' she suggested. 'If anything goes wrong, improvise.' Dodo nodded warily. Catherine stepped back and made to go, but Dodo caught her sleeve. She looked back, but with Fantômas's features. His face was hard and impatient, so she let him go. He swaggered back onto the stage, shooing the remaining friars away. They tumbled from the stage, desperate to escape his wrath.

'Citizens! We are well and truly finished!' the director boomed, his voice breaking slightly. Fragments of Catherine Arouette slipped through, tingeing his arrogance with something shapeless, fragile and human. 'First Deputy!' He bowed, mustering all the tricks and flourishes into a hateful, mocking sweep. A murmur filled the hall, passing from actor to actor as they recognized the first unexpected note of the address. The second note was the pistol which appeared in Fantômas's hand, slipped invisibly from the folds of his cloak. It aimed simply, steadily at Minski's head.

'*J'accuse*,' he finished. No more flourishes, no more bows, no more mockery, only the words, only the undiluted voice of Catherine Arouette rolling from the director's tongue. She stripped off her disguise quickly, spitting the syllable that released her own face from

224

within the living mask, but never once letting the gun waver or slip. Dodo found herself grinning, enjoying the stage-craft that underpinned the drama.

Eventually there was only Catherine Arouette surrounded by the ruins of Fantômas, his props and tricks and masks scattered dust-like across the stage. Across the auditorium the actors were sitting up, their hushed tones filling the chamber. Someone close behind Dodo began to clap enthusiastically. She looked over her shoulder and was not in the least surprised to see Dalville winking down at her.

Only Minski himself seemed unmoved.

'Catherine Arouette,' he said at last, blinking slowly.

'Yes.' She gave him a brief, formal curtsey. The pistol remained.

'You were the first of my experiments, the first of my failures,' the First Deputy drawled, his eyelids half-closing, as though tired. 'I won't pretend I remember you. Your name is written on a piece of paper somewhere. You were a whore I sliced open once. No more.'

'No.' She shook her head. Face and voice were steady, undamaged by his barb. 'I rejected your surgery. I'm a new kind of person, of the kind which will always elude you, of the kind which your tyranny has suppressed. I'm a human being, Minski. Neither the first nor the last. *Human*. Nothing more.'

The tyrant smiled. It sat strangely on a face that seemed unused to pleasure. He raised a cautious hand, but made no effort to rise.

'I see a human being,' he said, finally. 'It offends me.'

He spoke again, a single non-sound in the non-language of the aliens. Dodo had only heard it from Catherine's tongue before, and it had sounded strange and comical, struggling in the limits of a human voice. Minski delivered his non-word in a perfect voice. It growled and hissed from his tongue, lingering in the air before him, shifting and mutating as it went. It rose in pitch and volume, billowing outwards to fill the

225

auditorium before bursting in an explosion of non-silence.

Dodo sensed something new in the auditorium. All around her, actors were sitting up in their seats, suddenly tense and alert, listening carefully. Once again, she felt excluded. The players were as one. She was another.

'Mastery,' Minski whispered, almost to himself. Dodo had to strain to hear. 'At last, perfect control.'

The pistol wavered in Arouette's hand.

'Be savage, vicious, bestial,' Minski said quietly. 'Kill Catherine Arouette.'

The actors leapt from the seats and rushed at the stage, howling as they went. Catherine's arm swung downwards, the pistol flicking from face to face never certain, never settling. She glanced up, finding Dodo and offering her a doomed stare. She swung her arm round and tossed the flintlock across the stage into Dodo's waiting arms. It was only there for a moment, cold and heavy against her palms, before Dalville stepped out from behind her, smashing the pistol away. It hit the floor, skidding into an empty corner out of her reach.

Dalville seized her and swung her round. He was smiling blissfully.

'What's wrong?' he asked kindly. 'Once we've killed her everything will be fine.' He squeezed her shoulder, adding a thoughtful, 'It's what Minski wants,' as though that explained everything.

Out of the corner of her eye she saw Catherine disappear under a mass of writhing, clawing bodies. She was silent, the only part of the mass that wasn't screaming. Dodo squeezed her eyelids tight, crushing the sight out of her mind. She could still hear the howls of the crowd, seeming all the more horrible for being detached from the scene.

A pistol barked in the distance, in the darkness. The screams vanished into an instant silence. Dodo was afraid to open her eyes, terrified of what she might find outside the dark. She managed it in the end.

Minski was sprawled back in his chair, his head lolling on his shoulders, a raw wound seeping blood over his heart. On the stage, the frenzy of the actors had dissipated. They were no longer screaming, but wailing and moaning, their faces cast downwards. Their hands clutched desperately at their faces and their eyes and they shuffled away. As they pulled back, Arouette pulled clear of them, her frail skin slashed and torn – bleeding in a dozen places. She saw Dodo and offered her a genuine toothy grin.

'It must have been in the food,' she said absently, spluttering and spitting lumps of dust from her mouth. 'You didn't eat did you? You must be very hungry.'

Dalville was leaning against Dodo's shoulde:. He was a dead weight, but she was happy to prop him up. He was sobbing against her ear – a child's tears not an adult's, baffled and betrayed by the cruelty of the world.

'Mad for a minute,' he droned between sobs. 'For a moment. I'm sorry, really I'm sorry, really.' She left him apologizing, rambling the same handful of sorrys to himself. He was beginning to sound like Bressac, like Bressac before he'd died and lost his name.

The final figure on the stage was an old man, dumpy and balding with a watery, helpless face. Dodo had seen him before, had stumbled across him with Dalville when they'd looked round the dressing room. There was a ruthlessness in his soft blue eyes that belied his feeble appearance. The flintlock that smoked in his hand was testament to that.

He glared at Dodo, clutching the gun defensively.

'He was a tyrant and he would have killed your friend,' he said reasonably. 'That's the only excuse I can offer.'

'No one's accusing you,' Catherine said, stepping forward and laying a kind arm round his shoulder. She led him to the edge of the stage and sat him down. He eyed her suspiciously, but seemed comfortable, dangling his legs over the edge and kicking aimlessly at the air.

'Do you know me?' he asked gently.

'I saw you once,' Arouette replied. 'I know who you are, who you've always been. I remember you very well.'

'That's good,' the old man nodded. 'I've been imprisoned for so long, trapped behind masks and numbers, I was beginning to worry that I was someone else altogether.'

'Monsieur le 6!'

Dodo swung round, startled by the familiar bark, by a voice she hadn't heard for days. The Doctor was striding down the central aisle of the auditorium. His walk was triumphant, his hair falling in arrogant waves, shining under the stark theatre lights. He was perhaps a little shabbier than when they parted, but otherwise he seemed improved and strengthened by his time away from her. She called his name and waved. He acknowledged it with a brusque nod of the head.

She looked again with a calmer eye, seeing not only his strength, but also the hollow weakness that lay beneath it. This was a temporary renewal. It wouldn't last. She raised her hand, covering her eyes with shadow.

The Doctor reached the edge of the stage. For a minute, he and the old man were silent, matching each others cold stares.

'I am *not* Monsieur le 6,' one said.

'No,' replied the other.

'*She* knows' – the one jabbed a long, bony finger at Arouette, who sat beside him, grinning secretively – 'but she won't tell me.'

'You've not given me a chance,' she replied.

Le 6 snorted.

The Doctor nodded respectfully and spoke. 'You are Citizen Donatien Alphonse François de Sade, formerly the Comte de Sade, best remembered as the Marquis de Sade.'

'Yes,' the old man agreed. His mouth cracked open, a

crescent of shining teeth forming between his lips. He fell back onto the stage, curling silently into a bundle, tightening into a foetus. 'I am,' he mumbled, his voice emerging somewhere near his knee.

The rumble came again. The walls of the Bastille trembled.

10

The Misfortunes of Virtue

The Doctor hefted Sade's head in his arms, displaying it shamefully like an embarrassing trophy. It rattled as he shook it, dislodging shards of clockwork that rained from the bottom of its clean-cut neck. Something twisted inside his skull and the eyeballs popped from their sockets to dangle comically on coiled metal wire.

The Doctor dug his fingers into the cavity in Sade's temple, probing deeper through layers of synthetic skin into polished metal and intricate mechanisms. He found a misshapen metal lump wedged into the machinery. He caught it between delicate fingertips and tugged it loose, bringing it out of the head and into the light.

'Ah,' he said, recognizing it as a fragment of the ball from a flintlock. The automaton had put it there himself, before the Doctor could stop him.

'It's not a very good likeness,' Monsieur le 6 commented. 'I hope it's not.' He put his hands against his face, testing the flesh. Satisfied by what he had found, he placed tentative fingers on the cheeks of the clockwork face, prodding and stroking.

'Still warm,' he hmmed, rolling his eyes up into the Doctor's face. 'This isn't me. It wouldn't have fooled anyone who knew me.'

'I imagine Minski disposed of your family and friends soon after taking power. He probably thought he had disposed of you as well.'

Sade – the genuine Sade – nodded, his face twitching into a cool and unreadable expression. He stalked away, wheeling round the stage in an ever-decreasing circle, casting his eyes rapidly between the ceiling and the floor. Dodo fell back out of his way, joining the Doctor and Dalville on the theatre's edge. Her hands brushed against the hollow forehead of the fake Sade, fascinated and afraid.

The Doctor closed his eyes, trying to block her out of his sight. He felt more than a little guilty for bringing her here, then abandoning her in the middle of this perverse parody of human history.

'Why did he bother with this?' she asked, tapping a finger on the head.

The Doctor dampened his thoughts, turning to lecture her in a calm, unfeeling voice. He couldn't allow her to see anything else.

'I can only guess. Minski told me that once he had perfected them, he realized the automata were a false trail. It is possible he wanted to provide himself with a personification of this twisted philosophy he had absorbed – a perversion of the creator as well as the creation. Maybe he needed a figurehead who could articulate everything he could not.' He clapped his hands together and giggled, pleased with this line of speculation.

'Look around you. Look at the Bastille tower, or that murderous labyrinth of his. Look at the architecture of this entire world and you see everything unspoken in his philosophy, given external form. Like *so*,' he snapped, dropping the head onto the stage, where it broke apart. Lumps of false flesh and hair scattered across the stage, drowned in a sea of shattered metal. The fake Sade's soft eyes rolled over the edge of the stage and dropped the short distance to the floor where they burst open, steel pins jutting out of shapeless white mounds.

'Ouch,' the true Sade said. He had adopted the cruel smile of his imitator, but it was softened and warmed by his small lips. The auditorium shook once again and his smile vanished while he steadied himself. The Doctor felt the ground teeter beneath his feet, but Dalville reached out and clasped his arm, holding him still until the tremor passed.

'Thank you, young man,' the Doctor said kindly. The actor nodded emphatically but seemed too nervous to say anything. Dodo slid up alongside him, a wide smile beaming off her countenance. The Doctor nodded to himself thoughtfully, certain that Dodo had been looked after well during his absence.

He killed the thought. The latest tremor was an adequate reminder that the problem – that history itself – was still unresolved. He swung round, staring out across the sheer cliff-face of seats. Most were occupied by dazed players, watching haplessly as the real world unfolded on the stage before them. Catherine Arouette flitted between the rows, comforting each player in turn. Dressed in her long, dark cloak, her eyes peering down coldly from their fleshless hollows, she must have seemed a grim healer.

The Doctor found himself pulling his coat tighter, without knowing why.

'Citizen Arouette,' he called. She looked up slowly, but he was prepared to wait. From what he had seen of her, and what he had learned from Dodo, she was deserving of his patience and respect. 'We have little time left. We have to shut down the world-machine.'

'Be my guest,' she called. 'I'd like to stay with my people. Catherine didn't know many of them. She'd like to learn and remember them while she has the chance.'

The Doctor nodded thoughtfully, turning to Dodo.

'I have to say goodbye,' she said, putting a hand on Dalville's high shoulder, struggling to make it seem casual. Again, the Doctor nodded.

'I'll go with you,' Sade called from the back of the stage. 'I'm the last of the architects of this world. The machine knows me.'

'And?' the Doctor said, spotting more here than was being said.

'And, yes, I feel responsible,' Sade continued smoothly, 'and I feel guilty, as uncharacteristic as that may seem.'

The Doctor shook his head, offering him a silent smile. Sade snorted but couldn't quite meet his stare.

'Now!' The Doctor brought his hands together in a decisive clap. 'We might need Minski's corpse. Who moved the body?'

The silence deafened him. It was replaced by a horrible, sticky sensation of suspicion and realization. He wheeled slowly to stare at Minski's seat, now abandoned with only flecks of blood left to mark his passing. Sade rushed forward to join him, his soft eyes wild with disbelief.

'I shot him!' he insisted, hard conviction in his tone. 'I shot him through the heart.'

'Minski,' the Doctor replied quietly, 'is simply a mass of biological tissue mimicking humanity. You may have punctured him. You might even have hurt him, but you wouldn't have killed him by shooting him through the chest!'

'He hasn't a heart?' Sade's voice hummed with cold realization.

'He has no heart,' the Doctor echoed.

Citizen Juliette Picard remained defiant at her post, a solid anchor in the ocean of madness and anarchy around her. She drew a small measure of satisfaction from being the last soldier to hold true to her orders. The chain of command was the steadfast outcrop to which she clung. Around her, cowardly little officials were running, volunteer soldiers in their ragged clothes were running, even Minski's bodyguards in their precise uniforms were a part of the turmoil. They had no faith, Juliette thought, so they panicked.

Occasionally one of the mob would stumble into her, seize her by the shoulder and give voice to their hysteria. They spoke of the black ships that rained death on the city; of the British attack force massing at the gates of the tower, killing everyone they met; of the blast that had destroyed the upper part of the Bastille, sending thousands plunging to their deaths. One had even said that the First Deputy had been assassinated, or had died when the black ships sliced through his tower.

They were fearful droplets, trying to smash her away from the shore. She endured them, faithful to her orders and to Minski, as she had been during the night with Minski's hateful father. She had experienced one moment of weakness, during a lull in the panic when the crowd had played itself out. She'd leant forward to look through the nearest window, gazing outwards in horror at the devastated city and the solid black clouds that had made it so. Other than that, she was determined.

She would remain at her post. She would remain. She would.

She looked up and saw Citizen Minski stumbling down the corridor towards her, dragging himself against the nearest wall for support. He had one hand clamped over his chest, scarlet fluid seeping between his pale fingers. His face – normally so serene – spoke of pain and betrayal. Juliette Picard considered her orders and found them outweighed by a higher loyalty. She abandoned her post, rushing forward to meet the Last Frenchman, catching him in her arms as he fell.

'Citizen,' he slurred, raising a weak hand. 'Citizen . . .'

'Sir?' she asked, tears glistening on her eyes.

'Carry me.'

She nodded mutely, not willing to trust herself with words. She picked him up, marvelling at how light and how warm he felt in her arms. She had never been closer to him, but her exhilaration was mixed with icy fear. His blood had already made a dark stain on her blouse, and she knew that he was dying. She stood, holding him tight in her arms and quaking with indecision.

'Where to?' she asked at last.

'Down,' he hissed. 'Down. Take me to my laboratory.'

Then he passed out. Sobbing with fear, cradling his precious body against hers, Citizen Picard hurried to the nearest elevator.

Dodo took Dalville's hands in her own and studied them, forcing herself to memorize every detail, from the criss-cross patterns on his soft palms to the vivid red patches on his knuckles. The half-dark of the dressing room made her task so much more difficult and her effort so much more intense.

She looked up, surrendering with her eyes. He accepted, pushing his face into hers and kissing her, on the mouth briefly, once on each cheek, slowly on her forehead, then returning to linger on her lips. Silent tears trickled down her face. He caught them with his fingertips, smudging them into her skin.

'I'm glad I didn't tell the Doctor,' she said, disturbing the quiet of the room. 'I don't think he would have understood.'

'No,' Dalville said starkly. 'You know, when he first came down the aisle in the theatre, I could see his face perfectly as he recognized you, and yours as you responded to him. I knew he was coming for you.'

'Yes,' Dodo replied quietly. 'He was.'

Dalville nodded. 'It's a good thing –' His voice cracked, but he continued smoothly after a pause. 'It's a good thing we didn't let it get complicated.'

'Yes.' Dodo nodded, unfeeling. 'We weren't ever going to settle down.'

'No commitment,' Dalville agreed. 'Nothing permanent. Just a brief acquaintance, a couple of nights bouncing around in bed, a little bit of fun.'

'It wasn't love, ever.'

'No, not love.'

'It *was* fun. I liked you.'

'I liked you.' It sounded like the inscription on a tomb. 'I liked you.'

'If it's any consolation,' she murmured, reaching out to brush his face with her knuckles. 'I doubt I'll be with the Doctor for much longer. I'm not a great traveller. Sooner or later . . . *sooner*, I'll stop.'

'I don't suppose . . .' Dalville ventured, though with little hope.

Dodo shook her head sadly. 'It wouldn't work. When this is over, you won't remember me. The past ten years will cease to have happened. And look at me – I'm just a part of your last three days!'

'Ten years ago, Bressac . . . Jean-Louis was alive.' His voice purred out of the dark. 'It's strange, I believe everything you've said except that. I just keep thinking of that grave breaking open and spitting him out right as rain. It's a stupid idea, and I don't know whether to laugh or cry.'

Dodo shrugged.

'What about you?' he continued. 'What will happen to you?'

'I'll remember everything,' she said. 'I'm no more a part of this world than the Doctor is. I'll remember you. I'll cherish the memory.'

'But you won't get your cherry back?'

'No. I don't think so.'

Dalville grinned at her, his eyes glowing in the dark. She returned the smile and pulled closer to him, swinging one leg over his thigh. Together they leaned back on the bench, savouring the peace and the shared warmth of their vile, subtle bodies.

The earth moved, but it was only another explosion rocking the tower.

'So,' Dodo asked curiously, 'what does happen to my eyes?'

He coughed, his cheeks darkening, apparent even in the gloom.

'They shine.'

Juliette lays Citizen Minski's body on the ground–flesh,

on the edge of the chapel of steel and bone. Her arms are aching with the effort of carrying him so far, but the pain is good. It reminds her that she is still real, that everything around her is real and she is not dreaming. Her head feels swollen and limp on her neck.

She casts her eyes upwards, following the curve of bone arches to the flesh ceiling, but the sight stirs only a little fear in her, nothing else. She is acutely aware of herself, tiny and frail in the vastness of this place. At her feet, Minski is frailer still, his body twisting awkwardly on the uneven floor, his head rolling at a painful angle. Juliette kneels to move him into a more comfortable shape. Her hand fumbles over the raw wound on his chest. Her fingers brush cautiously round its edges; they come away stained red. The First Deputy raises his small head. His eyes blaze.

'What is this?' Juliette asks, untamed fear in her question.

'This is my birthplace. I started out as a nucleus swirling at the heart of a pool of rich fluid. I sucked the life from the pool, drawing cells and strength to make my body.' His voice trails away and he looks round, losing interest in Juliette. 'Minski came later. Minski grew out of other things.'

He fixes her in his sights once again. She stiffens proudly, feeling complete in his gaze. By looking, he defines her.

'Go to the heart of the machine,' he orders. 'You'll find a creature trapped in the cage of bones. Kill it, then return to me.'

She responds with a mindless salute, rising and turning to carry out her task. She sets out across the bonescape, her heart burning with a certainty that runs lower with each new step. It's only a short distance to the heart, but she loses track of time as she goes, each footfall lasting a second and an hour. The walls and the ground fade around her, losing clarity and shape, but she continues. Her orders make sense of everything, even in this confusion.

She reaches the cage of bone beneath the machine's spine. There is – as her orders specify – a creature here. It hangs loose among the maze of shafts and ribs and wires, its head and limbs rolling as though it no longer has the strength to hold itself up. Its flesh is riddled with cracks, each fault oozing a liquid with the colour, smell and texture of curdled milk. Juliette controls the urge to retch, but makes no move for her pistol. She is content to stare, and to wonder.

Moments later she is back at Minski's side.

'Did you kill it?' he asks.

'No.' She shakes her head. His lips twitch, forming a question. 'I didn't know how,' she admits. 'I'm sorry.'

'No matter,' Minski concedes. (She breathes again.) 'It's dying anyway.'

'Yes.'

'I'm dying too,' he suggests. Juliette gasps and falls back shaking her head defiantly. The First Deputy gives her a callous stare.

'You're one of them,' he spits, contemptuously. 'Aren't you? You're part of the Minski cult, the followers of the Celebrity? I suppose I should feel flattered. The dust worships the sole of the boot. Arrogant dust.'

'We want you to live through us,' Juliette protests, though with no great strength. The corners of Minski's mouth tremble and a spot of blood rises to his lips. He's trying to laugh, Juliette thinks. She has never thought of him laughing before – it seems foreign to his nature.

'If that's what you want,' he says. 'Do you have a knife?'

She nods, reaching to touch the handle that rests against her ankle.

'Good,' Minski replies. 'Make a wide, clean cut from your breastbone to your navel. I need to hibernate for some years. Your body will be my vessel and my sustenance. I'll live through you.'

'Is that all I'm good for?' Juliette asks, vaguely. She draws the knife from her boot and stares at the blade, fascinated by the patterns of light she finds reflected along its biting edge.

The Doctor pressed his key into the air of the laboratory, humming with little patience as the gate formed around it.

'You realize that Minski is probably in there already,' Sade warned him, hovering at his shoulder. 'In fact, I'm surprised he hasn't sealed the gates.'

'He probably doesn't realize I have a key,' the Doctor replied. He glanced across the laboratory to the shattered head of the traitor, thoughtfully giving it a nod. It had long since fallen silent. Its cold eyes bulged beneath drooping lids and blood and skull-shell still dripped from its wound to the floor. The Doctor remembered his promise and willed the gate to form faster.

They stepped through together, into the dark.

They step out together, into the machine.

The first thing the Doctor sees as the machine-flesh coughs him into its heart is Minski lying on the ground. Kneeling beside him is a woman in the blood-stained uniform of a revolutionary soldier, the dominant red squeezing out the white and the blue. She has a knife in her hand, its blade tarnished with blood. The Doctor moves cautiously towards her, his arms outstretched.

The blade slashes down. The Doctor flinches involuntarily. When he looks again, the hilt of the knife rises erect between the soldier's rib.

'Ah,' she says calmly. 'For a moment, I wasn't sure —'

The light in her eyes grows dim. Her head falls forward, rolling limp on the end of her neck. Gradually her dying twitches fade and she is still, a corpse making prayer over Minski's body.

The Doctor kneels and touches the woman's skin. Certain she is dead, he turns to Minski. The First Deputy's body lies like a discarded toy on the pulsating ground, his flesh mutilated by frenzied slashing. Viscous crimson liquid licks from the torn wounds in his neck and stomach. It looks and smells like human blood. The Doctor chooses not to inspect it any closer.

His hand wavers on the handle of the blade protruding from the woman's chest. It is lodged hard, immovable. His palm comes away red and sticky. He wipes it on his handkerchief, then turns away. He guides himself through the ambiguous time and space of the machine to its heart.

Citizen Sade is already there, staring up at the crucified alien with something close to pity, something akin to awe in his eyes.

'Angels,' he whispers. He swings round, out of the Doctor's gaze, his shoulders rounding and his head held low.

The Doctor grants him his privacy and calls out to the creature in the machine. 'Robin Goodfellow? Can you hear me?'

The masked head rolls upwards, its chin splitting as it rises, dribbling more fluid into the mesh of machinery that snares it. 'Doctor,' it replies softly.

'Is there enough power to restore the Earth to its original position in time and space?'

'Perhaps,' it murmurs. 'Do you have a slide rule?'

The Doctor nods, patting his pockets. He passes the object through the intricate layers of machinery into Goodfellow's waiting, shaking fingers. They fumble with the disc, twisting it rapidly through frantic calculations.

'There is enough,' it concludes. 'So many have died, and their spirits have nourished the machine. There is enough power.'

'Then stop the machine,' the Doctor barks.

Goodfellow shakes his head. 'I'm sorry Doctor,' he croons, raising his ragged fingers to his face. The Doctor can't tell whether this is shame or a simple, desperate effort to hold his skull together. 'The system recognizes only the operator.'

'Minski,' the Doctor clicks his tongue, casting his eyes back across the machine to the shrunken corpse of the system operator. His eyes flash and his back straightens. For a second – no longer – he accepts defeat.

Then he looks round and finds a solution.

'Sade,' he snaps, reaching forward and seizing the man by his shoulder. The bones seem thin and brittle in his grip. Sade looks round, his eyes hooded by shadow.

'The system might know you,' the Doctor suggests. Sade nods and steps forward to address Goodfellow.

The alien's voice cracks across him, leaving his command unspoken. 'You are recognized as the operator base, but you cannot override the operator's instructions. The best you can do is try and jam the mechanism.'

The Doctor and Sade exchange glances. Both pairs of eyes fall onto the pistol tucked into Sade's belt. He pulls it out, hefting it carefully in his palm before hurling it into the heart of the world-mechanism, above Goodfellow's head.

For a moment there is near silence, disturbed only by the hiss and grind of the machinery. In that moment, the Doctor imagines that the pulse of the mechanism is growing slower and harder – that they have succeeded in stopping the world. Then there is an explosion, a burst of sound and colour but little force between the crushing pistons and manically spinning cogwheels. The machinery spits out a blackened, steaming lump of metal. It lands at the Doctor's feet, twitching forlornly, then falling still.

'It's no good,' Goodfellow observes in a voice which the Doctor finds disquieting, a tone of solid defeatism. 'The material isn't compatible.'

'They were always like this,' Sade points out. 'They picked the finest nits imaginable.'

The Doctor doesn't reply, barely hears what has been said. He gazes down at his hands, at withered skin and useless fingers, unable to accept the certainty of defeat. It doesn't seem fair, to be brought back from the edge of Change in order to be dragged down by the slowness and indecision of this frail body. He realizes he can leave.

Alone among the people in this artificial world, he can escape, back into a universe without an Earth. He could even take Dodo, if she wanted it.

He doesn't want it.

Sade draws up close behind him, a hand stretching round his shoulder and his face nudging close against the Doctor's.

'I know where we can find some compatible material,' he says.

The Doctor swings round and blasts him with the full force of his sudden rage. 'Well, why didn't you say so before?!'

'I didn't think you'd approve,' he replies. His lips twitch, as if to add something new, but then they fall still. 'I'll fetch it,' he says, a slight smile dancing on his pale lips. He moves away, out from beneath the machine's spine. The Doctor turns away, taking the last opportunity to stare up at the full majesty, the full *obscenity* of the world-machine. It soars upward towards the apex of the flesh-chamber, every tiny wheel and gear and piston working ceaselessly, mindlessly towards its own tiny goal, each essential to the roar and grind of the vast machinery. The Doctor is tempted to follow the outline of each component, peering in ever closer detail. He resists, certain that were he to be drawn into that game, he would never escape.

Calm, measured breaths at his back alert him to Sade's return.

'Did you get it?' he calls.

'Yes,' is the muted reply. 'I got it.'

The Doctor turns.

Sade stands on the edge of the cage of bone. Cradled in his arms is the diminutive, bleeding corpse of Citizen Minski, First Deputy of France, system operator of the world-machine. The Doctor stares, his mouth opening to speak but finding nothing he can possibly say. The Marquis de Sade bows his head slightly and manages an inscrutable smile. For an instant, the Doctor believes he is seeing another Sade automaton, one of a different size and shape but with the same expression, the same face of dark humour.

'I'll need a hand,' Sade says gently.

Pausing only slightly, the Doctor joins him, taking half the body from him. They swing it together, building a steady rhythm. Then, as one, they hurl it into the heart of the heart of the world-machine.

And then everything stops.

Paris ceased to burn. The fire that licked through its streets froze into static columns of light and heat. The victims of the conflagration jammed still, solid flames erupting from their hair and clothes, no longer burning. The soldiers in red ground to a halt, their bullets growing still in mid-air. Their victims teetered between life and death. Everywhere expressions of hate and of fear were captured by the frozen moment.

Paris held its breath, a city caught in tableau.

Outside the city, across the world, everything stopped.

The black ships still breathed, pulsed and moved, but they no longer fired. Cautiously they glided to the ground, stepping out of the sky onto solid, unmoving earth.

Dodo sat naked and alone in the darkness, listening to the silence that had blossomed suddenly around her. The walls had stopped shaking – or perhaps had been caught in mid-tremble. It didn't really matter. She glanced to one side of her, at Dalville who lay stretched out across the bench, his eyelids frozen half-closed, the yawn trapped as it formed on his lips. She wasn't certain whether she was alone, while he was here. She wasn't even sure whether he was alive or dead.

No, he was alive. He simply wasn't moving or breathing and the helpless twitches of his muscles had ceased. She drew her palm across his chest and found he was still warm with life. All the same he seemed dead, trapped in the oblivion between moments and memories.

Footsteps trailed along the passage outside the dressing room, the last thing she expected to hear. The door clicked open and a shaft of light fell into the room, a clean glowing line that impaled the darkness. Held in the door frame was a silhouette – a shadow the shape of Fantômas.

No. It was a shadow the shape of Catherine Arouette.

'Dodo?' Her voice sounded husky in the dark.

'Hello Catherine,' Dodo called back, still cowering on the edge of the light. 'I wasn't sure whether you'd still be . . . well, moving.'

'Neither was I.'

She pushed the door wider open, spreading the light further across the room. It struck Dodo on the face and was warm across her body, but she let it pass over her. She allowed herself to rise, legs trembling beneath her – nervous but not afraid, embarrassed but not ashamed.

Arouette blushed ashen-grey. Her eyes were dark, the shadow driving her smouldering pupils further back into her skull. Her face wavered between smile and grimace. Her eyes shuffled between Dodo and Dalville, drawing in the scene, not certain where to look. Dodo took Dalville's coat and spread it across his motionless form, ending her conflict.

'Oh,' Arouette said softly. 'The two of you?' she asked.

'Yes,' Dodo replied calmly.

Arouette stepped forward, her face a picture of concern. 'Dodo,' she whispered. 'Dalville was infected with Minski's virus.'

'I know,' Dodo replied. 'And now I am.'

'You realize' – Dodo wasn't certain but she thought she heard a quiver in Arouette's voice, maybe disgust, maybe fear, maybe excitement – 'that you'll pass it on to all your future lovers, and to your children.'

'Yes,' Dodo responded numbly, 'but I have to take something with me.'

Arouette nodded simply.

'You'd better get dressed,' she suggested. 'The Pageant has arrived.'

If anything, she felt more self-conscious as Arouette watched her dress than she had been before. The woman's eyes were cool and haunted.

'Is something wrong?' she asked as she pulled her T-shirt on. It was a horrible thing, a garish shade of red decorated with black rings. She'd liked it once – no longer. She resolved to burn it at the earliest opportunity.

'Your skin,' Arouette said sadly. 'It's very smooth.'

'Thank you,' Dodo snorted.

'When he touched you,' the woman continued, her voice shrinking to a whisper, 'it didn't hurt?'

'No, of course not.' Dodo giggled slightly.

Arouette nodded and coughed affectedly. 'I didn't think so. I'll wait outside.'

The Doctor and Sade look up, startled by the appearance of three new creatures, three of Goodfellow's kind. There is no warning of their arrival. It is as though they have stepped out of nothing to be here. At their backs, in the tortured labyrinth of metal, in the heart of the still machine, Goodfellow's breathing grows hoarser.

The aliens bow. Sade replies in kind but the Doctor only nods.

'I am Liberty,' says one. 'I have come to release Masksmaster Goodfellow from bondage.'

'I am Equality,' says one. 'I have come to restore the lost souls of Tyll Howlglass and Larkspur to their vile bodies.'

'I am Fraternity,' says the last, 'and I have come for the corpse.'

Unimpressed, the Doctor steps forward into their path.

'And what will you do then, hmm? What will you do about this world and its people?'

'We will reverse the machine,' Liberty replies. 'We

245

will rewind the false history of this world and restore it to its place in real-time.'

'To the humans,' Equality continues, 'it will seem as though nothing has happened. Their history will unfold as though seamless.'

'We can't say that theirs is a good history,' Fraternity ends, 'or one better than this, but it is theirs and they'll have to live with it.'

The Doctor nods curtly. He is still not satisfied.

'There must be no more experiments of this kind,' he says gravely. 'If there are, they will be ended swiftly and efficiently. As will you.'

'Do you threaten us,' Equality protests, 'my Lord?'

'No.' The Doctor shakes his head. 'I warn you. Nothing more.'

He turns on his heel and stalks out of the heart of the machine. Sade follows him out, silently. The Three Graces watch their backs recede, then return with a modest amount of pride, to carry out their tasks.

Catherine led Dodo down through the levels and passageways of the New Bastille, past soldiers and officials frozen in mid-flight and corpses, crushed by falling blocks, frozen in death. The first body she saw had been staring into space, caught in time at the moment of death, its eyes staring into an unknowable terror. The sight had left Dodo shaken. Arouette had put an arm round Dodo's shoulder and squeezed protectively.

'Don't worry,' she said. 'They're not really dead. They're only acting.'

Somehow, that made things seem much worse.

As they reached the subterranean levels, they began to encounter movement. The aliens of the Pageant were there, forming rents in the fabric of reality in order to inspect the machine. Their voices echoed through the corridor, blending into a chorus, a song of subtle beauty that set Dodo crying inside. It affected Catherine even harder, the tears bursting from her eyes like water rushing through a cracked dam. A hand went up to hide her face.

The first thing Dodo heard as they reached Minski's laboratory was Sade's voice, spitting through the dusty silence.

' . . . what you may feel, I wouldn't trust them to keep their word. Angels aren't bound by promises or morals. They do as they please.'

'They have made no promises,' came the rejoinder. It was the Doctor's voice, hard and commanding. It was a sign that their time on this world was almost over. At once, Dodo felt a thrill of excitement and relief, a little disappointment and a strange, hollow sense of loss.

'That's the only reason I'm inclined to trust them at all,' Sade snapped. The pair of them glided into Dodo's view, two angry old men arguing together by the door of the TARDIS. Dodo broke free of Arouette's grip and leapt into the Doctor's arms, almost bowling him over in her haste. He put his cold, old arms round her, pulling her into a limp cuddle.

'Oh Doctor,' she said, the words rolling thoughtlessly from her tongue. 'I'm so pleased to see you. And the TARDIS –'

'There now, child,' he replied. 'It's all over now.'

Child, she thought. It wasn't meant as an insult – she hardly felt stung by it – but it was there. It felt as though a little more space had opened between them, another inch added to the gap.

Child!

'The Doctor and I were just discussing endings,' Sade said. 'He believes they can be happy. I believe they can be unsatisfactory at best.'

'There *are* happy endings,' Arouette replied. 'I've directed one or two.'

'On the stage,' Sade hissed, leaping on the point. Dodo found herself looking up from the Doctor's embrace, watching the argument twist and grow.

'And in life,' the director insisted. 'Look around you.

247

No one died today. No one has died in the last ten years. They'll all live again, the memory of their pain erased.'

'Then they've suffered for nothing, and that's *tragedy*,' Sade riposted. 'If suffering has a virtue it is in our memory of it. Who will remember the pain of this world? Even you and I will only recall it in dreams and fevers.

'This world is not a true one. When a lie ends, where is the virtue? If the truth is that men and women and children and all manner of creatures continue to suffer at the hands of others, where is the happy ending?'

'It's there, in pieces,' Catherine said softly. 'In the real history of the world, my brother will outlive the Terror. He'll be happy to be alive.' She spoke without pleasure, her eyes and her voice dropping like lead to the floor. 'He'll be alive because you spared him, Citizen Sade.'

'I remember your brother,' Sade whispered. 'He wasn't guilty of the charge, y'know. But I remember him very clearly.'

Catherine nodded and lapsed into dull silence and stillness. She looked, Dodo thought, exactly like one of the corpses she had seen during their descent – still and dead eyed, infinitely pitiable. Sade too had seized up, his heart darting furiously while his body remained at rest.

'I think we should say our goodbyes,' the Doctor murmured.

The Doctor stood hunched over the TARDIS console top, his hands blurring as they manipulated the instruments that would activate the dematerialization sequence. How much of it was bluff Dodo couldn't tell, but the Doctor moved confidently, as if the past few days had washed away his illness and his age.

The roar of the TARDIS engines as they lurched into life left her drained and despairing. The sound marked an end to her life on this world, a place of bad memories and some good ones, a time she could never return to. She wasn't sure what there might be to look forward to.

'Are you all right?' the Doctor asked. He was looking

up from the controls, a kindly and patronizing smile playing on his face.

'Hmm, yes,' she replied absently. 'I'm fine.'

'Good, good,' the Doctor mumbled, lowering his head once again. 'I would hate to think that you had been left tainted by that terrible place.'

Dodo thought of the virus eating through her nervous system and her brain. The image didn't stir her. It meant nothing, nothing at all.

'What happens to those two?' she asked. 'To Catherine and Sade.'

'History doesn't say what happens to Catherine Arouette,' the Doctor droned, without looking up. 'She dies, long before your time.'

'What about Citizen Sade?' she insisted quietly.

'That I do know. In the last days of the Terror, Sade is imprisoned pending execution. A mistake is made on the day he is scheduled to die, an error in the paperwork, a slip of the pen. Such things happen, and the execution is postponed. Hours later the architects of the Terror are deposed.

'Sade is released. He lives as normal a life as any eighteenth-century aristocrat, until the new regime becomes embarrassed and locks him away again. He spends the rest of his life in relative comfort in an asylum at Charenton, where he directs plays. He dies there.'

'Poor man,' Dodo said softly. It might have been a distortion in the glass column at the console's centre, but she thought she saw the Doctor nod with her. She smiled, bounding across the console room to the trellis wall where the Doctor kept his elegant, antique clock. She tapped its pendulum playfully.

Behind her, the Doctor gasped. Dodo swung round in time to see him slump forward across the console, in time to leap forward and steady him before he fell backwards. As she helped him, she saw his face, recognizing the lines of weariness and pain written across his forehead.

'Are you all right?' she mouthed.

The Doctor nodded, and even that seemed an effort.

'I'll help you,' she said, drawing her arm round his shoulders and half-leading, half-dragging him across the room to his chair. He slumped there, mumbling to himself, his flesh growing pale and thin on his bones.

'Soon,' he muttered. 'Very soon.' Then he covered his face with his hands and fell silent. Dodo stood still, watching him from a respectful distance, watching him age, watching him die, moment by moment. The clock ticked on the edge of the room, marking each of them.

Dodo waited until she was sure the Doctor was sleeping in peace. Then she strode from the console room, pulling the door closed quietly behind her. She ran the rest of the way to her bedroom, where she locked herself in and escaped into a dark and peaceful silence.

Available in the *Doctor Who — New Adventures* series:

The next Missing Adventure is *The English Way of Death* by Gareth Roberts, featuring the fourth Doctor, Romana and K9.